Wildflower Wedding

With a

Killer Reception

The Sisters, Texas Mystery Series, Book 8

BECKI WILLIS

Special Thanks
Cover design by dienel96
Editing by SJS Editorial Services

ISBN: 978-1-947686-17-5
ISBN: 1-947686-17-8

TABLE OF CONTENTS

1

Gloved hands handled the charge with care.

The black powder nestled inside the canvas bag wouldn't detonate like dynamite, but it was highly volatile, nonetheless. A single spark of static electricity could set off a fast, hot flash and burn. For that reason, protocol demanded accurately weighing and measuring the powder before dispensing.

The special ingredient required equal reverence. Too much, and the tampering would be obvious. Too little, and it would be ineffective. It had to be perfect.

With the ingredient added and the bags secured once again, the charges went back into the limber chest, and the lid carefully lowered.

Easy does it.

One misstep, and the surprise could blow up in just anyone's face.

Pun intended.

ഃഔഃഔ

The Texas sun was intense for this early spring day,

adding to Bobby Ray Erickson's discomfort.

It was a cumbersome and exacting task, dressing the part of an 1836 Texian. Despite the chafing, he wore the authentic period clothing with pride. Bobby Ray knew that his was a choice. His great-great-great-great-grandfather hadn't been so lucky.

Ever efficient, the long-tailed muslin shirt served as both underwear and outerwear for the would-be pioneer. Without pants, the shirt's hem would hang all the way to his knees, and easily transformed into a nightshirt for sleeping. With pants, the excess material bunched up around his privates and rubbed in a most unpleasant way, but it did offer some barrier to the coarse wool fabric of his pants. True to the period, the simple brown pants were shapeless and stiff, with a buttoned flap and no belt loops. Bobby Ray held his britches up with galluses and wooden buttons, just like his ancestors had done. His waistcoat was made of leather and held the heat of the day against his chest. Under the sun's powerful rays, the tanned hide seemed to fuse into his own. The final insult was the heavy wool coat.

Despite the day's warmth, Bobby Ray wore the dark coat with pride, for it identified his rank as captain within the militia. Like the volunteer army before him, his coat was made of homespun wool, but the two white loops of cord dangling from his shoulder made the cumbersome cloak worth it. A crimson sash about his waist tied on the right, further marking his accomplishment. Officers in the United States Army tied their sashes on the left, but Texians were different.

On this day, it wasn't just the uniform that brought the large man such distress. His allergies were increasingly getting worse, exacerbated by spring pollen. Budding trees and new grasses always made breathing conditions worse, but this year's winter awakening was particularly troublesome. Add in his sensitivities to certain foods and the way everything seemed to tighten his airways these days,

Bobby Ray was truly miserable as he marched onto the parade grounds.

Never mind the chafed privates. His entire upper body felt abraded, rubbed raw by thousands of unseen ants marching across his skin. He could feel the welts forming beneath the scratchy wool of his pants, imagined the rough muslin sticking to the splotchy hives that surely crisscrossed his chest. His throat felt tight and close. His chest was heavy. Bobby Ray felt his cheeks grow warm and his ears burn, but he held his head high and marched on.

Today was Texas Independence Day, and no Texian worth his salt would put his own personal comfort before the most sacred day in their state's illustrious history. As a captain within the Texian Militia, Bobby Ray would never shun his celebratory duties because of a little thing like being unable to take a deep breath. No matter how much his wife scoffed at his dedication, Bobby Ray took his responsibilities seriously.

Every year on the weekend closest to March 2, Texas Independence Day, people across the vast state paid homage to their forefathers and the brave pioneers before them. And where better to celebrate the day than Washington-on-the-Brazos State Historic Site, best known as The Birthplace of Texas? The main attraction of the complex was a carefully constructed replica of Independence Hall, a long, unpainted, humble wood building where the Texas Declaration of Independence was signed in 1836. Drafted just days before the fall of the Alamo, the auspicious document had been the first step in declaring Texas a sovereign nation, independent of Mexican and Santa Anna's dictatorial rule. For the next nine years, the Republic of Texas was a nation unto itself, and did not annex to the United States of America until 1845.

The two-day celebration included a variety of fun activities and hands-on experiences, food and crafts, speeches from state and local dignitaries, music, plays, and more, but the crowd favorites were always the live reenactments of the Texian Militia and, on Sunday afternoon, the cutting of a massive Texas-sized, Texas-shaped birthday cake. Bobby Ray was proud to be a part of the celebration and to walk in the footsteps of his forefathers.

This was the last reenactment of the day. Twenty more minutes, and he could slip off the coat and loosen the vest, if only for a few minutes. After he cooled off and took a few deep breaths of unrestricted air, he might have a piece of that cake. Collette didn't usually come with him when he performed, but she was here today, and she had brought along a picnic lunch. He had looked forward to indulging in all the fine foods of the day—turkey legs, curly fries, frozen lemonade and funnel cakes from the vendors, cornpone and hoecakes cooked over open fires, jellies and honey on hardtack biscuits, and jerked meat from the live demonstrators. With his wife along, he wouldn't be able to indulge in such delicacies. Collette fed him a special diet these days, but so far, his allergies seemed to be getting worse, not better.

What he wouldn't give for some of those golden fried fish fillets he saw earlier, or another taste of that popcorn shrimp. Petey had slipped him a tiny curl when Collette wasn't looking. Much more than one piece, and he would start wheezing for sure. He might even break out in new welts. But from his way of thinking, it couldn't be much worse than it was right now. He knew his face must be purple by now. His body itched like it was on fire. A crunchy, perfect piece of fried catfish and a handful of shrimp might just be worth dying over. It would sure beat whatever food Collette rationed out to him, and it dang sure wouldn't come with a side of nagging.

It would get him out of this coat, and out of his misery. For the first time he could remember, Bobby Ray considered shucking his wool coat.

He managed to fumble his way through the first reenactment. His contribution in the musket firing was minimal, giving him a few extra minutes to breath. After the Sergeant's brief introduction to the crowd, Bobby Ray stepped forward. He pulled out his sword and issued the solemn orders for 'ready,' 'aim,' and 'fire.'

The black powder muskets were loud. Their sharp reports left the stench of gunpowder in their wake and white puffs of smoke hanging in the still midday air. The ammunition might be impotent, but the gunpowder was real, and it rattled a cough from Bobby Ray's already tight throat. He stepped back to avoid the worst of it, as the soldiers reloaded for a second round.

On the other side of the safety rope was a family of five. The tall, slender woman looked vaguely familiar, as did the man by her side. Bobby Ray thought he might have been a sports figure, back in the day. The two teenage girls beside them looked borderline bored, but the exhibition fascinated the lanky blond boy by their side. Bobby Ray managed a tight smile around his next fit of coughing.

It was gratifying to see the youth of today taking an interest in history. The teen might only be intrigued by the weapons now, but it was a start. That was what first hooked Bobby Ray, too, before he came to love every aspect of reenacting.

After another two rounds of musket fire, it was time for the dual cannon exhibition. As discreetly as possible, Bobby Ray pounded on his chest to clear his clogged airways. Maybe sneaking that piece of shrimp hadn't been such a smart idea, after all. Hadn't he had a similar reaction the last time he ate seafood? The doctor warned his reaction could get worse with every encounter. He cautioned Bobby Ray against eating fish of any kind, particularly shellfish, but sometimes—like today—he just couldn't resist. The only thing Bobby Ray loved more than eating seafood was *catching* seafood. Man, did he love to fish!

Bobby Ray thought about his next fishing trip as the sponge man cleaned the gun's bore with a wet swab. For the first firing, Bobby Ray was acting as Number 4 gunner. Wearing a heavy leather thumb stall, he pressed his thumb to the vent hole to prevent a draught from fanning any unwanted flames. Once the Number 3 man had inserted the powder bag and the projectile, Number 2 rammed them in tightly with the reverse end of his swab. Bobby Ray then pricked the canvas bag through the vent hole, releasing the gunpowder. At Number 1's command, the fifth member of their crew lit the charge with his slow match.

Within a moment, the mighty gun boomed out its report. The reverberation shook the ground, rattling even the cannon's framework. As the crowd behind him cheered, Bobby Ray coughed and curled up his nose. This charge had a strong and peculiar odor about it. He eagerly stepped away from the first cannon and made his way to the second one.

He must have moved too fast, he decided, because for a moment there, he felt disoriented. Darkness blurred the edges of his vision, and his head felt light.

For the second demonstration, Bobby Ray was in the Number 3 position. He hoped his hands were steady as he carefully removed the powder bag from the limber chest and loaded it and the impotent projectile into the big gun's barrel. Assuming his position beside the barrel of the cannon, he leaned away and covered his ear when the sergeant gave the command to fire.

The resounding boom was fierce and loud. Smoke swirled thick and dense, tainted with that same odd odor. As close as he was to the barrel's end, Bobby Ray felt as if the polluted vapor went straight to his chest. It clogged his airways and filled his throat. He struggled to pull in a breath of air, no matter how shallow. Darkness gathered in his mind.

He stumbled a few feet away, vaguely aware that the

crowd cheered and hollered, ignorant of his distress. He almost made it as far as the safety rope, where the family of five was no longer cheering. They now eyed him with concern.

With no warning whatsoever, Bobby Ray Erickson crumpled to the ground like a lump of coal.

2

Madison Reynolds slid into her favorite corner booth at *New Beginnings Café.*

"You look tired." Her best friend's candid appraisal came with a cup of steaming-hot coffee. Pouring another cup for herself, the café owner slid into the seat opposite Madison. "Did you have fun yesterday at Washington-on-the-Brazos?"

"Yes and no," Madison replied. "The weather was gorgeous, the celebration was great, and the period crafts and demonstrations were awesome. There was even a massive birthday cake."

"I hear a 'but' in there," Genny wisely detected.

"But I saw a dead man."

Her friend threw her hands up in disbelief. "What is it with you and dead bodies!"

"Genesis Baker! You know I have no control over any of the bodies I've found!"

"Montgomery," the blonde corrected, flashing the sparkling rings on her finger.

Genny still wore the rosy glow of a newlywed. Three weeks married, she and Cutter were learning to share their lives with a significant other and to fit that person into their already-established routines. It was a first marriage for both the forty-year-old entrepreneur and the man eight years her junior, but judging from the perpetual smile on her friend's face, the couple was mastering the art of compromise. Madison only hoped she and Brash could do it as well as the Montgomerys.

"So, how did you find this one?" Genny asked.

"I didn't exactly *find* it. It just sort of... dropped, right there in front of me. In front of all of us. It was one of the gunners for the militia demonstration."

"How horrible! He just fell to the ground?"

"Yes. As the last round was fired, there was a huge *boom!* And a few seconds later, he just dropped to the ground. Just a few feet in front of us."

"Heart attack?" Genny guessed as she sipped on her coffee.

"Maybe."

"I hear another 'but.'"

Madison sighed. "But Brash thinks it wasn't quite so simple. He's trained as a first responder, you know, so he naturally ran to help. I guess his police training kicked in, because even before park security or the DPS officers arrived, he was already conducting informal interviews with the man's co-actors." She stopped for a moment to frown. "Or, are they called co-reenactors? Anyway, for whatever reason, he felt like something was off."

"Brash is usually right," Genny agreed. "He's the best chief of police this community has ever had. If he suspects foul play, it probably was."

"I'm not sure what he saw that tipped him off," Madison said, envisioning the scene again in her head. "The girls giggled about the troop's clothes as they marched in, imagining if boys these days wore homespun shirts and shapeless wool pants. His coat was so tight, he looked a bit like a stuffed turkey," she admitted. "His face was red and splotchy, like he couldn't take a deep breath. And then, on the second blast, he just fell to the ground."

"What happened then?"

"Brash checked him for vitals and asked if there was a doctor in the crowd. A woman came forward and worked with him for a few minutes, but about halfway into Blake's little show, she blurted out that he was dead!"

"Wait. Back up. What little show are you talking about?"

Madison nervously fingered the coffee mug. "The crowd was curious and kept pushing forward, trying to get a better look. So the kids and I tried to run interference and get them to back away. Someone in the crowd recognized me. Well, they recognized Brash first, from his NFL days, and his days as a college coach. After the rounds of *Gig 'em Ags* and *Go Bears,* someone recognized me from *Home Again.* Things sort of went downhill from there," she admitted.

"The gift that just keeps on giving," Genny mumbled in agreement.

"They keep showing those silly reruns all the time! How can people forget about us and let us live in peace, if they keep rerunning those shows on national television?"

"I think that's the point," Genny reminded her. "Your renovation was the highest-rated reality show *ever* on HOME-TV. They don't want people forgetting."

"Mission accomplished, because no one has," Madison sulked. "The good news is, the crowd forgot about the dead man after that. Someone spotted my engagement ring, and then everyone wanted details. That's where Blake and the girls came in. Blake tried to distract them by suggesting they go have cake. When that didn't work, he talked about things that make Texas great and reminding them why they came out to celebrate in the first place. Megan's a Texas trivia buff, and Bethani likes details, so between them, they put on quite the show."

"Dare I ask?"

Madison waved her hand in the air. "You know, trivia like how, technically, it's against the law in Texas to curse in front of a corpse. Details like how El Paso is closer to California than it is to Dallas. Or how there's a privately owned wind farm in West Texas that's four times the size of Manhattan. Blake added his own spin, like how it's proof we Texans are full of hot air. He conducted it a bit like a game show. They had quite an act going, until the doctor blurted out the news a bit louder than necessary."

"You gotta admit, the kid's a natural entertainer."

"I know." Madison continued to finger the mug. "And he did it for all the right reasons, and I'm very proud of him. All three of them. But Blake had the crowd laughing when the wife came up. She doesn't normally come with him to his reenactments, but this time she did. It was bad enough she had to see her husband lying there on the ground. But with my son entertaining the crowd..."

"Ouch. That's not good. But seeing her husband die! That's even worse."

"She wasn't there yet when he actually... fell. But she came right after. I just feel so bad for her. I keep thinking about the shock on her face. The guilt."

Genny gasped. "You think the *wife* killed him?"

"What? No. Why would you..." Realizing why her friend drew that conclusion, Madison hastily explained, "No, not the guilt of killing him. The guilt of ... well, the same guilt I felt when Gray died. Guilt for not feeling the things you know you should be feeling. Guilt for not being completely and utterly devastated by the fact your husband is dead and never coming back." She looked down into her coffee. "Like mine, I don't think hers was a happy marriage."

"Why do you say that?"

"Brash and I stayed there until DPS took over the scene. The kids were like self-appointed ambassadors for the park, urging the crowd to follow them to the cake cutting ceremony. Even after three turkey legs, mind you, my son was starving. I stayed with Collette in one of the renovated cabins, and I did the only thing I knew to help. I listened.

She talked about how Bobby Ray—that's the dead man's name, Bobby Ray Erickson—loved doing reenactments all over the state, even though it meant sleeping in a tent and roughing it, just like they did back in the days of the Republic. She told me how much he loved sports and hunting, especially archery. How he loved to deep-sea fish but was allergic to shellfish. She told me he was a good worker and a good son, but she never mentioned he was a good husband." Madison lifted a shoulder as she concluded, "It was more of what she *didn't* say, than what she did."

"Like wondering how she would ever function without him? How she would never see his gorgeous hazel eyes again or feel his strong arms around her?" Genny stared off into the distance, obviously imagining how she might react, should the worst happen to Cutter. "How he'd never leave his sooty bunker gear in the hallway again, or track cow manure across a newly mopped floor? How he'd never eat another batch of hot apple turnovers, all by himself?" Tears swam in her baby-blue eyes as the terrible thoughts flooded through her.

Madison patted her friend's hand in a gesture of comfort, but memories made her smile bittersweet. "Believe it or not, that's not always the first thoughts through your head," Madison said. "I know Gray and I were estranged at the time of his accident. Little more than polite strangers, living in the same house for the sake of the children, but that doesn't mean I didn't love him, on some level. Still, I remember thinking such random thoughts when I first got the news. Was my sweater still in the backseat? Was he wearing his good watch, the one I gave him for our fifteenth wedding anniversary? Who would preach the service? I needed to cancel my dental appointment the next day. Clean out the refrigerator for the many pies and casseroles that would soon arrive. Remember to rotate my tires on the schedule he kept for me. Silly things, really, but things I could wrap my head around." She pushed out a sad breath. "I couldn't wrap my head around his death. And I don't think Collette could wrap her head around her husband's death, either."

Genny shook her head in empathy, sniffing away the traces of her overly emotional reaction. "That's just so sad."

"It is. And on top of all that, thinking it could be deliberate. I can't imagine the horror of knowing your husband was murdered." Her mind was busy turning gears. "It makes you wonder," Madison continued, "how someone could have orchestrated that. I mean, he's from Marlin. Their group is completely volunteer, and they do these reenactments across the state. So, it would have to be someone who knew his schedule. Someone who knew he would be there this weekend. It's most likely someone within his own regimen, wouldn't you think?"

"It could be," Genny agreed. "But I'm not like you, Maddy. I don't really think a lot about murder and suspects and motive. That's your thing."

Madison couldn't help but laugh. "I guess it's because I'm about to marry a lawman, slash special investigator for the sheriff's department."

"That, and because half your clients seem to think you're some sort of private investigator, yourself!"

"There is that," Madison agreed with a slight grimace.

When she moved back home last year, she started a temporary service to make ends meet. Before acquiring her house and her own dedicated business space, the corner booth at *New Beginnings* had been the unofficial office for *In a Pinch Professional Services*. Over the course of the last fourteen months, her business had slowly outgrown the corner booth, but Madison couldn't help but recall some of the more challenging jobs accepted at this very table.

It was amazing, really, some of the things people hired her to do. While pharmaceutical runs and taxiing outpatients back and forth to doctor appointments provided a meager income, they were only a small portion of the services she provided. She had temporarily worked at a car dealership, insurance company, surveyors' office, the police station, a commercial chicken farm, and at various other businesses around the sistering towns of Naomi and Juliet. People hired her to spy on cheating spouses, to find a missing chair and missing Christmas presents, and to prove a teetotaler didn't die of alcohol poisoning; not naturally, at any rate. She walked dogs and walked chicken houses and took on the formidable task of proving a man innocent of murder. It was a far cry from the charitable work she did in Dallas, or the receptionist job she held with her late husband's investment company, but it was oddly fulfilling. Madison enjoyed the challenge of learning different jobs, and she found great satisfaction in helping others.

"Have you given any more thought to getting your PI license?"

"Not really. At the moment, I'm a little preoccupied, getting ready for a certain upcoming wedding."

Genny struck a shocked pose. "Really? And whose could that be?" She feigned total innocence.

"Let me see... Oh, yes. Mine!"

They both gave an excited squeal, gripping one another's fingers in the middle of the table in a throwback from their teenage years. The two had been best friends since they were in junior high.

"How are the plans coming? What can I help with?" As always, Genny was the first to volunteer for anything Madison needed.

"I think everything is on schedule. Between Granny Bert and Mrs. de, I don't have a very big part in the wedding."

"Uhm, except for the fact you're the bride," her friend pointed out.

"I'm not sure that matters at this point!" Madison laughed. "Between my grandmother and his mother, not to mention his sister—and even Shannon, his ex-wife—I don't have a very big role in preparing for this thing."

"*This thing* happens to be one of the most important

events in your entire life."

"It rates right up there with giving birth to the twins," Madison agreed. "You know I loved Gray when I married him, but let's face it...I've been half in love with Brash for over half my life! He was my high school crush, and now he's my soul mate." She gave a dreamy sigh. "As long as I come away from the day with his ring on my finger, I really don't care much about the details. It's the happily ever after I want.'"

"And you shall have it, my friend. But don't give up all rights to planning your wedding. This is y'all's day. It should be about the two of you, and what *you* want."

Madison propped her elbows onto the table. "You know what I want? I want a wildflower wedding. Just Brash and me. The twins, of course, and Megan. Only our closest friends and family. Outside, at the ranch, in our spot by the river." She used her hands for emphasis. "Small and simple."

"Then that's what you should have."

She made a face. "It may be too late. The invitations are at the printers."

"So make it an invitation to the reception. Let Granny Bert and Mrs. deCordova throw the party *they* want, but you and Brash have the wedding *you* want. You deserve it."

A hopeful light came to Madison's eyes. "You think I could get away with it?"

"Of course you can. You're the bride. You can do anything you want."

When her phone buzzed, Madison dug through her purse to find it. "What I want is to find a phone that floats," she mumbled. "Right to the top of my purse, above all the other stuff I have crammed in here."

"I have a better solution. Don't cram so much stuff in there."

"Ah, easy for you to say. You're not the mother of two busy sixteen-year-olds." She began pulling things out of her purse, setting them on the table in the quest for the elusive cell phone. "See this? It's my emergency sewing kit. I never know when Bethani might pop a seam on her cheerleading outfit or rip the hem out. And this is Blake's backup to his backup inhaler. He doesn't have an asthma attack often, but with all the sports he plays, it's best to be prepared. This is the trash from his breakfast snack this morning, the one he ate in the car on the way to school, *after* I fed him waffles and sausage this morning. These are the papers I need to fill out for their driver's permits. And this is... well, I'm not sure what this is, but I'm sure it's important." Her fingers made contact with her vibrating phone. "Ah, here it is!" she cried in triumph.

She frowned when she saw the message scrolled across the screen.

"Bad news?" Genny fretted.

"No. Just Mr. Barrett again." She tucked the phone away with a sigh. "Remind me. *Why* did I take on a new client, less than a month before my wedding?"

"Do you want the short explanation—money—or the long one, where we talk about feeling sorry for the old man, knowing he's trying to find his family before he goes to that big ranch in the sky, and how he was always nice to us when we were teenagers, never complaining when we had all those pasture parties on his land?"

"Let's go with the short one."

"You needed the money." Genny flashed her friend a smile before giving the short explanation a long clarification. "Even though Brash has repeatedly offered to support you, you feel it's important to maintain your financial independence. After the stunt Gray pulled, leaving you widowed and penniless before your fortieth birthday, you feel the need to show your children that *you* can provide for them. That a woman must be strong enough, and resourceful enough, to stand on her own two feet. Even if Brash helps with the bills *after* the wedding, you want to contribute your fair share. And that means taking on new clients, even at a time like this."

"So you're saying I should call him back."

"That depends. What did he want this time?"

"*This* time, he wanted me to track down his niece's son. Thirty minutes ago, he wanted me to track down his niece. Thirty minutes before that, he texted me to say he just discovered he had a niece." She tried not to look as exasperated as she felt. "You're right. I'd like to help him, but I wish to goodness he hadn't bought one of those DNA kits!"

"I know," Genny commiserated, "but it's kinda sweet, and kinda sad, all at the same time. He never had children of his own. Who's he going to leave all that land to? He's getting on in years, and it's only natural to start thinking of the importance of family, and the connections he never made. Time's running out for him."

"But he's hired me to track down all those leads, and my time is running out, too! I hoped to finish this up before the wedding, but with him adding new relatives every thirty minutes, I may never catch up!"

Genny wagged her eyebrows, grinning mischievously. "Someone in his family was very prolific, weren't they?"

Glancing at her phone, Madison sighed. A new message popped up, with another possible family connection.

"More than you know," she sighed.

3

After leaving *New Beginnings*, Madison drove out to Nigel Barrett's place. The older gentleman lived only a few miles from the deCordova Ranch, in an old house near the Brazos River.

The house reminded Madison of the one they had toured yesterday as part of the living-history farm at Washington-on-the-Brazos State Historical Site. The centerpiece of Barrington Farm was the carefully restored home of Anson Jones, the last president of the Republic of Texas. The typical 1800s dogtrot style of the old home amused the kids. Blake had joked about hoping the Wi-Fi worked on both sides of the house, and Bethani had grimaced at the thought of having no Wi-Fi, at all. Brash explained the purpose of the wide, covered space, perfect for additional living space and air circulation, but he lost all three teens when he spoke of life without electricity.

Like the Jones' home, a wide 'dog trot' divided Nigel Barrett's house neatly in half. But unlike the historic two-story Jones home, his was a single story, painted barn red instead of white, and had been upgraded with electricity and plumbing. Window units, two satellite dishes, and numerous wires and electrical poles spoiled the authenticity effect, even though Madison was certain it was built well before the turn of the twentieth century.

Looking at the ramshackle house, one would never know the old man had two producing oil wells on his property.

Oddly enough, Madison mused as she took the steps up to the porch, both the Barrett home and the Jones home sat along the winding Brazos River, separated by several miles and a county line.

There were two doors on each side of the house, all four opening into the dogtrot. Madison knocked on the first one on the right. "Mr. Barrett? Are you home?"

Across the wide space, a door opened behind her. "Over here, Ms. Reynolds," the older man said. "That's the night side of the house. This side is for day living."

She supposed that translated to bedrooms on the right, living room on the left. As she stepped through the door he held for her, Madison was a bit apprehensive about the home's interior. To her surprise, the inside was fully modernized and quite comfortable looking. Even though the style was dated—the wood paneling had a 70s feel, and the sofa was a throwback from her childhood—a flat-screen television took center stage in a very modern-day entertainment center.

With a voice command, Nigel Barrett turned off the television.

"Nice," Madison commended him with a smile.

"If you think that's something, you should see my TV room. It's on the night side of the house. Surround-sound speakers and three flat-screen televisions, all voice controlled. This one is just for day viewing."

Not sure how to respond, Madison went with, "Oh. Well, that's convenient, I guess."

"Not really," the old man grunted. "How would you like having to go outside, every time you wanted to go from your bedroom to your living room? Or to your kitchen? Ended up having to put in a kitchenette on the night side of the house, in case I get a hankering for a midnight snack. It's like having two houses, one on either side."

"It's a wonder you didn't build a new house, one that had all the conveniences in one spot." *Or*, she thought to herself, *closed in the dogtrot.*

He gave her a disgusted look. "Now, why would I go and do something like that, when this house is still solid? That would be a waste of good money, and good lumber. No, ma'am, this house was good enough for my grandpappy, and it's good enough for me. I see no need to move, not after all these years."

"You're happy here, and that's all that counts." Eager to change the subject, Madison motioned to the couch. "Do you mind if I have a seat?"

"Nah, let's go to the kitchen. That's where my computer is."

He led her across the room and through another door. The kitchen was a strange mix of old and new. A shiny stainless-steel refrigerator stood next to an ancient gas-powered cast-iron stove. The fancy brushed stainless faucet cost ten times as much as the aluminum sink beneath it. Madison knew. She had the same faucet at her house, compliments of HOME-TV.

From the looks of his home, it appeared that Nigel Barrett never replaced anything until it was worn out or broken. At least he had no qualms about buying quality replacements.

His kitchen table was long and cluttered. Madison suspected he ate his meals at the far end, the only spot not littered with papers, notebooks, and such. A laptop took residence on the opposite end of the table, with an ergonomic chair and a flowered cushion.

"This is where I do my work. Here are the notes I wanted to show you."

"How long have you been working on your family tree?"

"Just a few months. But I found the old family Bible, if that helps. It has the birth records in it." He pointed to the thick, leather-covered tome. "You can take that with you."

"Are you sure? I wouldn't want anything to happen to it while it was in my possession."

"Unless you plan on coloring the papers or ripping them out, I reckon you can't do it too much damage."

"Of course not. I'll take good care of it, and bring it back as soon as I'm finished," she promised.

He motioned to one of the chairs. "Take a load off. You can tell me what you found out about my niece and great nephew."

"Nothing!" Madison cried in surprise. "You just sent me the information this afternoon. I haven't had a chance to look them up and confirm the relationship yet, Mr. Barrett."

"But you looked up the first names I gave you, right?" He gave her a sharp look.

"Yes, sir, but you do realize these aren't guaranteed matches, don't you? Just because you share DNA doesn't mean they are close relatives. They can be cousins, many times removed."

"Still, check them out and get back with me as soon as possible." He practically barked the words.

"I'll do my best."

"That's what I'm counting on, young lady. You came highly recommended, or else I wouldn't have hired you. But I figured being Bertha and Joe's granddaughter, you must be okay."

Madison murmured the right responses, thanking him for the opportunity, but silently she wondered if the man could get any more cantankerous. She didn't remember him being so crotchety when she was younger.

"I'd like to ask you a few more questions for clarification purposes." She pulled out her notebook and pen. "Please tell me your parents' names and dates of birth."

"It's all there in the Bible," he said.

"Okay. And your siblings?"

"That's all there, too."

Madison stared down at her empty page. So far, he hadn't given her a single tidbit. "What can you tell me about your siblings? Where are they now?"

"Most of them are in the family plot up on that hill yonder. Three of them died during the blizzard of '34."

"We had a blizzard? I didn't know it ever snowed that hard here."

"Not a snow blizzard," he corrected. "A dirt blizzard. I was just a babe, but they tell me it was a mighty storm. A bone-dry summer, and then a strong wind came out of the west. The fields were fresh plowed for fall crops, and that wind came in and flattened it like it was West Texas. The winds blew so hard, and stirred up so much dirt, there were dirt drifts four feet tall. The twins were buried alive, and one of my sisters couldn't breathe, the air was so thick with dust. My granny went blind, and so did their best mule."

Madison stared at him in horror. If he didn't have such a set look on his face, she would think he was joking. "I've never heard of such. That's horrible!"

"Another brother went off to war and never came home. That just left Eli and Earl, and little Betty Jean."

Madison did a quick tally in her head. "You mother had eight children?"

"No, nine. Who'd I forget?" He scrunched his face and thought about it. "Oh, right. The baby girl."

"Baby girl?"

"That's all the stone says. Baby girl."

"Your poor parents," Madison murmured. "They had more than their share of tragedy."

"Times were hard back then. We didn't have fancy doctors and fancy medicines. I never saw a doctor until I enlisted in the Army," he boasted.

"That's amazing. Now, about your three living siblings."

"They ain't living no more. Eli choked to death before he

could sign up to serve. Like me, he never married. Earl left home when he was fifteen and went to work for the railroad. Died a few years back. It's all in the Bible, too."

"And your sister?"

"Ran off with a traveling salesman. Never saw or heard from her again, but Mama recorded the marriage in the Bible, just the same."

"So of nine children, you were the only one to remain here?"

"That's right. Born and raised on this land. And I plan to die on it, too," he said stubbornly.

"So any collateral relatives you have would be from Earl or Betty Jean, is that correct?"

"Depends on what a collateral relative is."

"A direct relative would be your ancestors or descendants, such as children or grandchildren. A collateral relative would be an aunt or uncle, niece or nephew, etc."

"Yep, then I reckon they would come from Earl or Betty Jean."

"Do you want to expand the search to include first cousins? Your parents' siblings and their descendants?"

"Not necessary. Both were an only child."

Madison bit back her initial response. It was on the tip of her tongue to say she was sorry. Her heart went out to him, knowing he had no family of which to speak. Coming from a huge family herself, Madison couldn't imagine being alone. Half the community was a Cessna or a Hamilton, much to her son's consternation. When they moved here last year, he had quickly discovered that all the prettiest girls in school were related to him, in one way or another.

That was one of the things that made planning their wedding so difficult. The guest list was huge, with her family alone. Add the deCordovas and the McCormicks, and the list seemed endless. The thought of a small, intimate ceremony appealed to her more every moment.

Pulling her thoughts back on track, Madison asked

several more questions, but found Mr. Barrett wasn't much help.

"I made a profile on that MyFam.com site and started my family tree. You can look at it online."

"Is there anything else you can think to tell me? Something that may help me find your relatives?"

"Can't think of anything."

After a few more dead-end questions, Madison gathered her notebook and the old family Bible, surprised at how heavy it was. Promising to be in touch as soon as she knew anything, she bade him goodbye and got into her car. As she drove away, she saw Nigel Barrett cross the breezeway to enter the night side of the house.

Apparently, the man was ready to settle in for the evening, and it wasn't even six o'clock yet.

4

Collette Erickson shut the door and slumped against it. Her purse slipped from her fingertips and hit the floor, scattering its contents at her feet.

She was home now. It didn't matter that her coin purse rolled beneath the coffee table or that a crumpled *Long John Silver's* bag spilled out around her. It didn't matter that her clothes were wrinkled or that her mascara left muddy streaks down both her cheeks. It didn't matter that yesterday seemed like a bad dream, or that she had spent her first night as a widow in a cheap motel, waiting for daylight to come so she could claim her husband's body from the morgue.

She was safe now, tucked away in the doublewide trailer house where she and Bobby Ray had lived for the past seven years. At least here, there were no pitying glances from his fellow reenactors. No empty promises of support. No questions from state troopers. No curious stares from the onlooking crowd, and no empty echo of the hospital's lower corridors. No forms to fill out.

Best of all, here in her own home, there was no need to pretend.

The shock Collette felt was real. But the grief had been for *their* benefit. Faced with her husband's untimely death, it was how the public expected her to act, but it wasn't how she felt.

She felt free.

After nine years of marriage, Collette felt as if she could finally breathe. Whatever love and happiness she imagined with Bobby Ray had evaporated long ago, stifled by his boorish ways and his unnatural obsession with history. During the first blush of new love, they talked of traveling the world. Bobby Ray promised to take her to Paris for their first anniversary, and like a fool, she thought he meant France. Little did she know he meant Paris, Texas. His idea of a romantic weekend was a paltry picnic beneath the town's own version of the Eiffel Tower, followed by a tour of historic homes in the area. It proved to be only one of many disappointments in their life together.

As the blush faded, the pallor set in. That was how she often thought of their marriage. Weak and pale. During the first few years, she hadn't thought of herself as *un*happy, so much as indifferent. She had been complacent, content to rock along with the steady drone of a ho-hum life. While she finished college and launched a career in the medical field, Bobby Ray worked in a tire factory and played dress-up soldier with his friends.

In truth, as long as Bobby Ray kept his collection out of sight and didn't expect her to share his enthusiasm, she could tolerate his obsession. He insisted on buying a four-bedroom trailer so that two of the rooms could be dedicated to his endless assortment of period costumes, ancient weaponry, and so-called 'historical treasures.' In turn, Collette claimed the largest bedroom, the one with the walk-in closet and the sunken garden tub, for herself. Sometime between their fourth anniversary and the increasing number of weekends he spent on the road doing reenactments, Bobby Ray moved into the spare bedroom, and the slow descent of their marriage continued.

Collette wasn't sure when it happened, but over the past few years, the pallor slowly darkened. The colorless shell of their relationship—the one that started with the healthy blush of hope and promise before it completely bleached out—turned murky and dim, morphing into a dark, ruddy red. The color of anger.

She had been angry with him for so long now. Angry with him for spending all his time and money on his hobby, instead of on her. Angry with him for leaving her home alone, while he traveled; perhaps not abroad as they had once dreamed, but away from the mundane sameness that had become their life. Angry with him for having something he loved and truly enjoyed, when she had felt stifled in her chosen career. And now she was angry with him for dying too soon. She was finally free, but that, too, made her angry.

Collette peeled her limp body off the door and stooped to collect the scattered mess at her feet. Her mind was already racing through the things she had to do. Call her boss and take the rest of the week off. Contact the funeral home and confirm cremation. Find an appraiser to look at Bobby Ray's collection, and hope it was at least half as valuable as he always claimed.

Her cell phone rang, helping her locate the half-hidden device beneath Bobby Ray's recliner. That was something else to add to the list: buy new living room furniture. This western leather had never been her style.

Seeing Marjorie's name flash across the screen, Collette answered. For once, her co-worker's mindless chatter would be a welcome diversion from the madness twirling round in her head. Knowing the other woman's affinity for gab, Collette would be lucky to get a word in edgewise, and her friend would never notice.

"Hey, girl, how's it going? Did you have a good weekend? Ours was awesome!" Without waiting for an answer, her co-worker launched into a one-sided conversation.

"We took the kids to the Texas Independence Day celebration at Washington-on-the-Brazos. Wasn't Bobby Ray there this weekend? Dressed like they are in those get-ups, it's hard to tell who's who. I waved at one guy in the infantry, thinking it was Bobby Ray, but I'm not sure it was. He never waved back. We saw the first couple of musket and cannon demonstrations, but we missed the final one of the day. I hear there was some sort of commotion over there, but I'm sure it was nothing compared to where we were.

"We were in line for cake, and you'll never *believe* who we saw there! You remember that show that came on last year, *Home Again?* The one where the woman inherited that huge old house from her grandmother and had it remodeled by that hunky carpenter? People in town called it the Big House, and that was *before* they added that third turret! Can you even imagine having a three-story house like that, with all those bedrooms and bathrooms? Just think of how much toilet paper so many bathrooms would require!

"Well, anyway, the kids from the show were there. You know, those adorable blond twins that drew in all the teenage viewers? Bethani, the girl who wanted to go back to Dallas at first, before she made the cheerleading squad and became besties with the policeman's daughter, and her brother Blake, who's just about the cutest boy you've ever seen, and who's into all sorts of sports and the drama club and hunting and fishing? You should have seen him yesterday, telling jokes and leading a huge long conga line over to the cake. The other girl was there, too. The policeman's daughter with the long, auburn hair and the cute glasses. Now Lauralee wants to get the same kind of frames. We've got an appointment this Friday to see the ophthalmologist, so I'll have to leave work early. I told her they won't look the same on her, not with her round features and her light coloring, but she wants to be like the pretty girl on TV, so what's a mom to do? I'll take her to get the same glasses, of course. At least she gave up the notion of contacts."

While Marjorie rattled on about teenagers and their whims, Collette digested the first part of the conversation. She had been too stunned yesterday to make the connection, but she knew she had recognized the teenagers and their mother. It hadn't dawned on her, until now, that the sympathetic Madison was the same woman she had watched on her favorite television makeover show last summer.

Collette spoke for the first time since saying hello, interrupting her friend to ask, "Weren't they from The Sisters?"

Having long since moved on in the conversation, the question confused Marjorie. "The eye doctor's parents? No, they were from down somewhere near the coast. Oh, wait. You mean the kids from the show. Yes, yes. Juliet and Naomi, better known as The Sisters. That's not too far from Washington-on-the-Brazos, you know. We were going to drive through there on the way home, but Troy needed to get back in time to mow the grass. Barely March, and already our lawn needs cutting! Speaking of grass, I wonder if Blake cuts their lawn, or if Madison hires it done? Or maybe that good-looking policeman does it for her. Everyone yesterday was talking about their upcoming wedding and wanting to know if the reception was open to the public. Can you imagine if it was? I'd love to go, wouldn't you?"

Marjorie imagined scenarios where the public might be chosen on a lottery-type system, or by contest participation. As soon as they hung up, she would get online and see if the radio station was sponsoring a contest for special invitation seats to the big event. She'd let Collette know what she found out and tell her tomorrow at work.

"I won't be there tomorrow," Collette broke in again. She added an abrupt, "I have to go now."

"You're okay, aren't you? Come to think of it, you do sound a little tired. Good thing this is your day off, and you can get some rest. Okay, talk to you later. I'll let you know about the contest. Bye."

Conversations with Marjorie were always like that. They required little effort on the listener's part, other than an occasional murmur of agreement. Some hint of an audience was all the woman needed for mindless minutes of endless chatter.

But today, her inane babble had served a purpose. At least for a few moments, Collette had forgotten reality.

Angry with him or not, Bobby Ray had died too soon.

5

Texting the twins to let them know where she was, Madison stopped by her grandmother's house before heading home. Bertha Cessna, known affectionately by the community as Granny Bert, had just returned from one of her water aerobics classes.

Seeing her grandmother in her sagging swimsuit, Madison recalled a similar scene from about a year ago. With the swimming pool where they normally met out of order, the geriatric class convened at Granny Bert's for a 'dry run,' and the twins had the misfortune of witnessing it.

"They came in their exercise clothes, Mom. Their *swimming suits!*" her son had wailed. "The things we saw. I may be scarred for life."

"I didn't know it was possible to have so many wrinkles." Bethani's voice had been a blend of horror and awe.

"And believe me, Mrs. Shanks should not be wearing a two-piece swimsuit!"

A year later, and Madison still laughed at her children's descriptions of the day. In a way, that scene had prompted her to move out of her grandmother's rambling craftsman-style home and accept the gift of the Big House.

Technically, of course, she had purchased the stately old mansion left to her grandmother by the town's founder, Juliet Randolph Blakeley. Madison paid the token sum of five thousand dollars for the three-story Victorian, payable in one-hundred-dollar increments, to make the sale legitimate, but they both knew the house was a gift.

There had been times, Madison dared admit, she thought the house to be more of a curse. It was in dire need of updating and repairs, but the renovations would cost a small fortune. She barely had a penny to her name. Desperation drove her to accept the deal with HOME-TV, allowing them to film the makeover and turn her private life into a public spectacle. At first glance, Granny Bert's conning to get the renovations done free seemed another magnanimous gift, but the downside was that Madison had to sacrifice more of her privacy. Life, as Granny Bert always said, comes with stipulations, and some of the stipulations had been steep. The curse continued when a skeleton was discovered in the basement of the old mansion, and when someone tried to scare her away from continuing the remodel. Not to mention times like yesterday, when random people recognized her and thought her life was still for public consumption.

In the end, however, the house proved a blessing. Fully restored and more beautiful than she ever dared imagine, it was a permanent home for her and her children. The twins would go away to college before long, but the house would always be there for them to come home to. No one could take this home away from them, unlike the house in Dallas. The one Gray had mortgaged to the hilt and then reneged on. The one Madison was forced to sell at a loss and leave behind when she came running back home to live with her then eighty-year-old grandmother. This, she knew, was their forever home, and very soon, she would share it with Brash and his daughter Megan.

Shaking the memories of Blake's exaggerated rendition from her head, Madison helped herself to a glass of sweet tea while her grandmother changed into dry clothes. She was thumbing through a magazine when Granny Bert came out, wearing black slacks and a button-up shirt. Glancing down at the similar outfit she was wearing, Madison reminded herself to go clothes shopping. A vibrant forty-year-old bride-to-be shouldn't dress like her grandmother.

"What brings you out today? You don't usually visit on Mondays," Granny Bert noted bluntly.

Madison couldn't help but frown. "Am I that predictable?"

"More predictable than a strong dose of Castor oil," her grandmother nodded. "With that, it's not a matter of *if*, but of *when*. But not you, Maddy girl. I can set my clock by you."

"You make that sound like a bad thing." Madison was more than a little miffed.

"Not bad. Dependable."

"Yeah, well, having people depend on you all the time isn't all it's cracked up to be. They expect entirely too much from you, because they know that somehow—even though you don't have the time, and you don't have enough information, and you don't want to hurt anyone's feelings—you'll come through for them in the end. Because, one way or another," her voice rose in exasperation, "you couldn't dare let someone down."

Her grandmother eyed her with shrewd observation. "That came out of nowhere," Granny Bert said, noting how the agitated younger woman squirmed in her seat. "You want to tell me what's going on in that head of yours?"

Madison avoided looking her in the eyes. "I don't know what you're talking about."

"That won't work with me, missy. I raised you. I know when you're upset, and you, girl, are upset."

"Maybe a little."

The older woman harrumphed. "Try again."

It burst from her, coming out in no particular order. "It's

just that the wedding is getting out of hand. Even Annette is pressuring me to invite all these people from Dallas. For a woman who was so against my marriage to her son, my former mother-in-law is suddenly all excited about my marriage to Brash. I don't know how—well, actually, I do, because it's just the way he is—but Brash has managed to charm that woman and has her twisted around his little finger. She has all these ideas about fancy cakes and proper dinner settings and things that neither one of us care about. All we want to do is get married. But if we have the wedding we *really* want, we'll let so many people down. You, and Mrs. de, and Annette, and Laura, and the list goes on and on!"

Her grandmother sat back and leveled her gaze upon her. "Whose wedding is this?" she boomed.

"Mine and Brash's, of course."

"So have the wedding you and Brash want. Don't worry about the rest of us. We've all had our own weddings. We don't need to be meddling in yours."

"I wouldn't call it meddling." Madison squirmed in her seat again. "Exactly."

"Do you want proper dinner settings?"

"No. We want a buffet. Maybe even a barbecue. Or a crawfish boil."

"Then tell Annette no. Do you want five miles of tulle and those little sparkling lights everywhere?"

"The lights might be nice, but I'm not a fan of tulle."

"Then tell Lydia no. She's the mother of the groom, not the wedding designer. Same for Laura. She's his sister, not the coordinator. Do you want Dolly Mac Crowder at the wedding?"

"Well, no, not really. But she's your friend..."

"Ha!" Granny Bert cackled. "That woman and I haven't been friends since 1950. We're what you call friendly adversaries. The only reason I wanted to invite her is to rub her face in the fact you're marrying the most eligible, sought-after bachelor in town. With Cutter married, Brash is the only decent catch left, and the last hope for her horse-faced granddaughter Hillary. That woman has been after Brash deCordova since he set foot back in this town!"

"Granny, you can't talk about people that way. She's not horse-faced, she's..." Madison searched for a better description for the long-faced, homely woman. None came to mind. With a slight giggle, she admitted, "Okay, so she's horse-faced. But you can't say that out loud."

"We're all thinking it. Someone hollers 'hey,' and that woman comes at a gallop!"

"Granny, you're incorrigible!"

"I hear she buys her shoes at Tractor Supply, in the farrier department."

"*Granny!*"

"I can go on all day. Or you can tell me to take Horse Face's grandmother off the guest list."

In a small voice, Madison said, "Take Horse Face's grandmother off the guest list."

"Done." She nodded smartly but held up a bony finger for one concession. "But don't ask me to take Jolene Kopetsky off the list. Sticker will be back in town in time to be my date, and I want to parade him in front of Jolene. Would you believe that hussy had the gall to call him while he was out in Wyoming?"

Madison let out a long-suffering sigh. "Granny, would you just marry the man already? You can't expect him to keep waiting on you his entire life—"

"Waiting! That man has *waited* on me with six wives!" her grandmother huffed.

"Only because you were happily married to Grandpa Joe. But it's been nine years, Granny. It's okay to marry someone else."

"I kept my marriage vows for fifty-three years," she boasted stubbornly, "and I'm not about to break them now, especially for the likes of Sticker Pierce!"

"Then let the man go and let him see who he pleases!" Madison cried in exasperation. "You can't keep stringing him along like this."

"It's worked all these years," she pointed out with a sniff. "Why change things now?"

Madison threw her hands up. "You're impossible!"

"And you were telling me what else is bothering you. This is about more than the wedding."

Her grandmother did, in fact, know her too well. Madison made designs in the condensation on her tea glass. She got as far as "Nigel Barrett h—" when her grandmother interrupted.

"You said it all, with just the name. That man has become downright ornery in his old age."

She didn't point out that the two of them were roughly the same age. "He hired me to do some research for him," she said instead, "but he's not making it easy. I don't remember him being so hard to get along with, back when we were in high school. We used to sneak out to his pasture and have—" she stopped in the middle of her sentence, unsure of whether or not to go on. Even though it had been over twenty years ago, she was clearly incriminating herself.

Granny Bert laughed. "I know all about your pasture parties, girl. There wasn't much that got past your grandfather and me. You forget, we raised four boys, your father among them. You were a breeze to raise, compared to my Charlie."

"Mr. Barrett had to know it was us. We made a point to pick up our... trash, but—"

"Beer cans," her grandmother corrected.

"—but I know we must have left ruts. We even built bonfires out there. I'm surprised he didn't make us leave."

"Your grandfather always made sure the fire was out after y'all left. More than once, he plowed over your ruts, too."

Mouth agape, Madison stared at the older woman. "You mean to tell me... We thought we were so cool, and so smart, sneaking out like that. You knew all along?"

"A dozen trucks bouncing across a field in the dark? All that hootin' and hollerin', and the loud music? Everyone knew! Andy deCordova's place backs up to Barrett's. He'd call your grandpa and tell him how the field looked, and between the two of them, they took care of it."

"You're telling me that my grandfather and Brash's father knew a bunch of underaged kids were out drinking in a pasture, and they just let us? And they cleaned up after us?"

"It kept you off the roads and out of mischief. Gave you a sense of freedom, even though we all knew where you were and what you were up to." She tapped the table with her bony fingers. "Remember that, when your kids pull the same stunt."

"But—" she was still sputtering, trying to comprehend this revelation from the past.

"Focus, girl. We were talking about Nigel Barrett. And you're right; he's gotten more cantankerous through the years. It may be because he's been forced to sell off pieces of his land, bit by bit, to pay the taxes. Made him a bit spiteful."

"But he has two oil wells on his place. Why can't he pay his taxes?"

"Those wells haven't always been there, you know. About fifteen years ago, he had to sell a couple of hundred acres. A few years later, he sold even more."

"Who to?"

Granny Bert gave her a sharp look. "You don't know?"

"No. That's why I asked you."

"You may want to ask your bridegroom that question."

"*Brash* bought Mr. Barrett's land?" she squeaked in surprise.

"It butts up to his family's property." Her grandmother studied her again. "You really didn't know?"

"We really haven't gotten around to discussing finances and assets yet," Madison admitted. "Of course, my side of the conversation won't take long."

"Barrett sold a tract on the west side of his place, too, to an outsider. Then they struck oil, and he never had to worry about money again. I hear he has a TV room that would put even your fancy media room to shame."

"He told me about it. It sounds like that room alone is worth more than the rest of his house."

"'Course, he was smart and kept full mineral rights to the land. With all this talk of new oil and gas activity in the area, he stands to make another fortune."

"There's talk of new activity?" she asked in surprise. The local economy always enjoyed a boon when oil and gas production was up.

"A landman came out last week to talk to me about leasing your grandpa's farm. I turned over the day-to-day operations to your Uncle Joe Bert years ago, but I still control executive and royalty rights on the minerals. The first company made a fair offer, but I have a meeting with another one next week. I'm holding out for top dollar."

"Remind me. What's it mean to keep full mineral rights on your land?"

"It means you make money on the minerals when you lease it for oil or gas exploration, no matter who owns the surface. Smart move on Nigel's part." She thumped the table again. "So what did he hire you for?"

Long ago, Madison learned that Granny Bert had no respect for client confidentiality. Not only did she eventually worm the information out of her, but the older woman was an invaluable source of information and insight into the workings of the local community.

"He bought one of those home DNA kits and is set on tracking down whatever family he may have left. Every time he gets a hit, or even just an inkling that someone may be related to him, he sends me their names and expects immediate results."

"I reckon he feels there's not a lot of time to squander.

Besides fighting old Father Time, I hear he went to see his VA doctor a few weeks ago."

"How did you hear that?"

"Oh, the usual way. Somebody told somebody else, and that somebody told me. You know what they say around town. *If Bertha Cessna don't know it, it ain't worth knowing.*" She punctuated the claim with a proud smirk and another thump of her fingers.

"So, did he get a bad report or something? Is that why he has a sudden interest in finding his next of kin?"

"My sources couldn't say for sure, but that would be my guess."

"Your 'sources' wouldn't happen to know where I could find his niece, would they?"

"Would that be Earl's daughter, or Betty Jean's?"

"Earl's, I suppose. He lost track of Betty Jean."

"He may have, but that doesn't mean the rest of us did," Granny Bert snorted. "That poor girl was just trying to better herself. Her parents did nothing but use her as an indentured servant. She saw a chance to get out, and she took it."

"Where did she end up?"

"Up the Brazos River, around Waco. Betty Jean's gone now, but her daughter still lives in the area."

Madison perked up. "That's great! Do you have a name?"

"I'd have to make a couple of phone calls, but I could get it for you."

"That would be perfect."

"Earl settled not far from there, around Crawford, I seem to recall. I always think of him when they mention George W's ranch."

"Even more helpful."

"So, now that you're feeling perkier, tell me about the dead body you found yesterday."

"How did you... oh, never mind." Would she never

become accustomed to her grandmother's uncanny knack for knowing *everything?* "And for the record, I didn't find it. It sort of found me. Me, and about seventy-five other spectators, gathered to watch the demonstration. The man just dropped dead, right there in front of us."

"Leave it to you, girl. Leave it to you."

6

As she watched her fiancé jog deftly up the steps to the Big House, Madison's heart ached with fullness. How could something as small as her heart hold all the love she had for this man?

It wasn't just that Brash deCordova was so undeniably handsome. His intense brown eyes and chiseled features turned heads the moment he strode into a room. The few strands of silver weaving through his dark-russet hair only enhanced his good looks, lending him a noble, dignified air.

It wasn't just that he was incredibly virile. He was six feet, one inch of solid male. Two hundred and twenty some-odd pounds of muscle and brawn, conditioned as an athlete and a lawman. Long legs and long, sensual fingers. He had only to run his hand along her arm, and she was lost.

It wasn't even that he was so downright *sexy*. His rich, deep voice and bedroom eyes were the stuff of fantasies. Brash had turned kissing into an art form. And he had a way of smiling at her, of trailing his eyes slowly along her body without physically touching her, that left her shaken to the core.

It was none of those things, and yet it was all of them.

Most of all, Brash deCordova was a *good* man. A good, honest, hard-working man who gave generously of himself and who made it his life's mission to help others. He was a dedicated officer of the law, he worked with several charities including his own football camp for underprivileged youth, and he was always the first to help in an emergency. He was an excellent father to his sixteen-year-old daughter and had already developed a special bond with Blake. He had even won Bethani over, who had been a devoted daddy's girl, reluctant to join the Brash deCordova fan club. Not only that, but Brash had a strong sense of right and wrong, and he rarely wavered in his convictions. He was dependable and trustworthy, and loyal to a fault.

There were times, like now, when her feelings for this man frightened her. Except for her children, Madison had never known such all-consuming love before. As a teenager, she had been infatuated with the boy. She was impressed with his good looks and charm, dazzled by his prowess on the football field and his leadership abilities. When she came back to The Sisters last year, it hadn't taken long to become impressed with the man. She found herself turning to him for support, appreciating the way he handled even difficult situations in a calm and rational manner. He quickly became her rock. Madison considered herself a strong and independent woman, but she often felt like an impostor; somehow, she had become dependent upon this man. Not for her happiness or for her sense of worth; no man had that power over her. But she was dependent upon him to be whole. He was the other half to the jigsaw puzzle of her life, the final piece that made her complete. He was, in every sense of the word, her soul mate.

"Hey there, gorgeous," he said as he approached, in that sexy voice reserved just for her. It was decadent and warm, and set off a host of inappropriate thoughts for the situation at hand.

The situation was that she waited for him on the porch

swing, in clear view of anyone passing by on the street. The situation was that the twins were home, holed up inside. The situation was that they had agreed to wait until their wedding night to consummate their relationship. Some called it old fashioned, but they called it setting an example for their impressionable teenagers.

"Hey there, yourself." She smiled, patting the seat beside her.

He leaned down for a kiss, and then slid in beside her, his knee popping as he did so. "What are you doing out here on the porch swing?" he asked. "What thoughts are going through that beautiful and intelligent head of yours?"

"I was hoping we could take a ride."

"Anywhere in particular?"

"I could use a session of your patented river therapy."

His smile was indulgent. "Anything for you, sweetheart."

"Let me tell the kids."

She stepped inside to use the intercom, informing the kids of their plans. After locking the door and setting the alarm behind her, she walked hand in hand with Brash to his pickup truck. They made small talk as they drove out to his family's ranch and took a winding dirt road through cotton fields and hay meadows, past grazing cattle and pumping oil rigs, to reach "their spot" on the river. Madison wondered if she'd ever get used to the momentary panic of backing up as close as possible to the riverbank, but she put her trust in Brash. He always braked in time, just as they crested the edge of the steep riverbanks and had an excellent view of the water below.

They got out and lowered the tailgate, so they could spread a blanket and sit comfortably upon the cold, hard metal. They sat in silence for a long moment, his arms around her, and her listening to the strong and steady thump of his heart. The sun was setting just beyond the trees, allowing the coolness of evening to slip in behind it. On the air rode the sweet scent of fresh grasses and newly budding leaves.

It was springtime, the time of new life and new growth. The perfect time to start a new life with this man beside her.

"I know you're waiting on me to say something," she finally said.

If he was impatient, he didn't let it show. "Whenever you're ready."

She turned to look at the fields, just now beginning to show a bit of color. "The wildflowers will be out soon," she predicted.

"Another couple of weeks, and they should be in full force."

"Even the bluebonnets should be popping up by then."

"Probably," he agreed.

"Spring time is so beautiful in Texas. Especially here at the ranch."

"I've always thought so."

After another lull in conversation, Brash gently nudged her. "Pick out a log, Maddy, and lay your troubles on it," he murmured into her ear.

They had been here many times over the course of the year. When troubles loomed, or when life began to weigh them down, they came out to engage in Brash's self-devised 'river therapy.' The idea was to spot a limb or some other debris floating below in the Brazos River, and to imagine putting your worries upon it. Whatever it was that troubled you, you visually piled it onto the logs below, and watched as the current of the river carried it away. As corny as it sounded, for Madison, it was a foolproof method.

"See that little limb over there?"

"The one passing the curve?"

"That's the one. I'm putting Dolly Mac Crowder on it."

"I think you need a bigger limb," he said, trying hard to keep the amusement from his voice. Dolly Mac was a large woman.

"Don't laugh at me," she warned in a sharp voice.

"Never."

"Good, because I just tossed her horse-faced granddaughter up there with her. I don't want either one of them at the wedding."

"O-kay," he said slowly, clearly wondering what they had done to cause such ire.

"And the log coming up right behind it? Annette's fancy-smancy plate settings are sitting smackdab in the middle of that one."

Together, they watched as the logs carried both problems downriver and, eventually, out of sight.

The next log was a bit harder to load. "And that one? The one twisting and turning its way downstream? Your mother's tulle is on it. And that huge stack of bridal magazines Laura brought over for me to look through. Gone."

They watched it until it disappeared around the bend. "Anything else?" he asked.

"Find me a big one."

"How about that one?"

"That'll do. I'm piling it full of the whole big mess that's become our wedding. Seriously, Brash, this thing has gotten completely out of hand."

She heard his sharp intake of breath. Felt his arms stiffen around her. "What are you saying?" he asked sharply. "Are you calling off the wedding?"

"No! No, never that!" she assured him, tightly squeezing his arms to her. "Well," she amended, "maybe the wedding itself, but not the marriage."

"Call me dense, but I don't think I understand."

"When you first asked me to marry you, we talked about what kind of wedding we wanted. We both said small and simple. But then everyone started adding their opinions. And they offered to help, which was fantastic, but before I even knew it, it had somehow mushroomed into something I didn't even recognize."

"So, what are you saying?"

"I'm saying I don't like all that frilly tulle. And I don't like fancy sit-down dinners, and I don't like other women coming onto you, even if they do buy their shoes at Tractor Supply."

"Huh?" He was clearly confused.

Maddy brushed her fingers through her hair. "Granny Bert," she said by way of explanation. "My point is, yesterday, Genny said something that's really gotten me thinking. She said that it was our wedding, and it should be the way we want it."

"I absolutely agree."

"Do you *want* a big wedding?"

His answer was simple. "I want to marry you. I don't care if it's in a church, a tree house, or down at the JP's office."

"What if it was here, at our spot?"

"Like we originally talked about."

"Exactly. Before everyone else took control of our day and spun it into something neither one of us actually wants."

"I just want you, Maddy." His voice warmed her, from the heart out.

"And I want to be your wife. Period."

"So, no fancy wedding?"

She shrugged. "See for yourself. It's about to make the bend, right about... now." She shook her head in feigned resignation. "Too late now. The fancy wedding is already gone."

"Now, see? That wasn't so hard, was it?"

"Your method always works," she agreed. "But I know our families will be disappointed, so I propose a compromise. Like Genny said, we could let Granny Bert and your mom throw the party *they* want, and you and I can have the wedding *we* want."

"Private wedding, public party?"

"It would work, don't you think?"

"I think it's brilliant, just like my bride to be." He

dropped a kiss onto the top of her head.

"Are you sure?" Experiencing a moment of doubt—she was always the dependable one, after all, and couldn't bear to let people down—she said, "I'm talking really small. Our three children and our parents. Assuming, of course, that mine are back from Uganda by then. Granny Bert, your grandparents, and Genny and Cutter. Your sister Laura and maybe, *maybe*, your other siblings, and Shannon and Matt. I know it will hurt Annette's feelings—"

"Hey, if my ex-wife can be there, why not your former mother-in-law?"

"Because Shannon is Megan's mother and Matt is your best friend."

"And Annette is Blake and Bethani's grandmother. And don't forget, she's taking all three kids skiing during our honeymoon."

"Okay, okay. Annette and Charles can come. But that's it."

"I insist on having the preacher present. I don't want you getting away on a technicality."

"Definitely the preacher. We're talking twenty, twenty-five people, tops. Think we can get away with it?"

"I don't know why not."

Madison took a deep breath and let it out on a satisfied sigh. "It's settled then," she said with a smart nod. "We're having a wildflower wedding."

Brash burrowed his face into her neck. "Two weeks and four days, Maddy," he murmured. "I'm marking them down, one cold shower at a time." There was just enough emotion in his voice, just enough tremor, to make his words ring with truth.

She didn't dare turn around in his arms. It would be too easy to push him back against the truck bed and have her way with him. Too tempting. Breathing heavily, she contemplated it for a moment longer, before swallowing hard and quickly changing the subject.

"So. Yesterday, Granny Bert told me something I did not know."

"Yeah?" It was a struggle for both of them, getting their desire under control.

"I was telling her about my new job with Nigel Barrett. Do you remember how a bunch of us kids used to go out to his pasture and have those parties?"

"Sure do."

"Did you know that your father, and my grandfather, and apparently half the town, *knew* about those?"

She felt him shrug. "It doesn't really surprise me. I usually know when the kids nowadays have their parties a couple of miles downstream. I pretend I don't know, but I always make sure the grass is mowed, so they don't have to worry about snakes, or the fire getting out."

She punched him in the arm. "You men are so sneaky!" she accused.

"It keeps the kids safe, and off the streets."

"She also told me something else. She said several years ago, *you* bought some of Mr. Barrett's land."

"That's right. I needed to invest my money from the NFL, and I can't think of a better investment than land. They're not making any more of it, you know."

"So, not all of the deCordova land is actually part of the ranch? Some of it is yours?"

"Only about two hundred acres," he shrugged. "Not a lot, in comparison to the rest."

"I had no idea," she murmured. "Where is your land?"

"You're sitting on it."

"This is yours?" she squealed, turning now to look at him. "Our spot is actually on your land? We're getting married on your land?" Her voice rose in excitement. "That's even better!"

"Not my land, Maddy. *Our* land. Our spot, our land. Everything I have is yours now." He sealed his promise with a deep kiss.

"I just want you," she insisted against his lips.
"You have me."

7

Lydia deCordova took the news of a wildflower wedding with grace and understanding. She wanted whatever the happy couple wanted, she insisted. She was merely thrilled to be getting Madison as a daughter-in-law and seeing her son so happy. She couldn't quite hide her pleasure, however, when Madison gave her full reign on the reception. According to Madison, she was leaving that to Lydia, Granny Bert, and, if they didn't mind too terribly, Annette. The only stipulation was no fancy sit-down dinner.

With that detail out of the way, Madison felt much lighter. She dropped by the police station to share the good news with Brash.

"He's in his office," Vina Jones said, without appearing to look up. It only went to prove what Madison had long suspected: the woman had eyes like a fly, seeing everything at once. The older woman of indeterminable age ran the department with impeccable efficiency and the iron rule of a military sergeant. One look from her withering gaze, and even hardened criminals fell in line.

For the longest time, the older woman had intimidated Madison, until she realized it was all a front. Away from the

50

office, Vina was a sweet and doting grandmother; her grandson Jamal was Blake's best friend. In a weak moment now and then, that same matronly attitude spilled over at work.

"To what do I owe this pleasure?" Brash asked, breaking out in a smile when he saw Madison slip into his office.

"I have good news. Your mom wasn't upset about the change in plans. She took it like a champ."

Brash chuckled but wasn't surprised. "She's married to a rancher and raised four kids. She's used to going with the flow."

"We were even able to change the invitations. Instead of inviting people to the wedding, we're now inviting them to the reception. I hope you don't mind, but there will be a slight time lag between the wedding at two, and the reception at six."

When he ran his slow, sexy gaze over the length of her body, she knew exactly what he was thinking. Her breathing quickened as he visually peeled away her clothing, one piece at a time. "That may be enough time," he drawled. "Or, we may be late to the reception."

Caught up in his fantasy, Madison murmured, "What reception?"

They stared at each other across the breadth of his desk, until Brash abruptly sat, muttering to himself, "Two weeks, three days."

"Should I go?" she offered.

"Too late. Besides, I wanted to talk to you about something."

"What's that?" She seated herself in one of the visitor chairs. After that sensual undressing with his eyes, she covertly checked for loose buttons.

"I've been in contact with the park rangers and the DPS, concerning Bobby Ray Erickson's death. They're ruling it natural causes and aren't requesting an autopsy."

"Did you share your concerns with them?"

"Yes, but you know the drill. The widow is refusing to grant a voluntary autopsy. Without her consent, and without probable cause, and with budgets being what they are, they can't formally request further investigation."

"You say formally?"

"Captain Petty suggested that if I wanted to ask some questions—unofficially, of course—he wouldn't stand in my way."

"So now what?"

He was slow in answering. "I hate to ask this. I know you're busy."

"Yes, I am," she agreed. "Mr. Barrett and two teenagers see to that. But it just so happens the time I allotted for wedding planning just freed up. Oh, except for next Tuesday. Derron is taking me shopping. What do you want me to do?"

Blue eyes gleaming, he let his naughty gaze trail over her again, but he kept the moment light. "That, my love, is a loaded question."

"Let me rephrase that. How can I help you with the case?"

He leaned back in his chair, the leather seeming to share his sigh. The answering pop could have come from his knee or from the tension springs. "I thought you might reach out to the widow. Her name was Collette, right?"

"Yes."

"You two seemed to have a connection. I thought that maybe you could check in with her, see how she's doing. Ask a few subtle questions. Get a feel for the situation, now that the initial shock has worn off."

"What am I looking for?"

"I'm not sure. There was something off Sunday, but I couldn't quite put my finger on it. According to the reports, he recently aced a health-screening test. Two weeks later, he supposedly drops dead of a heart attack. I'm not saying it doesn't happen, but something about this just didn't feel right. I'm hoping you might pick up on it. Unless, of course," he added, "it upsets you."

"What do you mean? Why would it upset me?"

"I thought it might bring back bad memories of when Gray died."

Tears misted her eyes. "Thank you for that. And yes, it did. I sensed that her marriage was as troubled as mine. I'm fine now, really I am. But I love you for worrying about my feelings."

"I always worry about you, sweetheart, and how you're feeling. We're a team. It's what we do."

"I guess I should go call her. I should have a few minutes, between Mr. Barrett's texts." She rolled her eyes to express her aggravation.

"That bad, huh?"

"It makes me wonder if he really did get bad news at the doctor. He's overly zealous about finding any living relatives that are out there."

"Whenever I need a local background check, I talk to your grandmother."

"One step ahead of you, big guy."

"Then use my backup plan. My mother."

"You know, that may not be a bad idea. She and Mr. Barrett are neighbors, of a sort." Madison twisted her mouth in thought. "Too bad you didn't mention that thirty minutes ago, *before* I left her house."

"You know she'd love to see you again. And with the wedding in less than three weeks, I'm sure she'll be checking in with you daily." An amused smile hovered on his mouth. "Just to see how much more tulle to order, that sort of thing."

"Funny." She wrinkled her nose at him. "I may have mentioned today—repeatedly—how I'm not a fan of frou-frou. I repeatedly used the words 'clean, straight lines.' I'm hoping she got the hint."

When Madison's phone buzzed, she glanced down at it

and frowned.

"Mr. Barrett?" he guessed.

"Actually, no. Believe it or not, it's Collette. She wants to meet for lunch tomorrow."

Brash flashed her a charming smile. "And just like that, another obstacle floats away."

8

Small towns had a special knack for making the best of consolidating spaces and resources, particularly when those resources came in the form of paying customers/clients/patients. Naomi and Juliet were no different.

The Sisters Clinic, for instance, was a multi-functional building that served many purposes. The Tuesday/Thursday Clinic was open two days a week to service the medical needs of the community. Mondays and Fridays were reserved for chiropractic needs, while on Wednesdays, the semi-retired Doc Menger, DDS occupied the space. The townspeople felt fortunate to have their own local dentist, if only for one day a week. Getting in to see the doctor was sometimes difficult, but it beat driving to Riverton or to the bigger city of Bryan/College Station.

On this Wednesday, Blake had a dental appointment after a close encounter with a baseball bat left his tooth chipped. The doctor would squeeze them in, but warned they would probably have to wait.

With most of the seats already taken, Madison and her son settled upon a stingily padded bench for the long haul.

"Looks like this could take a while," the teen remarked.

"At least he could see us today, and we didn't have to wait until next week."

"Yeah, I don't think I could work him into my schedule next week." Blake made it sound as if the dentist were making an appointment with him, not the other way around. "Way too busy. Baseball games on Tuesday and Friday, practice Monday and Thursday, Debate Team Wednesday, FFA Banquet on Thursday, track meet on Saturday." The teen consulted an invisible calendar just above his head. "Did I forget anything?"

"A little thing called school?" his mother suggested.

His shrug was nonchalant. "Eh. I'll squeeze it in if I have time."

"How's your project coming along for Mr. Perez's class?"

"Slow. You'd think he'd cut me some slack, seeing as we're related, but he's a stickler about nepotism. He almost failed Teryl last semester, and she's his own daughter!"

"In a small town like this, if he made an exception for everyone who was related to him, he'd never give a failing grade."

"Apparently, blood isn't thicker than ink," the teenager complained. "Looking at my last paper, I thought he had a cut on his finger. There was red ink slashed all over that sucker."

Madison arched a haughty brow. "Maybe if you spent more time studying, and less time on sports..."

"Nah, I doubt that would help." He quickly discounted the suggestion. "Is he on the guest list, though? Maybe I could soften him up with a big plate of barbecue."

"He's on the guest list for the reception," Madison confirmed. "Not even my first cousins are invited to the ceremony, and Carter is at least my third."

"How is it he's kin?"

"His grandfather was Granny Bert's brother." She ran the branches of the family tree through her mind. "Uncle Clyde, whose daughter was Theresa, whose son was Carter. Yep, my third cousin."

"Is that the same as first cousin, twice removed?"

"I think so. I'm trying to brush up on my understanding of how all that works. I have a client who's looking for his family, so I'm trying to learn about ancestry and family bloodlines."

"He should do one of those DNA tests."

"He did. The trouble is, of eight hundred and something potential matches, very few share enough DNA to be the nieces and nephews he's looking for."

"Why doesn't he just check with his sisters and brothers?"

"He lost contact with them years ago. Besides, all of them have passed away by now. Of nine siblings, he's the only one still surviving."

"Sounds kind of sad," the teen reflected. "Not just to outlive your entire family, but to lose touch with them, too. As annoying as my twin sister can be at times, I can't imagine not ever talking to her again."

"I know, honey. It's very sad." She patted the teenager's leg, thankful that both her children had such a strong sense of family and community. It had been their idea to do the Cookie Campaign at Christmas, and they had helped create a new family tradition to embrace starting over here in The Sisters. Despite being teenagers with very hectic schedules, they never grumbled about spending time with their large extended families.

An abundance of good food, she suspected, might be part of the reason why her son seldom complained, but it didn't matter. He willingly spent time with family, and she was a firm believer in giving children roots.

Thoughts of family and roots brought Nigel Barrett to mind. As Blake's phone snagged his attention, Madison considered her next move on finding the elderly man's relatives. Like it or not, a visit to the River County

Courthouse was probably in order.

After making a few notes in her phone, Madison tucked the device away and looked toward the reception window with a hopeful expression. Blake's name still hadn't been called. The receptionist wasn't at her desk, so Madison picked up a nearby magazine with lukewarm interest.

Even if she had an inherent interest in mountain climbing—which she didn't—it would have been difficult to concentrate on reading, given the loud discussion taking place back and forth across the room. She and Blake sat in the middle of the room with their backs to the door. Across from her against the far wall, Harry Applegate carried on a conversation with an unknown man seated behind her, near the door. Instead of moving closer to one another and continuing to talk in private, the men simply raised their voices to be heard. Never mind that one woman was on the phone, and two other people watched the television in the corner.

"I hear HighTop is back to leasing in the area," Harry said.

"I heard mention of it, but no one's been out to see me yet," the other man replied.

"I thought your boy was a landman for them?"

"He was, but when the industry went bust a few years ago, he had to find something else. He works over in Navasota now, selling cars."

They talked about cars for a few moments, lamenting the high price of buying new and the uncertainty of buying used, before Harry went back to the previous topic. "I heard HighTop offered Nigel Barrett a good price for his mineral rights."

"Did he sign with them?"

"Not sure. Knowing ol' Nigel, he's holding out for more, even though the old coot has more money now than he could ever spend."

"Maybe he needs it for his medical bills. I hear he's been

going over to the VA Hospital in Waco lately, seeing some high-tech doctor."

"What seems to be the matter with him?"

"If you ask me, all that's wrong with him is he's old and lonely. Got nothing better to do than to sit around all day in front of his television. Maybe he figured he'd go to the doctor for some social interaction."

"At his age," Harry chuckled, "that's probably about all he has to look forward to."

"Mr. Applegate?" The dental assistant appeared in the doorway with a chart in her hand. "Doc Menger will see you now." Her gaze roamed the room before she caught Madison's eye. "You're next, ma'am."

Madison flashed a grateful sigh and went back to her magazine. At least the room was quiet enough now that she could concentrate on the words.

Yet, she found herself unable to focus on their meaning. It wasn't just that she had no idea what *aid-climbing* and *stemming* were. Her mind had stalled on Nigel Barrett, and why he might be seeing a doctor. Was he terminally ill, as Granny Bert had suggested? It was sad enough that the man had lived his life alone; to die alone seemed even more tragic. She made another note in her phone, this one about asking her client if she needed to be aware of anything concerning his health. She was hardly an estate planner, but she could certainly help the older man record and vocalize his last wishes.

She was aware of the door opening and the rustling of fabric, suggesting someone stepped inside. The unseen man from behind her greeted the newcomer, who volunteered that he was there to pick up his wife.

"Had to have a little dental work done, did she?" the first man said by way of making conversation.

Madison acknowledged that her nerves were worn thinner than usual. Normally, small talk in waiting rooms didn't bother her. There was the occasional obnoxious party who talked too loudly on his or her cell phone (putting those calls on speakerphone was a personal peeve of hers) but Madison was able to tune people out. Never mind that waiting rooms were prime fodder for juicy gossip—case in point, Nigel Barrett's health status and his recent visits to the VA doctors. Not that she cared, but she also now knew that Harry's wife was considering buying a Toyota Camry and that the man behind her preferred Ford vehicles. The fact she had retained such useless information in her already-frazzled brain irritated her even more.

But today, with her anxiety high and her To-Do list growing longer by the minute, the mindless chatter around her chafed. Though she normally paid it no attention, today the small talk grated on her nerves like hot coals against a rub board.

Yes, the man's wife is having dental work done. She's not here to have her tires rotated! It was all Madison could do to keep from turning around and snapping out the sharp reply. Contrary to what the man might believe, he wasn't that fascinating of a conversationalist, and the entire waiting room didn't want to hear his opinions. The least he could do was lower his voice.

She managed to bite her tongue and keep silent, and with the next overheard words, she was glad she had.

"Say," the first unseen man said, "I hear you're planning to run for chief of police."

Sitting up straighter in her seat, Madison kept her face averted as she leaned slightly back, now eager to hear what the two men were saying.

"Well," the newcomer said, his words a bit of a chuckle, "I wouldn't say I was *running*. It's an appointed position, not an election."

"But you *are* trying to unseat Brash deCordova." The first man pressed for clarification.

"I think it's about time, don't you?" The second man's voice was smooth and practiced. He sounded every bit the politician.

Beside her, Blake stiffened and pressed his leg against hers, but he, too, kept his face averted.

"deCordova has been on the job too long," the man continued. "At any rate, he was never a qualified candidate for the position. His background is in chasing a football, not chasing criminals. Look at all the shenanigans that have taken place in the last year or so! A gambling ring, illegal drugs cooked and peddled right in the middle of town, kids trying to burn the school to the ground, that Santa Claus thievery. We need someone who can take a firm stand against crime and drive it out of our community."

Madison couldn't see, but she imagined the man standing on his soapbox, shaking his fist for emphasis.

"But he solved every one of those cases you mentioned," the first speaker pointed out. "Seems to me he's doing a right fair job."

"The real question is, why should we settle for fair, when we deserve the best?"

"And you think that's you, I take it."

"Absolutely. I have an impeccable record. I was a cop for over twelve years in Pasadena. I worked for another five years in the Walker County Sheriff's office. I know how to handle hardened criminals and wannabe thugs. Without a doubt, I'm the best man for the job."

"You came here from Huntsville, did you? My grandsons lived there when they went to Sam Houston." He referenced the university named for the first president of the Republic of Texas. "When did you move?"

"Two years ago this month. And I hate to say it, but we've noticed how things have steadily gone downhill since we've been here. That first year, there weren't any television shows and cameras making a spectacle of our town. In my opinion, that's what half of the problem has been. The cameras revealed our weaknesses, like the lack of security in key places around town and the laid-back attitude of the police department. It's a wonder we aren't overrun with riffraff, trying to take advantage of our Barney Fife police force."

The woman who had previously been talking on her phone broke into their conversation. "It seems to me we have more of an Andy Taylor police force. Calm, rational, *firm* control. I think Chief deCordova is doing an excellent job."

If the woman noticed Madison sitting there, she never let on. Madison sent her a grateful look, just in case.

"That was fine in the 1960s," Mr. Politician said, "but we need to get with the times. There are people on both city councils, who happen to agree with me. I've expressed my concerns in recent meetings and found quite a bit of favorable response." Judging from his satisfied sniff, Madison imagined his nose stuck high in the air.

"Mom," Blake hissed through his teeth. "Say something!"

She shook her head, placing her hand on his knee in a gesture of restraint.

"With all the hoopla concerning his upcoming nuptials," the man continued, "I fear our chief isn't giving proper attention to the town. If I were chief of police, there wouldn't be *anything* more important than my job."

A well-dressed woman stepped from the inner office as he made his emphatic statement. Her face pulled downward in a grimace, but Madison wasn't sure if it was a result of the anesthesia or from overhearing her husband's claim. *Nothing like hearing you rate below his imaginary job.*

Madison didn't waste too much pity on the woman; she vaguely recognized her as one of Myrna Lewis's cronies. Myrna had long been a thorn in Madison's side, even though *In a Pinch* often filled in at *Lewis Insurance*. She couldn't ask for a nicer or more congenial client than Dean Lewis, but the same could hardly be said for his wife.

If this woman was a friend of Myrna's, it could only mean bad news for Brash. Myrna had a long-running complaint against the entire police force for not prosecuting anyone who dared walk near her beloved yard. She no doubt supplied Brash's would-be opposition with a litany of complaints and shortcomings against him.

Madison tried to remember the other woman's name. Sharon? Sharona? Sheila? It escaped her at the moment. Whatever her name, she didn't look pleased as she strutted across the waiting room. Her only words were in sign language. The graceful flip of her hand said it all. 'Get up, husband. We're leaving now.'

Just as the couple opened the door to leave, the dental assistant reappeared in the hallway. "Blake Reynolds? We'll see you and your mom now."

Heads held high, the two of them walked across the suddenly silent room and disappeared.

ଔଔଔଔ

As soon as they left the dentist office, Madison dialed Brash's number.

"Hello, my beautiful bride to be," his warm voice greeted her. "This is a pleasant surprise."

Her voice was cool and clipped. "Is there something you forgot to tell me?"

"Uhm, not that I'm aware of. But from the tone of your voice, I'm guessing I'm wrong. What did I forget?"

"You tell me!"

"Let's see. I told you about the bachelor party my brothers are throwing for me. An afternoon of fishing, followed by a rousing game of poker and maybe a few beers. My father, my grandfather, your son, and half the guys from church are going to be there, so I doubt they have anything too raunchy planned. I doubt that's what has your feathers all ruffled."

"I'm not a chicken, Brash," she said irritably. "And I'm not a delicate china doll who can't handle the truth. Why didn't you tell me about the last few city council meetings?"

"I had no idea you were interested in going to them, sweetheart. They post notices in the paper. I guess I just never thought to tell you when one was coming up."

"I'm not talking about attending the meetings, Brash. Although I will make a point to, from now on."

"Then what—" He broke off mid-sentence with a heavy sigh. "Is this about Misty? Because, honestly, I had nothing to do with it. I told them to leave me out of the entire process until they had found a qualified candidate as an officer. They had unanimously chosen her before I ever saw the application."

"No, I'm not talking about—Wait." Something in his voice sounded a bit too rehearsed. "Who's Misty?" she asked suspiciously.

"Misty Abraham."

"The blond bombshell you once dated?"

"I don't remember describing her that way."

"You didn't. You gave me the watered-down version. A female deputy from Navasota you dated a few times, before your schedules got in the way. You failed to mention her voluptuous figure and her big blue eyes. I had to discover them for myself, when I googled her."

"Sweetheart, the only figure I'm interested in is yours. I can hardly wait to—"

"Blake's in the car," she broke in hastily, "and I have you on speakerphone."

Did his chuckle hold a hint of embarrassment? She couldn't be certain as he smoothly changed his reply. "I've warned you about stalking people on social media, Maddy."

"Then she shouldn't set her profile to public. Especially since it still has photos of the two of you on it!" Her voice was an octave too high before she pulled in a deliberate breath. "And back up a minute. Did you say she applied for the job of police officer? *Here*?"

"Not only applied, but she's the number one candidate.

My approval is just a formality. Both city councils have made their decision and plan to offer her the job next week."

"And you're going to *approve* hiring her?"

"Why wouldn't I? She's an excellent police officer. I think she'll be an asset to the department."

"I just bet you do," Madison grumbled, half under her breath.

This time, amusement filled Brash's chuckle. "Blake, pat your mother's arm and tell her she has nothing to worry about."

Grinning, the boy did exactly as instructed.

"But wait a minute," Brash continued. "If you weren't talking about Misty, what were you talking about?"

"That's what I want to know! What's this about someone wanting to take your job? Didn't you think that was something you should share with me?" She was clearly annoyed. "Are we keeping secrets already? First Misty, now Mr. Politician."

"Given that you've already dubbed him with a nickname, I take it you've met Joel Werner."

"Not exactly." She gave him a brief recap of the overheard exchange. "Who is he and what's he up to?"

"He moved in here from the Houston area, via Huntsville, a couple of years ago. You know the type. Moved to a small town to get away from all the big city hullabaloo, then wants to drag all the rules and regulations with him. Thinks he knows everything because he served on a big police force."

"FYI, his wife is chummy with Myrna."

"Sounds about right," he snorted.

"Why didn't you tell me, Brash?" Her voice was softer now.

"There's nothing to tell. Someone's always taking an exception to something I do. Comes with the territory, sweetheart."

"But I hear he's been coming to the meetings and making

his complaints vocal. And that some of the members agree with him."

"Some probably do. That's beyond my control and has no bearing on the way I do my job. If they're not happy with my performance, they can replace me."

"You don't mean that!"

"If they want to replace me, babe, my opinion on the subject won't matter. But I don't think we have anything to worry about. There may be a couple of members who agree with him, but most think he's a pompous ass—semblyman. Assemblyman."

Blake laughed at the way Brash stumbled through the correction, belatedly remembering his presence in the car. "Nice save, Mr. de," the teen chuckled. "Real smooth, but I'm familiar with the terminology. And I wholeheartedly agree."

"I had to hold this one back," Madison told her fiancé. The pride in her voice was audible. "He wanted to jump to his feet and defend you."

Brash, too, was clearly pleased. "Thanks, buddy. But if you give them enough rope, guys like Joel Werner usually hang themselves."

"He also seems the type that would make a big deal of that very statement and claim you're a violent and dangerous man who advocates lynching," Blake remarked.

"Good point. I'll remember not to use that analogy in public."

Madison still wanted more details. "So, you're saying you're not worried about this man? And that I shouldn't be worried about Misty joining the force?"

"Darlin', all I'm worried about is getting through the next two weeks. Once we're married and officially a family, I can't imagine having another trouble in the world."

In answer, she quoted her son.

"Nice save, Mr. de."

9

"Thank you for meeting me." Collette Erickson's smile lacked any real pleasure as she extended her hand toward Madison.

"I'm so glad you called," Madison replied sincerely. She put extra warmth into her own handshake. "Let's take that corner booth. It should give us a bit of privacy." She motioned toward her favorite spot at *New Beginnings*, following behind Collette to the rear of the café.

Settling into the bench seat, Collette looked around with curious eyes. "This is the place from the show, isn't it?" She offered a sheepish expression. "I didn't realize who you were Sunday, until my friend pointed it out. Apparently, she saw your son holding reign over by the birthday cake."

Madison cringed. "About the kids. They meant no disrespect. I know you walked up on their little show, but—"

Collette interrupted with a flash of her palm. "No need to apologize. They did a wonderful job of distracting the audience and keeping the Lookie Lous busy. I appreciate their efforts."

"I'm so glad you understand. I worried we offended you."

"Not in the least," Collette assured her.

"And no need to apologize about not recognizing me. I can't tell you what a refreshing change that is."

"I was a huge fan of the show. If it hadn't been for... circumstances, I'm sure I would have made the connection."

"You did have a horrible shock," Madison agreed. Her tone softened as she asked, "How are you?"

Her answer was quick. "Still in shock. When my friend called to tell me about seeing your kids there, I couldn't bring myself to tell her about Bobby Ray. I just let her talk. She tells me you and the police chief are getting married?"

Madison recognized the change of topics for what it was—a sign of denial. For now, she would indulge the other woman and help distract her numbed mind.

"Yes." She held up her tastefully styled ring, unable to keep the smile from spreading over her face. "In two weeks."

"He was the one there, wasn't he?" Collette realized suddenly. "The hottie helping with... the body."

Madison was accustomed to women calling Brash hot, but it was the first time a new widow—four days new, to be exact—had referred to him as such. She resisted a frown as she nodded in agreement.

"Yes. I'm sorry. He tried to save him, but there was nothing he could do."

"I'm sure there wasn't. It was probably immediate."

"When will you get the results of the autopsy?" Madison knew there wasn't one scheduled, but it didn't hurt to put the suggestion out there.

Collette sat up straighter in her seat. "What autopsy?"

"You asked for one, didn't you?"

"Of course not. Why would I?"

A waitress came to bring menus and water. "Thanks, Louise," Madison murmured.

"I'll tell Miss Genny you're here. She's in the kitchen cooking and didn't see you come in."

"No rush. I'm visiting with my new friend."

The older woman smiled before moving away. "For a minute there, I thought you were doing business out of the booth again."

Seeing the concerned expression on her companion's face, Madison was quick to assure her, "Oh, nothing illegal. Before I had my own office, I often met clients here to take on new cases."

Still holding herself stiff, Collette asked warily, "What kind of new cases? Are you a social worker? Or some sort of private detective?"

Madison laughed away the notion, but a touch of irony lingered in her voice. "No, although I sometimes have trouble convincing my clients of that! They hire me for the strangest things, but in actuality, I have a temporary service. You probably heard it mentioned on the show. *In a Pinch.*"

"Oh, yes, right. Of course."

Madison steered the conversation back on course. "Do I understand that you *didn't* ask for an autopsy? You aren't curious to know what your husband died of?"

"Well, yes, but not enough to, you know... hack up his body."

Madison cringed at her crude way of expressing it. "I understand, of course," she murmured. "But I would think the uncertainty would be worse than the thought of—" She stumbled over the next part, concluding with a weak, "of conducting the autopsy."

"Why? Cutting him up won't change anything. He'll still be dead." Collette grabbed her menu and opened it, sticking her nose inside.

Reluctant to give up so easily, Madison pressed the issue, "Did he have a history of health issues?"

"He was overweight, if that's what you mean."

"Are the doctors thinking heart attack?"

Collette shrugged from behind the menu. "Your guess is as good as mine."

"But an autopsy would eliminate the guessing and put

your mind at ease," Madison pointed out gently.

Collette lowered her menu to glare across the table. "What are you, some sort of ambulance chaser? My husband is dead. Knowing what killed him won't bring him back."

Madison was duly chastised. "You're right. I apologize. I didn't mean to upset you. Please forgive me."

The distraught widow pushed out an uneven breath. "Did *you* ask for an autopsy when your husband died?"

"No," she admitted. "But Gray died in a car accident. The cause of death was rather obvious."

"Maybe, maybe not. Maybe he had a heart attack before he crashed. Maybe he had a stroke, or an aneurysm, or a spider bite. Something else could have caused the wreck, even if the crash was what killed him. Same thing with Bobby Ray," she continued stubbornly. "He could have died of a heart attack, or an aneurysm, or some sort of rare gastric disease that cut off his blood supply. It doesn't matter, because either way, he's dead." She stuck her face back into the menu. "Is the tilapia good here?"

Madison knew when to let a subject die. "Yes, it's excellent. Genny makes a special sauce to go over it with fresh dill."

"She really does the cooking? I thought that was faked for the show."

"Don't let her hear you say that!" Madison laughed, trying to lighten the mood. "She insists on preparing as much of the menu as possible. Most are her own recipes, tweaked to perfection and to a level only she can achieve."

After Louise returned to take their orders and to deliver a plate of assorted appetizers, compliments of the chef, Madison spread her napkin across her lap and leaned in to initiate a conversation. "Tell me more about yourself, Collette. What is it that you do?"

"I'm in medical sciences."

"Oh, really? Don't tell my kids, but science was always

my weakest subject." She wrinkled her nose in distaste.

"I thought I'd never get through with school," Collette admitted. "I specialize in genetic testing, particularly as it pertains to genealogical diseases."

"Wow, that sounds very... smart. And very involved."

"It can be," Collette agreed.

A new thought occurred to Madison. "Say. You may be able to answer a question I have about DNA testing."

"Maybe. What would you like to know?"

"For starters, how accurate are these do-it-yourself kits?"

"Actually, they're fairly accurate for what they test. Most use autosomal testing. Half of your autosomal DNA comes from your mother, half from your father, so a test can tell you that you're related to another person, but it doesn't necessarily detect which side of the family they come from. Some tests use Y-DNA, which is passed from father to son, and still others use mtDNA, to trace maternal lines. Mothers pass mtDNA to all their children, but only daughters pass it on to the next generation. So, it largely depends on what your goals are when determining how accurate the tests are."

"What if a person was looking for nieces and nephews? Next of kin, so to speak."

Collette pursed her lips and her eyes narrowed in thought. "It would help. But remember, most DNA testing is only as good as the shared data."

"Meaning?"

"A DNA test can reveal a trove of information on that particular person, but you must compare it to other people for a familial match. If other people aren't tested, or if there are no written records to trace their lineage and connect them to specific family lines, then you have nothing to base a relationship match on."

"So, you're saying it only works on other people who have done DNA tests?"

"That's not what I said."

"I guess I don't understand."

Collette tried to explain the science behind DNA testing, but soon lost her student.

"Give it to me in layman's terms. I don't speak science," Madison reminded her.

"You need to think of these tests as just one of many steps in genealogical research. They don't wave a red flag and say, 'Sally Smith is your sister!' They will tell you that you share a percentage of DNA with someone else in their system, and what they predict the relationship is... mother, sister, half-sister, etc. They tend to show degrees of separation—shared ancestors, if you will—rather than predict aunt or uncle, niece or nephew. Most matches are referenced as cousins. For an accurate confirmation, you need to contact the other person, if they're willing, or find written documentation to support the connection."

When Madison's forehead still crinkled, Collette continued, "It may be easier to explain how DNA can rule *out* someone being related. Let's say you and your sister both use the same company for testing. Your tests come back and reveal that you share no DNA, whatsoever. You are not biological sisters despite the way you were raised and what you were told. DNA doesn't lie."

Madison pulled in a deep breath and nodded. "Basically, you've confirmed what I already suspected. I guess I was hoping you knew a few shortcuts I wasn't aware of and could save me a few hours of research."

"Sorry. It doesn't work like that." Collette bit into a loaded nacho chip and spoke from behind her hand. "If you don't mind my asking, why are you searching for your nieces and nephews?"

"Oh, it's not for me. It's for a client. He's an older gentleman who never married, never had any children, and who was estranged from his only living siblings. Now he wants to find any family he may still have."

Collette's forehead knitted into a complexed pattern. "Why?"

"I'm not sure," Madison said. "Like I said, he's older. I guess he's feeling the pull of time."

"Is he rich?" Collette wanted to know.

Reminded of her commitment to confidentiality, Madison didn't answer directly. "Let's just say that if you judged him by his home, you would assume he was a pauper." She was relieved to see Louise returning with their meal. "Oh, look. Here comes our lunch."

After they bit into their food and both agreed their dish was delicious, Collette picked the conversation back up. "Have you found any of your client's relatives?"

"No definite matches so far. Anytime a name pops us, he assumes it's a niece or nephew. He calls a dozen times a day, giving me new leads and new suggestions. So far, none of them has panned out. That's why I hoped you knew a shortcut!"

"He's all alone, huh? No family?"

"I haven't had any luck, as of yet."

"I'm alone, too, you know." Collette made the announcement out of the blue. It was the first real thing she had revealed about herself.

Madison took encouragement from the admission. Maybe Collette was slowly coming out of denial. "You have no family?"

"Not really. I never knew my father, and my mother split as soon as I graduated from high school. Bobby Ray and his mom were the only family I had after that. His mom died a couple of months ago. And now Bobby Ray." A look of extreme sadness moved over her face, making her appear older. "I'm alone now. No family, whatsoever."

"I'm so sorry," Madison murmured. Again, with so many cousins, aunts, and uncles of her own, she couldn't imagine being alone in the world. "Is there anything I can do? Help you plan the funeral service, perhaps?"

"There won't be a funeral. Why bother, when there's no one to come?"

"Surely you and Bobby Ray have friends. Co-workers. People who would like to be with you in your time of need and pay their final respects to your husband."

"Why go to the expense and the bother, when cremation is so much simpler?"

"Are you certain you want to do that?" Madison asked softly.

Collette batted her big blue eyes. "Why wouldn't I?"

Madison knew she was pushing the issue, but if Collette had his body cremated, they would never know the full details of Bobby Ray's death. "Because if you should change your mind about the autopsy..."

To her surprise, Collette Erickson burst into tears.

10

"Madison! What a pleasant surprise!" Lydia deCordova hugged her future daughter-in-law before ushering her into the rambling ranch house. "Twice in one week, no less. To what do I owe the honor?" A wary expression crossed her face. "I haven't done something wrong with the wedding plans, have I? I promise. I cut back on the tulle."

"It's not about the tulle," Madison assured her. "Although I do appreciate it. I'm just not a tulle sort of girl." Not to mention there had been yards of it at her first wedding, much of it encrusted with twinkling rhinestones and dazzling glitter. She'd been too timid to stand up to Annette, but she felt comfortable enough with Brash's mother to be honest with her.

"Then we shall cut the tulle," Lydia assured her. "Would you like some coffee?"

"Sure."

They settled on the sun porch off the dining room, with cups of freshly brewed coffee and homemade peach cobbler.

"How are the plans coming for the revamped reception?"

Madison asked. "Any push-back from Annette, or any of the guests?"

Lydia's blue eyes twinkled. "I wouldn't tell you if there was. But, no, actually everyone seems to completely understand."

"How did Annette take the news of no sit-down dinner? I know I took the coward's way out, making you break the news to her." Madison had the grace to look ashamed.

"A brilliant play on your part, I must say. The new mother-in-law couldn't appear more understanding than the first. Annette had to agree, if only to save face."

"We just want a nice, relaxing evening with friends and family. Nothing fancy."

"With crawfish and barbecue, I don't think that will be an issue, dear."

Madison knew a moment of uncertainty. "Too redneck?" she worried.

"Only if you're inviting society's most elite to the wedding. Everyone else will think it's the best menu ever."

"Not that it's anywhere near high society, but you will never believe the call I got this morning. A radio station in Waco wants to know if they can offer a contest to win—mind you, *win!*—an invitation for two to our wedding! A listener called in and wanted to know if they were doing a promotion to offer 'tickets' to our wedding, since they do it for the Houston Livestock Show and Rodeo and all the major sports events. Can you believe the gall of some people?"

"And the radio station went along with it?" Lydia gasped.

"They thought it was a grand idea! They offered to send a live band for the dance if we allowed them to *sponsor* our nuptials! Can you believe it?" It still made Madison's blood boil, simply thinking about the ridiculous phone call.

"No, dear, I really can't." Lydia shook her head in amazement.

Stewing into her coffee, Madison finally cooled down enough to tell Brash's mother of adding another name to the guest list.

"No worries. We're ordering enough for an extra fifty people." Lydia reached for a notepad and asked, "Who's today's addition?"

"A new acquaintance, actually, but I just felt so sorry for her. Her name is Collette Erickson, and I've already invited her. She's the widow of the man who died at Washington-on-the-Brazos Sunday."

"Yes, you told me about that, but I didn't realize you had made such a connection with her."

"I didn't, really. She invited me to lunch yesterday, and she just seemed so... so pathetic. She has no family of her own, and even her mother-in-law recently died. I felt guilty being so happy and having so much to look forward to, when I know how bleak and miserable her own future must look. I was in the same position, not so very long ago. Before I quite knew what happened, the invitation just slipped out."

"You don't have to explain to me, sweetheart. It's your and Brash's wedding. You can invite anyone you like."

"In that case," she dared to say, wincing slightly in mock fear of pushing her luck, "I want to add one more."

Lydia smiled and picked up the pen again. "And that is?"

"Nigel Barrett."

"Our neighbor Nigel Barrett?"

"Well, he's all alone, too," Madison defended her decision. "And he's actually one of my clients right now."

Lydia wrote his name with a flourish. "Done. Anyone else?"

"Not at the moment. But I do have some questions for you."

"Yes, we mailed the invitations," she volunteered. "No, we didn't ask for RSVPs. It's too short of notice, and most everyone you're inviting is sure to come."

"That's good, but that's not what I wanted to ask. I wanted to ask what you thought about your neighbor Nigel."

"As a potential guest? Inviting him is up to you, dear."

"No, I wanted to know what you think about the man himself. He's a bit crankier than I remember him being when I was a teenager."

"You have to remember, he's aged, as well. Not everyone does so gracefully."

"Granny Bert said something about him going through a rough time financially a few years ago, before they struck oil on his place. She thought that might be the reason he's so grumpy now."

"It could be," Lydia agreed. "For years, Nigel refused to try anything new. He was determined to do everything old-school, just the way his pappy and his grandpappy had done it." She did a good imitation of his craggy old voice, making Madison smile. "Refusing to update your wardrobe and your carpet is one thing. But in farming and ranching, refusing to update equipment and fertilizers is something entirely different. He paid for his stubbornness with failed crops and a loss on his herd. He was forced to sell some of his land, just to pay taxes and his winter feed bill. I suppose that could make anyone bitter."

"What can you tell me about his family?"

"The poor man doesn't have any." Lydia clucked her tongue in an expression of empathy.

"I understand he may have some nieces and nephews in the McLennan County area?"

"Possibly. You have to understand, Nigel was brought up in different times. His folks were hard people. Hard workers, and honest to a fault, but they didn't believe in showing affection. If there was ever a family hit by hard times and hard luck, it was the Barretts. They had eight or nine children, but only half of those lived to see twenty. The ones that lived to adulthood couldn't wait to get away, except for Nigel. He was the only one to stay behind and take care of the farm. I'm not sure if he thought of the others as traitors, or if he resented them for leaving him behind, but he cut all ties with the two siblings he had left. They both married and started families of their own, so yes, I'm sure they have children and grandchildren, possibly even great-grandchildren, but Nigel never knew any of them."

"Do you know if Nigel got a bad report when he went to the doctor recently?"

"I don't know about recently, but before Christmas, he told me he was sick. He didn't elaborate, but I think it must be something serious. He normally doesn't go to the doctor but once or twice a year."

"Do you think it's something life-threatening?"

"The man is well into his eighties. A simple cold could become life-threatening," Mrs. deCordova pointed out. She arched her brow and gazed at the woman who would soon share the title. "Why all the questions? Surely, you don't screen all your guests this thoroughly!"

"Just trying to do a good job for Mr. Barrett. I thought if I understood him better, it might make my job easier."

"I knew his mother. I can't imagine the heartache she must have endured, but she never let it show. She kept it all stored inside, never missing a day of farm work, not even to bury her husband or her children, one by one. I remember her once saying that land was the one true thing you could count on. When all else failed you, you could depend on your land. I'm sure it was a hard pill for Nigel to swallow, being forced to part with some of that land. His mother drummed into his head that it was practically sacred."

"I only recently learned that Brash bought some of that land."

"Yes, it made perfect sense, since it butted up to our property. And I think it pleased Nigel, knowing it wouldn't be chopped into smaller parcels and sold off to a dozen different people."

"But Nigel sold some on the other side, too, I understand. What became of it? Do you know who bought it?"

"Of course. Tony Sanchez."

"Tony Sanchez, as in the man invited to our reception? The football legend?"

Lydia nodded as she explained, "He and Brash were good friends around that time. A few years after Brash bought his land, Nigel sold a hundred acres on the other side, and Tony bought it."

"Does he still have it?"

"Oh, yes. He and Nigel argue over the mineral rights on a regular basis." She said it with a weary sigh, as if it were an old and tired argument.

"What do you mean? I heard Nigel kept all the rights."

"He did, but there's a clause in the deed about what happens to the rights upon his death. Half will revert to the land owners—in this case, Brash and Tony—but the other half will go to Nigel's estate."

"But what happens to his estate if he has no heirs?" Madison wondered aloud.

"That's what the argument is about. Tony keeps pressuring Nigel to assign full mineral rights upon his death, or to sell them outright, so he can benefit from the money now. Nigel says he doesn't need the money, but Tony says if Nigel dies without an appointed heir, the state could wind up being the biggest winner. Even if someone comes forward and claims heirship rights after his death, the case could be tied up for years in court. It's a big mess."

"What does Brash say about it all?"

"He says he knew the terms when he bought the acreage, and that fifty percent of the mineral rights is better than none. He thinks Tony is being greedy and Nigel's being stubborn, and he's staying out of it."

"I always knew your son was a smart man," Madison grinned. "And speaking of smart men—or shall I say *sly* men—Granny Bert informs me that your husband and my grandfather are some of the sliest." She proceeded to rehash the pasture party tale, not at all surprised to learn that Lydia was in on the duplicity, as well.

"Sometimes, dear, you have to learn to go with the flow," the older woman said with a sage smile.

"I'll try to remember that," Madison promised. "You may have to remind me a time or two, but I'll do my best to heed your advice."

Brash's mother patted her hand. "Like they say, parenting isn't for the faint of heart. Or spirit."

 C&QC&Q

While she was in the area, Madison decided to drop by Nigel Barrett's house and touch base with the curmudgeon. It was almost five, so she tried the night side of the house. Sure enough, he opened the door at the far end on the right.

"Hello there, Ms. Reynolds. Wasn't expecting you today, 'specially so late in the evening. Might as well come on in, though. Excuse my stocking feet." He stood aside so she could enter his TV room.

The room was everything he claimed, and more. Three giant, flat-screen televisions wrapped two walls like a surround-sound theater, all blaring the same action movie. Speakers came out from every angle, promising ample capacity to wake the dead. A third wall boasted three additional monitors, lined up for maximum multi-viewing. In one glance, Madison saw a basketball game, a stock market report, and a cable news show.

When Nigel barked the word "Hush!" all screens went instantly silent.

"I need one of those for my kids. Does it work on teenagers?" Madison asked with a hopeful smile.

"Teenagers? Thought you weren't married yet." The scowl on his face spoke volumes.

"My first husband died almost a year and a half ago. We were blessed with twins."

"Sure moved on quick," Nigel grunted. Dressed in his customary blue jean overalls and his socks, he shuffled over to a row of three leather-bound theater chairs and plopped down in the middle seat. Behind him on the fourth wall, Madison saw the kitchenette he had complained about.

Uninterested in explaining herself to the grumpy old man, Madison had second thoughts about her visit there today, even when he told her to have a seat.

"I can't stay long. I came by to invite you to the wedding reception."

"Just the reception?"

"The ceremony is private, but we'd like our friends and family to help us celebrate that evening. Here's your official invitation." She handed him the ivory envelope.

"If I don't have a doctor's appointment, I'll try to come by."

"It's on a Saturday, so you should be good. We're having barbecue and crawfish and all the trimmings, so come hungry."

"I'm allergic to crawfish."

"There should still be plenty to choose from."

"I'll try," the old man said. "Do I need to bring a gift?"

Madison bit back a smile at his blatant gaffe. Subtlety was not his strong point. "Of course not, Mr. Barrett. Your presence there is gift enough."

"My presents? Now I have to bring more than one?"

"Your presence, as in attendance. You don't have to bring a thing. Just drop by and join us."

He abruptly changed the subject. "Have you found anything in that Bible I sent home with you?"

"I've started looking through it. I'm trying to sort out your family tree so we can do a cross-reference with some of the possible DNA matches." She hesitated a moment before asking, "Mr. Barrett, are we working with any time constraints?"

"What do you mean?" he demanded, but she noticed he

didn't quite meet her eyes.

"Are you in a particular hurry for the results?"

"Well, I don't want you dragging your feet, if that's what you mean! I'm eighty-six. Of course, there's a time constraint."

"I'll do what I can, as quickly as I can, but these things take time."

Before he could bark out a response—she could see it there in his face, all but bursting out—the telephone rang, and he jerked the receiver to his mouth. "Barrett here."

She heard a gruff male voice on the other end but couldn't make out the words.

"I told you I'd let you know when I decided, and not one minute before!"

Taking it as her cue to leave, Madison scooted toward the door. She waved over her shoulder as Nigel Barrett ground out another angry comeback to his caller. On her way out, she thought she heard the word 'deed,' leaving her to wonder if it was Tony Sanchez on the other end of the line. If so, she agreed with Lydia's assessment of their relationship.

Tony Sanchez and Nigel Barrett definitely had an old and tired argument going.

11

"That, dollface, looks gorgeous on you."

Madison stood in front of the mirror at a Woodlands department store, modeling the outfit Derron had selected for her. She would never have chosen the flared hem, but she had to admit, her assistant had great taste. The slight swish of fabric offered a hint of movement, softening the stiff lines of her tall, slender form. The rich, olive-green color went well with her skin tones but could have easily come off as dull, if not for the pearl necklace and ivory angora sweater he paired with it.

"Sleek and elegant, just like you." He turned to the saleswoman and said, "We'll take it."

Madison started to protest. "I didn't say—"

"Yes, you did." He turned so that Madison couldn't see him mouth the words a second time, but she saw him nodding vigorously to the other woman.

"Now trade those shoes for these, and the sweater for this jacket." He handed her a pair of black heels and a silky jacket with just a hint of that same olive green among its many colors. When she was done, he stood back and admired the results, clapping his hands together in delight. "And just like that, you have one dress, two completely different looks. Both stunning."

"I think you missed your calling," Madison told the man.

"You're saying I *shouldn't* be your part-time receptionist, part-time handyman, part-time public relations manager?"

"No, but maybe you should become my part-time stylist, too."

"I've been telling you that since we met, dollface. You're a beautiful, vibrant woman, but you dress like an old lady."

"I prefer to call my look classic," she sniffed, stepping back inside the dressing room.

"Try the peach-colored dress next," he called. "You really should wear more dresses, you know. I'd give anything to have legs as long and glamorous as yours."

With his artfully styled blond hair, lively blue eyes, and wide, charismatic smile, Derron Mullins was a handsome man, but he came in petite size. His head barely reached Madison's shoulder.

"The peach dress has *flowers* on it," Madison complained. "And some sort of gauzy layers. You know I don't like frou-frou."

"Put the dress on, dollface. You'll like it."

Two minutes later, she glared at the smug look on her assistant's face. He was an ungracious winner, loving it whenever he was right. So far today, he was three for three.

As Madison stepped back into the dressing room, Derron exchanged the outfits with new selections. "Try the pants on first, with all three blouses. Save the red blouse for last. It goes with the khaki capris, as well."

"You know I can't afford all of these outfits!"

"Just try the clothes on, Maddy. We'll work out the details later."

Later, they stood at the register with a huge haul. Three dresses, one pair of navy slacks, one pair of capris, three blouses, two pairs of shoes, and three sweater/jackets. Plus accessories.

"Will this be cash or charge?" the clerk asked.

They both answered at once.

"Charge," Derron said.

"I haven't decided which ones I'm keeping," Madison explained. "Can you give me a tentative total?"

"We'll take them all," her companion said.

Her voice was firm. "No, we won't." She turned to Derron and hissed, "I told you, I can't afford all these! I have to put back at least half of these."

Derron reached into his wallet and produced a black credit card. "Like I said, we'll take them all."

"Yes, sir!" the clerk said with a wide smile. She slipped the card from his fingers before Madison could make a grab for it.

"Derron, you can't do that!"

"Of course, I can. This is my wedding gift to you. Your trousseau, so to speak." He bent with an elaborate bow.

"I can't possibly allow you to do this. This is too much!" Madison sputtered in protest.

"Too much? Too much for one of my closest and dearest friends? Too much for my employer, the woman who gave me the opportunity to prove myself and my place in the community? Too much for the woman who allowed me to right some of my mother's many wrongs? Too much for my mentor? I say it's hardly enough, dollface!"

"You're going to make me cry," she accused.

When she dipped her head to wipe away an escaped tear, Derron motioned for the clerk to continue ringing up the purchase.

"You can't reject a gift, Maddy. And that's what this is. A gift from me, to you."

Her voice was a choked whisper. "It's too much."

"That's for me to decide, dollface." He batted his long lashes and flashed his trademark smile. "But if it makes you feel any better, you can treat me to lunch. Or to a

Chippendales show. Your choice."

His outrageous comment brought a smile, just as he had known it would. "I think we'd better stick to lunch. But I will let you choose the restaurant, to show you how much I truly appreciate your gift. How much I appreciate *you.*"

"Now you're going to make *me* cry!"

After a late lunch, they drove back to The Sisters, discussing the busy two weeks to come.

"Just eleven more days," Madison said with a dreamy smile. "I can't believe it's almost here."

"I can't believe we have so much to do during that time. Besides all the wedding stuff, we have to squeeze in jobs for Merle Bishop and Dean Lewis."

"You're taking the one for Bishop, right? I can handle filling in at the insurance office, since it's just one day. Did you finish typing the report for Murray Archer?" On occasion, *In a Pinch* did research and minor surveillance for a private detective based in Houston. Whenever he had a case that came near the Brazos Valley, he reached out to Madison for help. Not only did it come with a welcomed, if small, retainer fee, but if she ever decided to pursue her own investigator license, the experience would count toward her internship.

"I emailed it this morning," Derron confirmed. "How's the research coming along for Brash?"

"I think the official term is 'stalled.' I can't think of anything else to do. Brash ran financials and a criminal background check, but Bobby Ray Erickson came back squeaky clean. There's nothing in his past that hints at any reason to murder the man. I can't even imagine it as a retaliation killing. He never served on a jury, never sued anyone, never consorted with known criminals. From what I can see and from what Collette tells me, Bobby Ray spent all his time either at work or with his Texian Militia group, playing soldier from the days of the Republic. Hardly murder worthy."

"The widow?"

Madison sighed. "A little needy. I know I told her to call me whenever she needed to talk. Having been in her shoes, I meant it when I offered a sympathetic ear. I just didn't expect her to take me up on the offer. Every. Single. Day. I know she's lonesome, and I get it. But you'd think we were besties from way back."

"I'm sure it will taper off soon. Like you said, she's lonesome."

"Yes, but I don't think that's necessarily because her husband died."

Derron shot her a sharp look. "What's this you say?"

"Theirs wasn't a happy marriage. From what I can tell, they were more like roommates than husband and wife. She resented the fact he had a hobby he enjoyed, when all she does is work. I think calling me every day is more about wanting a friend than about needing emotional support."

"You'd think she'd find someone closer to her area. She lives like an hour and a half from us."

"I know, and yet she wants to come visit. We had lunch last week, she's coming for the reception, and now she's trying to talk me into giving her a tour of the house this weekend. I don't have time to be giving tours right now."

"Then tell her that."

"I did. But she can be very persuasive."

"No," Derron corrected, "you can be very easily suckered in."

Madison knew he was right, but she rolled her eyes anyway.

"Have you checked out his militia buddies?" Derron asked, his mind still in gear. "Maybe one of them had a grudge against him."

"I thought of that. So far, all I get is how upset the group is with Collette, for not giving Bobby Ray a proper funeral. They were looking forward to a ritualistic musket gun salute befitting a fallen comrade. Apparently, they go all out when one of their own dies."

"Hmm. I don't suppose someone would go to the trouble of committing murder, just so they could play with the big guns?" He made it a question.

"I should hope not."

"What about insurance policies?"

"He had a standard ten-thousand-dollar policy through his workplace and a token policy with the militia group. Nothing worth committing murder over."

"What do you remember about that day?"

"Besides the fact that a man died ten feet in front of me?"

"About him, before he died. Did you see him come on the parade field?"

"Yes, they marched toward us and took their positions just beyond the rope barrier. We were standing in the very front, so we had an unobstructed view. I remember noticing how red his face was. It looked swollen and blotchy, but I thought he was just hot from marching in those tight, itchy clothes. He was one of the few men wearing a uniform jacket, and it looked like it was made from wool. He did seem to be having trouble taking a deep breath, but again, I thought it was the clothes."

"Do you think he was having a heart attack?"

"Maybe, although Collette said he didn't have a history of such. And Brash still isn't convinced. He sensed something was wrong that day."

"That yummy fiancé of yours is usually spot-on with his instincts."

"I know. So either we're missing something, or it's one of those rare cases when Brash is wrong."

Derron thought over everything she had told him before asking, "So, where does that leave us?"

Madison hefted out a sigh. "Stalled."

12

It was Saturday morning, one week before her wedding, and Madison had a hundred things to do. Yet, here she was, working on finding Nigel Barrett's family.

The older gentleman had shared his login credentials to MyFam.com with her, making it easier for Madison to navigate the information provided there. With over eight hundred potential genetic matches, she was now attempting to sort through them and find the ones most likely to be his nieces and nephews, but the distinction was far from clear. Unfortunately, Collette was right; the matches referenced as 'cousins,' and most were distant. Of the handful that looked promising, most had ambiguous user names. 'Barb62', 'TXDancer', 'FlowerChild' and 'RR78' didn't offer much in the way of positive identification. The best she could do was send a request to connect and hope someone responded.

She typed Earl Barrett's name into several search engines. According to the online obituary, Nigel's only remaining brother died almost ten years ago, leaving behind two children and three grandchildren. His wife and a son had preceded him in death. It took another chunk of time to find leads on Earl's kids. Of the three most likely possibilities for James Earl, none looked promising—one was incarcerated in the Louisiana state penitentiary, one was a patient in the Veterans' Psychiatric Hospital, and one had passed away last year. Leads for Barbara Barrett vanished like a puff of smoke.

Finding Barbara's children was even more difficult.

Dialing Granny Bert's home number, Madison got the answering machine. Her grandmother answered her cell phone after several rings.

"Granny? What's all that noise? Where in the world are you?"

"For some fool notion, I let Sybil talk me into going to a garage sale this morning. Not that either one of us needs any more junk, but she's looking for a replacement to her canister set. I told her she should just buy a new one, but nothing doing; she's looking for avocado green."

"But what's that noise?"

"They're calling it music, but you couldn't prove it by me. It's some of that newfangled stuff. We're here at Hugh and Joyce Darby's house, and their grandson popped in for an unexpected visit and brought his band with him. Hugh thought it would be a good draw for the yard sale, so he talked them into doing an impromptu concert. They set up right in the carport, and now I can't hear myself think."

"Isn't his grandson Todd Darby? His band is actually sort of famous. *Cowboy Candyband.* The kids play their music all the time."

"That explains why they're here in the front row, screaming their heads off with the rest of the neighborhood."

"My kids are there?" Madison squeaked in surprise. She glanced around her office as if expecting to see them there, even though Bethani had spent the night with Megan and Blake had batting practice this morning.

She belatedly glanced at her phone, where she saw a message from Bethani.

Blake's swinging by to pick up Meg and me. Got a few stops before coming home. LYB.

"Plus about half their classmates, it appears," her grandmother confirmed.

"I guess that's why I can barely hear you."

"Nah, that's Sybil. She likes the music almost as much as the kids do."

"Maybe I should call you back."

"I've moved further away, so try again. What can I do for you?"

"Did you ever find a name for Nigel's niece?"

"Laura Jean."

"I thought that was her mother."

"No, her mother was Betty Jean, the one who ran off with a traveling salesman. They had the one daughter, Laura Jean."

"Last name?"

"I hear she's had a few. She was born a Thomas and married at least twice. Huddleston and Ruiz, but not necessarily in that order. Someone thought she married a third time, but I couldn't confirm it. The name may have been Winston."

"Well, that's a start."

"Oh, and one of the husbands was Eric."

"Thanks, Granny. At least that gives me something to work with. You said she lives around Waco, right?"

"The general area, anyway. One of my sources said she was connected to the Ruiz family who owns that big furniture store in Chilton."

"One of your sources, huh?" Madison couldn't help smiling, once again amused by the terminology.

"Poking around in people's lives can sometimes be a delicate thing," her grandmother reminded her. "If I want people to confide in me, they need to know I'll protect their identity."

"Is that like honor among thieves?" Madison teased. "But

in this case, honor among gossips?"

Granny Bert huffed out her indignation. "Do you want to know what else I found out, or not?"

"Sorry. Please go on."

"It so happens that Hugh Darby is a musician of sorts, himself. He likes to play the fife. Guess where he was playing on Texas Independence Day?"

Madison perked up, sitting up straight in her white leather chair. The decadent office piece had been compliments of *Home Again* sponsors. "Washington-on-the-Brazos?" She dared to hope.

"Yep. He was right there when that cannon fella dropped."

"Where do the Darbys live? I'd love to talk to him."

Granny Bert rattled off the directions. Just before hanging up, she issued a warning to her granddaughter. "Be prepared. Hugh is so tight he makes Scrooge look like Santa Claus. He'll expect you to buy something if you want any answers."

"As long as it's nothing avocado green, I think I can manage."

ଓଓଓଓଓ

Twenty minutes later, Madison had two paperback novels in her hand as she approached the man in the lawn chair. The band was taking a break, mingling with their fans and signing autographs, so it was no longer necessary to shout.

"How much are these?" she asked.

"Dollar each."

She bit back a protest. Most paperbacks went for half that at garage sales. But if he had any information on Bobby Ray Erickson's death, it would be well worth two dollars to hear.

As she dug in her purse for the bills, she broached the subject. "I understand your grandson gets his musical talents from you. I hear you play the fife."

"Sure do," the man said with a proud smile. "Taught the boy how to play his first instrument. Not many folks appreciate a finely tuned fife these days."

"And you play in a militia reenactment group? I probably saw you, if you were at the Independence Celebration a couple of weeks ago."

"I'm sure you did." The man peered at her a bit closer, his thin face wrinkling into a squint. "Say, you're the one marrying the chief of police. Ain't that coming up soon?"

"A week from today, as a matter of fact."

He nodded in remembrance. "I saw you there that day. Y'all tried to help Captain Erickson, but he was already gone when he hit the ground." He clicked his tongue in regret. "I thought for sure we'd have a proper burial for him. I already had a tune picked out that I could play on the fife. The sweetest, most haunting melody you ever heard. It would have been beautiful. 'Cept," he practically spat, his face contorting into an angry scowl, "his widow didn't give him a proper send off. And him a captain in the militia, and everything! It just ain't right, her disrespecting him that way!"

Madison recalled her conversation with Derron earlier in the week. They had assumed no one would stoop to murder merely for the opportunity to conduct an authentic militia-style burial service, but Hugh Darby's reaction had her wondering if they were wrong. He seemed genuinely irate.

"Did he act unusual that day? Did he seem distressed, or in pain?"

"Not that I recall. His wife came with him that day, which was unusual in itself. My Joyce goes to all my reenactments, but Captain Darby's wife is an odd duck. I remember he ate a quick bite with her before our last demonstration. It must've given him indigestion, because he seemed to have a little heartburn after that. Beat on his chest a time or two, and his face turned sort of red and puffy."

"Do you think he was having a heart attack?"

"It didn't strike me that way at the time, but ten minutes later, he was dead. So maybe so."

"Do you remember him ever complaining of chest pains? Even before that day?"

"Not that I recall. Seemed to be in good health, other than his allergies."

"He had allergies?"

"To just about everything, it seemed. Cats, dogs, horses, trees, grass. For a man who liked to be outdoors so much, he was mighty allergic to it."

"He was standing right beside the cannon when it went off. I'm surprised all that smoke didn't bother his allergies."

"Probably did, but that was his position. He's usually our Number 3 or Number 4 man. His job was to either load the cannon, or to cover the vent hole and prick the charge. Captain Erickson was a true professional, no matter his personal preferences."

"For a volunteer position," Madison pointed out.

"Being a professional can't always be measured by being paid," Hugh pointed out.

"What did you mean, Number 3 or 4?"

"We have a cannon crew of five men. Each one has a specific job, just like they did in 1836. 'Course, we don't use cannonballs, but we do use real gunpowder."

"Who prepares the charges for the cannons?"

"The gunner."

"I suppose the charges are prepared beforehand?"

"That's right. We prepare them the old-timey way, with black powder and canvas bags. We keep them in a special limber box so they won't be exposed to the elements or dampness. And so they won't explode, neither," he added with a grin.

"Always a plus," Madison murmured.

"Say, that'll be two dollars. Sure you don't want more books than just those?"

"I'll be lucky to find time to read these." As she handed

over the money, she asked, "If you don't mind me asking, isn't there a reenactment group you could join around here that was closer than Waco?"

"Sure, but I have buddies in that one. Royce Bazajou, Dom Ringer, and I go way back to our Army days at Ft. Hood. When they invited me to join their group, I jumped at the chance."

"Is there anything else you can think to tell me about that day? Did anyone have an argument with Bobby Ray, or hold a grudge against him?"

"Well, Petey Vansant wasn't too happy when Bobby Ray got promoted to captain. Sometimes he would make a snide remark about it, but I don't recall any arguments that day."

He said something else, but a deafening roll from the drums drowned out his words. Madison leaned in and asked him to repeat it, but when the steel guitar kicked in, she knew their conversation was over.

"Thank you for the help," she practically yelled.

"That ain't *The Help*," he yelled back, "but I think we got that book somewhere. It'll be two dollars, though, as they made a movie out of it, and it's one of my wife's favorites."

"No, thank you for the information."

"*Transformation?* Never heard of that title, but look through that box over yonder. It might be there."

Giving up, Madison simply waved and turned away.

13

As she pulled through the gated entry and into the driveway of the Big House, Madison saw an unfamiliar car parked along the curb. She was halfway to the front steps when she heard someone call her name.

To her surprise, Collette Erickson crawled from the waiting car and stood just on the other side of the foot gate, politely waiting for Madison to invite her forward.

"What a surprise. I wasn't expecting you today." With her To-Do list running through her head, Madison found it difficult to infuse any real warmth into her smile.

"I know we never finalized our plans, but I thought I'd take a chance and drive on down. I have nothing better to do today." Collette added just enough gloom in her voice to make Madison feel guilty.

"I'm afraid you've caught me at a very busy time."

Collette's eyes clouded, and for one terrible moment, Madison was afraid her uninvited guest might cry.

"But I suppose I have time for a glass of iced tea," she was quick to amend. "I hate that you drove all this way for nothing."

Derron was right, she acknowledged to herself. *I'm too easily suckered in.*

"It was a nice day for a drive." Collette shrugged. She was suddenly smiling as she followed Madison up the cobblestone path, her eyes taking in the splendor of the grounds and the stately old mansion. "This is just so lovely! My friend Marjorie will be so jealous when she finds out you invited me here."

Resisting the urge to point out the fact she *hadn't* invited her, Madison unlocked the door. "You'll have to excuse the mess. With the wedding just a week away, I still have so much to do."

While Madison had empathy for Collette's new status as a widow, she found herself growing short on patience. She readily acknowledged that much of the problem was timing. She simply had too much on her plate right now, without devoting excessive time and energy to a new acquaintance. She wasn't certain Collette even qualified as a friend just yet. She wondered if Collette Erickson weren't a bit like some relatives; visits on holidays and special occasions were nice, but anything more grew weary.

"Can I have the grand tour?" Collette asked, eagerly looking around the foyer with its stunning staircase.

"I'm sorry, Collette," Madison said firmly. "Now is not a good time. I'm working today, so that I can spend the rest of the week concentrating on the wedding. I barely have time for that tea I suggested."

Collette pouted prettily. "Not even a little peek?"

"You'll see the dining room and butler's pantry on the way to the kitchen," she relented.

"I can't wait to see the dining room mural! Is it really a Seymour Addison original?"

"That's what they tell me."

It took four times longer than normal to reach the kitchen at the back of the house. Collette stopped to snap pictures and exclaim over even the smallest features in each room. Madison quickly prepared glasses of iced tea and directed her back to the front parlor.

Normally, she and Genny would curl up in the breakfast nook just off the kitchen or take their refreshments through the back hallway into the family room. Even her office was more comfortable than the parlor, but this visit was less about comfort, and more about being polite.

No matter how poor the timing, no proper Southern hostess could turn away a guest without offering a quick refreshment and a cordial attempt at conversation. *And the woman has just lost her husband,* Madison reminded herself, not for the first time. She could afford to give her thirty minutes of compassion.

She led her back to the front parlor, the one they seldom used because of its stuffy formality. Unlike the cozy family room, or even the ladies' parlor tucked away at the foot of the stairs, the formal setting did little to encourage long, comfortable talks. For today's visit, however, the room was perfect.

"How's your search coming along for your client?" Collette asked. "Have you located his family?"

"I'm making strides," Madison conceded, settling onto the velvet sofa beside her guest. That was another reason she avoided this room. The pale blue, brushed-velvet pile was much too prone to stains and signs of everyday use. "No definite connections yet, but getting closer."

"My mother-in-law was interested in ancestry. She came from a small family, but she wanted to know more about her ancestors."

"Did she do a DNA test?"

"Yes. I tried to help her understand how it all worked, but I'm afraid we didn't get very far before she passed away."

"I've been using a combination of DNA results, online birth records, and a healthy dose of small-town nosiness," Madison admitted. "So far, it seems to be working, slowly but surely." She would like to be working on her newly acquired information now, but manners dictated she at least give her guest time to finish her tea.

"I'd be happy to help, if you like," Collette offered.

"Thank you, that's very generous of you. But I'm sure I'll muddle my way through."

"You do realize when it refers to someone as a second or third cousin, it could just as easily mean aunt or uncle, or niece or nephew."

"So I've realized." Madison hesitated, wondering if what she considered doing was a breach of confidentiality. Nigel, however, was searching for his family and posted on a public forum to find connections. Surely, it would do no harm to ask for Collette's help. Especially if she redacted his name from the papers.

"Actually," Madison admitted, "I could use your help on one particular area. Are you sure you don't mind?"

"I would be delighted."

"Wait here, and I'll get the papers."

"I can come with."

"No, you stay and enjoy your tea. I'll just be a jiffy."

She hurried to her office, where she quickly located the reports in question. She had printed them out earlier and took a moment now to make certain Nigel's name was not visible on them. Satisfied she was protecting his identity should he even care, she dashed back to the parlor. She found Collette busy taking selfies.

"Sorry," the woman said with an embarrassed smile. "I thought this might help me make up with Marjorie, after I kept Bobby Ray's death from her at first. She's a *huge* fan of your show."

Her smile a bit weak, Madison took a seat next to her guest again. "I thought you might be able to explain this to me. I'm not sure what all these percentages tell me, especially the identical and half-identical markers. Like on this person, for instance. The prediction is second cousin. Could that be a niece, you think?"

"Possibly. Let me take a look. Also, if you can look up the other person's profile and see her year of birth, it might give you a better idea."

The telephone rang as Madison handed over the papers. "If you'll excuse me, I'll grab that and give you a minute to look at these."

With no need for new health insurance, Madison wasn't on the phone for long. When she returned to the parlor, she found her guest with a stricken look upon her face.

"Collette?" she asked in concern. "Are you all right?"

"I—I—" At a complete loss for words, Collette shook her head. "I'm sorry, Madison, it was an accident."

"What was an accident?"

Belatedly, she noticed the soggy papers upon the table. The tea glass was empty and all but one of the printouts was destroyed.

"I'm such a klutz!" Collette wailed. "I don't know how I did it, but I managed to spill my drink all over your table and your papers. I don't think any got on the rug," she was quick to add.

"I'll get some paper towels." A quick trip into the butler's pantry, and she was back with a full roll.

"I'm so sorry," Collette apologized again.

"Don't worry about it. I can always print another copy of the papers, and the table doesn't appear to be harmed in any way."

"For what it's worth, I don't think those were very promising matches. Oddly enough, the only viable possibility was the one that didn't get destroyed." She pushed the single paper her way. "See these lines? That indicates a very strong familial match, more so than the others."

"Really? They all looked basically the same to me."

"Oh, no." She spouted off a mouthful of technical jargon, none of which made sense to Madison.

"You're saying this RR78 looks promising?"

"Extremely. I would say there's a strong possibility—at least 80% chance or more—that this person is a close relative of your client. Basically, you can forget those others and concentrate on this one."

"Okay. Thanks."

"Absolutely," Collette smiled, obviously pleased that she had helped.

"Oh. I didn't tell you where I was earlier."

"Where was that?"

"I was at Hugh Darby's house."

"Is that a name I should know?" Collette asked in puzzlement.

"You aren't familiar with it?"

"Should I be?"

Madison shrugged. "I thought you might. He's a musician with the same militia reenactment group your husband was a part of. He plays the fife."

"Oh. That's the flute thing that marches alongside the drum, huh?"

"Yes, I believe so."

"And he lives nearby?"

"Just outside of town."

Collette sniffed in derision. "Personally, I've never understood the appeal. A bunch of grown men, traipsing around the state playing soldier. They even sleep in tents and cook over an open fire. They like to be authentic, right down to their skimpy bedrolls."

Madison hid a smile behind her glass. "I have to agree. That part doesn't sound very fun."

"I always told Bobby Ray he was born in the wrong century. He enjoyed every minute of it."

"It's important to keep our traditions and legacies intact, though," Madison said. "He and his fellow enactors are doing us a service, keeping history alive."

"I suppose. But it's one thing to watch on special occasions. It's another to have to live with the props and the relics. Every. Single. Day." She rolled her eyes in exasperation. "I'll be glad when the appraisers finish, and I can clear out the bedrooms. That junk took up two whole rooms! Three, if you count all the stuff piled up in his bedroom!"

That one statement told Madison what she had already suspected—the couple had not shared a bed. At least it made that part of his death easier for the new widow. Collette was already accustomed to sleeping alone, just as Madison had been when Gray died.

Madison was still seeking information to support Brash's suspicions of murder. "I imagine some of his collection must be quite valuable," Madison remarked.

"If it's half as valuable as he always claimed, I should make a nice little profit off this whole ordeal." Collette looked so pleased, dollar signs all but floated in the air around her head. She never seemed to notice that 'this ordeal' was the death of her husband.

Generously overlooking the gaffe, Madison's inquisitive mind was busy. "Did other people know about his collection?"

"Yes." Collette rolled her eyes and hefted an exasperated sigh. "He was always bringing people over to the house and showing off his 'treasures.'" Air quotes suggested that was his definition, not hers.

Madison debated on how to proceed, but she ultimately decided to tell Collette what was on her mind. Previously, she had remained silent in deference to the woman's all-too-fresh grief. She knew everyone had their own grieving process and timeline for healing, but Collette seemed to be handling the situation better than most. Surely, she was strong enough to handle the truth.

"There's something I haven't told you, Collette."

"And what is that?"

"I know it's not pleasant to think about, and I didn't mention it at first because I knew you were still in a state of shock. But Brash... Brash is very good at what he does. And for what it's worth, Brash believes Bobby Ray didn't simply die of natural causes. He believes your husband was a victim of foul play."

Collette stared at her for a long moment, her eyes wide with surprise. "You're saying he thinks someone murdered Bobby Ray," she finally said, her voice blunt.

"Well... yes."

"Why on earth would he think that?" Instead of sounding shocked, she sounded irate.

"I'm not sure. In fact, *he*'s not entirely sure," Madison admitted. "But he has a gut feeling about it, and believe me, his hunches are rarely wrong."

"They are this time."

"How can you be so certain?"

"Why would anyone want to murder Bobby Ray? The man was as dull as tarnished silver, but he was completely harmless. He didn't have a single enemy. No money, either, at least none I ever saw. What would anyone have to gain by killing him?"

"I'm not sure. Perhaps to gain his collection? If several of the pieces were authentic, it truly could be worth a fortune."

"Then someone would steal it," Collette pointed out, "not kill him."

"Maybe they hope to buy the collection when you put it up for sale."

When Collette stared at her as if she had lost her mind, Madison tried a different angle. "Hugh mentioned that one of the men in their group was envious of his promotion. Perhaps it got out of hand."

"They're volunteers, Madison." Her voice was hard. "It wasn't a paid promotion. Hardly something worth killing a man over."

"Jealousy makes people do strange things. I'm not accusing his friend, of course, but it might be worth looking into."

"It's not," Collette said flatly.

"Aren't you even a little curious? What if someone did kill your husband? Wouldn't you like to see justice served?"

"Just like an autopsy, it wouldn't bring him back."

"No, but it might give you peace of mind." Madison used a gentle tone to point out the obvious.

"I had peace of mind," Collette said coldly. "Right up until you shared your boyfriend's silly notions." She stood, grabbing her purse from the sofa cushions. "The investigating officers were satisfied with their findings. They said Bobby Ray died of natural causes. Stop trying to grandstand and make this into something it's not."

"I'm not grandstanding," Madison insisted, biting back a flash of anger. She reminded herself that Collette was still hurting. Perhaps she wasn't strong enough to handle Brash's theory, after all. "I'm concerned. And I'm just trying to help."

"I didn't ask for your help."

Madison made one last effort. "I think you should reconsider having that autopsy done."

"You're not listening to me," Collette ground out. "No one killed Bobby Ray. He was fat and lazy, and the only exercise he got was marching around in his scratchy old clothes, playing with a bunch of overgrown little boys and their precious old guns. He ate one too many burritos, and it killed him. End of story."

She stopped at the edge of the porch and took a deep breath, clearly trying to calm herself. "Thank you for the tea." Collette's voice turned contrite. "I'll see you at the wedding."

14

It wasn't that she had an abundance of time on her hands. She didn't.

It wasn't that she had nothing better to do. She did. Her wedding was now just days away. As impossible as it seemed, the To-Do list seemed to grow, rather than shrink.

It wasn't even that an impromptu trip to Waco allowed her to kill multiple birds with one stone. It did. Driving Nigel Barrett to his doctor's appointment qualified as a good deed, filled her car with gas (the least he could do, he claimed, if she wouldn't accept pay) and allowed her ample time to grill him along the way.

However, the spur-of-the-moment trip did give her the perfect opportunity to question some of Bobby Ray Erickson's friends. With the investigation stalled, Collette refusing to ask for an autopsy, and time running out, Madison suspected it was now or never.

It so happened she chose a perfect day to perform her good deed. The local reenactors had a meeting scheduled at a restaurant not far from the hospital. With a bit of cajoling on her part, they agreed to meet her after their business concluded. She had ample time to drop Nigel off at the clinic, drive to the restaurant, question Bobby Ray's peers, and still return in time to pick up the older gentleman.

"Thank you for agreeing to meet with me," she told the group. Judging from the empty seats and dirty dishes littering the table, several members had left before her arrival. She hoped they weren't her key witnesses.

"A few of the fellas had to leave." A heavyset man noticed her eying the vacated chairs and offered an explanation. "Some come on their lunch breaks and have to get back to work. I'm Royce Bazajou." He nodded to the other four men and two women still seated at the table, introducing each by name.

"As I explained to you over the phone, I'm a consultant for The Sisters Police Department, and was actually an eye witness to Bobby Ray Erickson's death. My condolences on the loss of your friend."

There were murmurs around the table of what a fine man Bobby Ray had been. Some mentioned his dedication to the group, others his finesse on the faux battlefields. One admired his knowledge of Texas history and his collection of artifacts and antiques.

"I understand he has quite the collection," Madison said, turning to the person who spoke. She thought his name was Dennis.

"Very impressive. He has a letter that was signed by Stephen F. Austin himself, and a cane that once belonged to ole' Sam. General Houston had a bum leg, you know, and had to use a walking cane."

"I take it you've seen his collection?"

"Oh, many times, many times," Dennis assured her. "He even loaned a few pieces to the university from time to time, and to the state museum in Austin. Bobby Ray had an eye for authenticity."

"I imagine some of those must have been quite valuable?" She posed it as a question.

"He never confirmed it, but I heard he paid over six grand for a knife rumored to be a Jim Bowie original."

Madison's brows pulled together. "I understood Bobby Ray worked at a tire factory. I didn't realize they paid so well."

Another man laughed and nudged the man talking. "Tell her about Stony."

"Stony?" Madison asked.

"Bobby Ray's stepfather. He bought a scratch-off ticket and hit pay dirt. Nice fella, but he blew the whole thing within a couple of years. Spent most of it on Jeannie, Bobby Ray's mother, but gave plenty to the boy. Stony was part of our group, you see, before the cancer got him. They shared a love for history, so when Bobby Ray found the knife, Stony was more than happy to give him the money to buy it."

Madison jotted down a few notes before asking, "Were all of you present the day Bobby Ray passed away?"

When even the women nodded, Madison tried to remember if she had seen them there. "You were on the parade grounds?" she clarified.

"I tuck my hair under a cap and play one of the soldiers," the thinnest of the women supplied. With her athletic build and rather plain features, and under bulky, nondescript clothes, Madison imagined she could pull off the charade quite convincingly.

"I was back at camp," the other said, "so I didn't see the incident."

"But the rest of you? You all saw Bobby Ray fall?"

Of the remaining six, only two had actually seen him stagger and fall.

"I was standing on the other side of the cannon from him," Royce Bazajou confirmed. "When he turned away so quickly, I knew something was wrong. It wasn't like Bobby Ray to abandon his post."

"Did he say anything?"

"Not that I recall, but standing so close to the cannon like we do, my ears ring for a good five minutes after a blast."

"Was there anything different about that day? About that particular blast?"

Royce bunched his lips together in thought, reminding Madison of a bulldog. "I do recall there was a peculiar odor that day. Both cannonballs had it, come to think of it."

"What did it smell like?"

"Can't rightly recall," he said, "just that it wasn't normal. To be honest, I remember thinking Bobby Ray had passed gas. Forgot all about it, until just now."

"You smelled this odor both times?" she confirmed. "What did it smell like?"

He threw his hands into the air. "Like the farts!" he huffed.

Madison noticed a tiny line form between his bushy brows, even as some of his friends chuckled. "You remembered something else?" she asked hopefully, recognizing the expression of doubt appear in his face.

"Yeah," he said slowly. "Maybe. I do remember thinking it smelled like someone had eaten crab legs. It was pretty rank."

"Couldn't have been Bobby Ray," Dom Ringer pitched in. "He was allergic to fish."

"I saw him eating shrimp off Petey's plate," the thin woman contradicted.

"Would that be Petey Vansant?" Madison asked. "I was hoping to speak with him."

Dom nodded. "He had to get back to work. He drives over from Marlin, just like Bobby Ray did. They work together at the tire factory."

"Worked," someone reminded him.

With a slow, mournful shake of his head, the man murmured, "I still can't believe Bobby Ray is gone."

Though she empathized with him, Madison had more questions. "Were the two of them good friends?"

"Well, sure. We're all like family."

"I understand that Mr. Vansant may have resented the fact Bobby Ray was promoted to captain."

Seven pairs of eyes turned to her with skepticism. "Who told you that?"

"Uhm, I heard it somewhere," she said vaguely.

"Must have been someone from a different brigade," the man identified as Louie supplied. "No one from this brigade would say such a thing."

Madison noticed he stopped short of saying the two men got along well, just that no one from their group would deny it.

"So, *did* Petey resent Bobby Ray?" she asked pointedly.

"You'd have to take that up with Petey," Royce told her. There was a note of finality in his voice.

"Do you have his telephone number?"

"What exactly," he asked, eyes narrowing, "are you looking for?"

"The truth."

"The police said Bobby Ray died of an apparent heart attack."

"I take it that all of you had known Bobby Ray for several years. Was anyone aware of any issues he had with his heart?" Madison's gaze slowly traveled around the group, waiting for each person to deny or confirm the question. Every single person shook his or her head with a negative response.

"Generally speaking, would you say he had been in good health?"

"Other than being a little overweight like the rest of us, I'd say he was," Royce volunteered.

"Other than his allergies," Dennis volunteered. "He always seemed to have a stuffy nose and itchy eyes."

"So, if he was in good health, and didn't have known problems with his heart, there's a possibility he didn't have a heart attack," Madison pointed out. She stopped short of suggesting he had been murdered. "But something killed him, and we're trying to find what that was. Does anyone remember anything odd about Bobby Ray's behavior that day? Did he seem to be having trouble breathing... difficulty concentrating... staggering when he walked..." She threw out the suggestions with hand gestures. "Anything out of the ordinary?"

"Besides his wife being there?" Dennis quipped. "That always seemed to irritate the heck out of him." He and the man beside him chuckled.

"The two of them never did seem like a matched pair," the second woman agreed.

"How well do you know Collette?" Madison asked the group.

"Well enough." It was the tone of the statement, not the words themselves, that expressed disapproval.

"I understand she seldom came to your events?"

"I don't recall her being at more than two or three reenactments in all the time Bobby Ray was a member," Royce confirmed. "She came to about as many meetings and banquets."

"She did come to Bobby Ray's promotion ceremony," the thin woman recalled.

"Yeah, but she won't even give him a proper burial!" Dom Ringer grumbled, setting off a round of similar murmurings along the table.

"It's not right," Louie all but whined, echoing Hugh Darby's sentiments, "not giving a captain like Bobby Ray a proper send off."

"We believe in honoring our fallen." This came from Royce. "When Stony passed on, we gave a three volley salute with our muskets. We would've done no less for Bobby Ray."

"Last question, and I'll let you ladies and gentlemen go about your day. Is there *anything* you can think of that might help us solve the mystery of Bobby Ray's death?"

When no one could offer a single suggestion, Madison thanked them and left.

As Granny Bert would say, there was no use in beating a dead mule.

15

Madison arrived back at the clinic to find Nigel waiting for her outside on a bench.

"I would have come in," she told the man as he settled in and buckled his seatbelt. "You didn't have to wait out here."

Instead of complaining as she expected him to do, the elderly gentleman shrugged. "I didn't mind, it being a pretty day and all. My nurse came down with me, made sure I got out here."

"It is a lovely day," she agreed. "I just hope the weather holds for this weekend."

"What's this weekend?"

"My wedding, remember? You're planning to come, aren't you?"

"You say you'll have something other than seafood? Because I don't eat anything that swims under water."

Madison bit back a smile as she pulled into traffic. That was the cantankerous old man she had come to know and tolerate. "There will be plenty of other choices, including barbecue brisket and chicken."

"Like I say, seafood and me don't get along. Especially

crawfish and the like. Looking back, I think that's what killed Eli."

"That's your brother, the one who choked to death?" Madison clarified.

"Mama thought he stuffed his mouth too full, but later on, I came to realize he was probably allergic to shellfish, same as me."

"I've heard allergies are often inherited." Madison nodded in agreement, as she switched lanes and prepared to turn at the next exit. "Did any of your other brothers and sisters have sensitivities to anything?"

"Not to food, that I recall. But I seem to remember a lot of sneezing and huffing and puffing from just about all of them."

Given that three siblings died during a dust storm, asthma seemed a likely culprit. Her heart ached at the thought of losing a single child, much less three at one time. She focused on asking her next question, rather than mourning the ancient deaths.

"What happens when you eat shellfish? How does it feel?"

"That's what I'm telling you. I don't eat it!"

"Yes, sir, I understand that. But if you were to take a bite, what would happen? You must have had a reaction in the past, to know you have an allergy. Do you remember how it affected you?"

"Well," Nigel said, scrunching his face together as if to squeeze out the memory, "I recall my throat getting all tight. My chest hurt a bit, and my breath came out sounding like a strong north wind through a poorly chinked log cabin. Seems I was a mite dizzy, too, but I'm not sure. It didn't take but two times for me to realize what was causing it. I haven't touched seafood in over sixty years."

Hearing his description, it seemed reasonable that Bobby Ray Erickson could have died from anaphylactic shock. Maybe there hadn't been foul play involved, after all.

Lost in her thoughts, Madison pulled onto Highway 6 and headed south toward home. The divided four-lane highway wasn't busy this time of day, so she set the cruise control and adjusted the lumbar support on her seat. On the other side of the car, her passenger was already nodding off.

Not for the first time, she wondered how sick he truly was. It wasn't uncommon for a man his age to sleep during the day, particularly in a car, but his face was paler than usual. That, too, could be attributed to fatigue or giving blood, but she worried it was something more serious. From what she understood, his trips to the doctor were becoming more frequent, and she suspected he came to this particular clinic because he needed a specialist.

Perhaps, she decided, she could bring him to his next appointment and do some research in the McLennan County Courthouse archives while she waited. If his sister and brother had settled nearby, at least some of their offspring probably lived in this area.

A flashy burnt-orange sports car came up in the other lane, traveling faster than the posted speed limit. It slowed as it drew up beside them, and Madison glanced over to see it had dark-tinted windows. As dark as they were, she idly wondered if they were legal, but soon the car sped up, moving out of sight and out of mind.

After passing through the small town of Riesel, they were the only vehicle on the southbound road. When they came upon an older model pickup truck pulling a trailer, Madison moved into the left lane to pass. She stayed there when she saw rough patches in the road ahead. It wasn't like there was anyone else on the road to need the passing lane.

Within a few miles, a car appeared in the rearview mirror. Madison started to move over, but the same orange sports car from earlier approached at a high speed and already occupied that side of the road. She wondered if the car had gotten off in town and was now back on the road, trying to make up for lost time. It was certainly driving fast enough. She would let it pass before moving back into the right lane.

Another glance into the mirror revealed the car veering into her lane. Madison pressed her foot on the accelerator to scoot out of its way. Once she was clear of its bumper, she could get over and let it have as much of the road as it wanted.

Apparently, it wanted the entire thing.

The car kept coming, crowding into the lane with her. Madison wasn't sure how it missed nicking her bumper, so she floored the gas pedal and tried moving into the right-hand lane. The sports car jerked back to the right, so Madison whipped left.

"Crazy driver!" she shouted.

Nigel Barrett awoke with a start, grumbling about all the swerving.

"That orange car is all over the road!" Madison defended her driving. "I'm trying to get out of their way, but they can't decide which lane they want to ride in."

"Looks like they want to ride smack dab in the middle of the road," the old man said, peering into his side mirror. He turned around in the seat, twisting his body to get a better look. "Too close to even see their license plate number." He glared over at her as he turned back around. "What'd you do to piss them off?"

"Nothing! It passed us earlier but must have gotten off at the last town." She put on her blinker, indicating her effort to move right, but the sports car ignored it. It still straddled the line, refusing to relinquish either lane.

"Make sure your seatbelt is on," Madison cautioned.

"It is."

"This may get bumpy." The warning came seconds before their left tire hit the rough strip of pavement edging the road. The twins called them 'drunk bumps,' claiming they were there to keep drunk drivers between the white lines. If the orange car wouldn't let her move right, she would move left and give it plenty of room to pass.

The orange car moved left with them, pressing ever closer. When it rammed her bumper, she cried out and almost lost control of the steering wheel. "Hang on!" she warned her passenger.

With the orange car pushing them, Madison's car left the pavement altogether and hit the grassy median between the lanes. She wrestled with the steering wheel, fighting to avoid the ruts from a previous vehicle. Getting stuck meant the orange car would ram them for sure, but crossing the median meant being thrown into the oncoming lane. She didn't need to see the approaching eighteen-wheeler to know that was a bad option.

"Cut back to the right!" Nigel advised. "Get back on the road and floor it!"

"I'm trying!"

"Try harder!"

The car's wheels churned in the grasses, plowing through a thick blanket of bluebonnets. "It's illegal to pick them. Hope it's not illegal to run them over," she muttered darkly, as the car bounced up and down, chomping its way across the state flower.

Behind them, the orange sports car barely grazed her bumper. Matching her bump for bump through the flowers, it stayed steady on their tail, not allowing more than a few inches between them. Any moment now, she expected it to pitch upward and come down on top of her.

"Watch out!" Nigel cried. "There's a bridge ahead. Pick a side of the road and floor it, girl!"

"There's an eighteen-wheeler on that side!"

"Then cut it sharp to the right and get back where we came from. Do it before the guardrail starts. Take your foot off the gas while you turn, then gun it as you come out of the fishtail."

"What about the orange car?"

"They can fend for themselves!"

There was no time to think it through. Madison jerked the steering wheel with all her might, sending them into a careening skid. She struggled to keep the wheel turned deep. It took every bit of her strength, but, with a helping hand from Nigel, she fought to control the helm. Her locked wheels slid atop the grasses, skating ever closer to the traffic on the northbound side of the highway. The eighteen-wheeler driver blared its horn and moved into the far lane, just as she felt her back driver-side tire scrape against the lip of asphalt. Her car jerked at the resistance, but it was enough to stop their forward progress. The second her tires bit into the earth with a hint of traction, Madison stomped her foot onto the gas pedal and straightened out the steering wheel.

Madison gunned the motor just in time to avoid a direct hit by the orange car. Its grill scraped against her back bumper as it lurched forward, seconds too late. The force worked to their advantage, helping aim Madison's car in the right direction.

She was too busy trying to avoid the sudden drop-off on her right and keep them out of the water below to see what became of the other vehicle. She barely missed the guardrail as she bounced out of the median and onto the pavement of the southbound lane.

"Don't slow down now!" Nigel scolded her. "Go, go, go!"

"But—"

"Don't give 'em a chance to come back and finish the job!" he snarled. "Get the hell out of Dodge!"

"But..."

"The orange car made it across. Do you want them to come back?"

"I—I'm leaving the scene of an accident," she protested, but not enough to slow the car. "I need to call 9-1-1."

"Give me your phone."

"I'll have to find my purse. I don't know what happened to it."

They located it on the floor at Nigel's feet. While he

reported the incident, Madison kept a close watch in her mirrors for any flash of orange.

Dispatch advised them to continue to the next town, where a local deputy would meet them and escort them to the police station. By the time they exited the highway in Marlin, Madison's nerves were strung taut. The excitement and brush with near death seemed to have energized her passenger, but it had the opposite effect on her. Walking into the station, Madison's legs were wobbly and weak.

After taking their statements and hearing the full story, the officer had them wait in his office. He returned with questions. "And you have no idea what prompted the other driver's road rage?"

"None."

"You didn't get the license plate number, is that correct?"

"I couldn't even see the plate, the car was so close."

"Fortunately for us, other drivers reported an orange sports car driving erratically and a truck driver called in the incident, corroborating your story. As it turns out, the orange vehicle is registered to Cornelius H. Booker from Mart. Does that name mean anything to either of you?"

Madison shook her head. "Not me."

"Never heard of him," Nigel echoed.

"Less than an hour ago, the car was reported stolen from the Department of Veterans Affairs Medical Center in Waco."

"That's where we just came from!" Madison exclaimed.

"Do you recall seeing the car there, Mrs. Reynolds? Did you perhaps cut it off as you were exiting the parking lot, or provoke the driver in some way?"

Perhaps it was her nerves, but Madison bristled at the wording of his statement. "You make it sound as if this is somehow *my* fault, Officer Denton. The fact that the other person was driving a stolen car should tell you something."

"I'm not accusing you of anything, ma'am. Just trying to make sense of what could have been a very ugly situation."

"Wasn't too pretty, the way it was," Nigel harrumphed.

"You're right, Mr. Barrett. Are you sure neither of you need medical attention?"

"Are you kidding? My blood hasn't flowed this good in twenty years!" the elderly man claimed.

"I asked a deputy to take a look at your car, Mrs. Reynolds. Other than some damage to your back bumper and a broken tail light, it appears to be fine. Do you feel comfortable driving, or do you need to make arrangements for someone to pick you up?"

Her hesitation was slight. "If I can have just a moment more, I should be fine."

"Feel free to wait here as long as you like, ma'am. Can I get either of you some water? Coffee? There's a vending machine around the corner."

"I'm fine, thank you. But, may I ask you a question?"

"Certainly."

"I'm working as a private consultant for The Sisters Police Department in Rivers County. I was in Waco to speak with friends of Bobby Ray Erickson, who I believe was a resident of your town. Did you know Mr. Erickson?"

"Bobby Ray? Sure. It was a dang shame, him dying so young." The officer squinted his eyes. "Why are you investigating his death? I heard Bobby Ray died of a heart attack."

"There's no official investigation," she was quick to say, "but an eye witness to Mr. Erickson's death did raise some questions."

"What kind of questions?"

Madison didn't give a direct answer. "I spoke with his militia reenactment group earlier. They suggested I speak with Pete Vansant, who also lives here in Marlin. Do you know how I would get in touch with Mr. Vansant?"

"They didn't give you his number?"

"No." She didn't elaborate as to why. "Do you know him?"

"I know Petey Vansant."

It was the way he said it. Slow, with an abundance of caution. A sliver of disapproval.

"You have his telephone number?" she asked hopefully. There was no listing for him in the phone book.

"I have his number, all right. Zero. You'd be better off asking your questions elsewhere."

"Fine. I'll ask you. If Petey Vansant had a problem with someone, would he be the type to act on it?"

The officer looked her over, taking in her disheveled hair and her still-trembling hands. "Ma'am, you just had a dangerous and stressful experience," he reminded her. "Do you really want to take on another?"

Madison refused to be patronized. She lifted her chin and replied coolly, "Are you saying Pete Vansant is dangerous?"

"I'm not saying anything." He stood from his chair and walked around the desk. "Feel free to stay as long as you need. As you know, the roads out there are dangerous."

"What was that about?" Nigel wanted to know. No longer sleepy, he had listened to the exchange with open curiosity.

"Come on. I'll tell you about it on the drive home."

It was his turn to eye her skeptically. "Are you sure you're up to driving just yet?"

"Just come on. The sooner we get back home, the better."

Once they were back on the highway, Nigel wanted to know who Petey Vansant and Bobby Ray Erickson were.

"Both men are part of a historical reenactment group. Bobby Ray was the man who died a couple of weeks ago at Washington-on-the-Brazos during a cannon exhibition. We were there when he dropped dead of what most people are calling a heart attack, but Brash suspected there was more to the story. Petey Vansant was his friend, but it sounds as if they may have been adversaries, as well. Petey resented Bobby Ray for getting a promotion, but no one will go into any particulars."

"You're thinking he may have had something to do with this Bobby Ray fella's death?"

"I can't rule it out, because I haven't been able to talk with him. He left the meeting today before I arrived, and no one will give me his number."

"Does he know you're looking for him?"

"I'm sure one of his buddies has told him."

"He don't drive an orange car by chance, does he?" Nigel half-jested.

Madison glanced into the rearview mirror, still leery of being in the clear. It was a possibility that hadn't occurred to her. If Petey Vansant had something to hide, would he go to such lengths to frighten her away? And what, other than hiding his involvement in murder, could warrant such dire means? No one needed to remind her that today could have ended much differently. "I hope not," she mumbled.

"So, if you're working on this other case, is that why you haven't found my kinfolk yet?" Nigel asked.

"No, sir, that's not it at all. I haven't found your kin because it's not as easy as you may think. I've reached out to a likely candidate, but he hasn't replied so far. But I do have a bit of good news for you. I discovered the name of your niece."

"I truly do have a niece?" His wrinkled face lifted, looking at least ten years younger.

"It appears so. Betty Jean had one daughter, Laura Jean. I'll do my best to find her for you."

"Let's hope your best is good enough," he growled. He fidgeted in his seat before making a reluctant admission. "That's wasn't bad drivin' back there. Not bad at all, girl."

From Nigel Barrett, that was high praise.

16

Genny and Cutter insisted on hosting the rehearsal dinner as one of their gifts to the couple.

The wedding party itself was small. Megan, Bethani, and Blake were the only attendants for their parents' nuptials. The guest list for the rehearsal dinner was only slightly larger, reaching out to include parents and grandparents, Matt and Shannon, and the preacher and his wife.

Cutter grilled steaks and bacon-wrapped quail outside, while Genny worked her magic in the kitchen, putting her warming drawers and dual ovens to good use. Even before the couple admitted their feelings for one another, Cutter had remodeled the kitchen with Genny in mind, seeking her input for the design. She had helped him create her dream kitchen, wondering what lucky lady would ultimately reign over it. A few short months later, here she was, and she had never been happier in her life.

On this night, she whipped up one delectable dish after another, and topped the evening off with red velvet cupcakes and her special rum-laced tiramisu. As they gathered for coffee and conversation, the three teenagers announced they had a special treat for their parents.

"Mom, Mr. de, we know you two have taken a long, twisted path to get to one another, but we wanted you to know that the three of us," Blake pointed to his sister, himself, and Megan, "couldn't be happier that you've found your way back together and that you'll finish your journey in life, side by side. Just in case you've forgotten some of the highlights, we thought we'd offer a little stroll down memory lane, as we so humbly interpret it." Wiggling his eyebrows, the show master flashed a bright smile. "Guys, welcome to our version of *This Is Your Life!*"

For the next twenty minutes, the trio had their family howling in laughter and wiping away tears of mirth. Taking turns as narrator and actors, the teens acted out the stories they told, using simple props and exaggerated facial and body expressions. Taking their cue from the silent movies of old, they gave a dramatic rendition of each tale. What they didn't know, they embellished with outrageous claims and lucky guesses, and pieced together a sometimes silly, sometimes poignant story of their parents' intertwining lives.

They had the most fun portraying Brash's prowess at sports, Madison's delight at giving birth to twins (matching pillows from Genny's sofa), the mad crush Madison had on Brash in high school, Brash's appointment as chief of police (and an imaginary shoot-out with villains that never really happened), and the tug of war with their emotions when Maddy returned to The Sisters, and they realized they were falling in love.

When the laughter died away and their audience continued to percolate with the occasional residual giggle, each teen took the 'stage' again to deliver their own heartfelt message. The tears started over again, minus the laughter.

Bethani was the first to speak. "It's no secret to anyone in this room that I was strongly against moving here. As far as I was concerned, our mother had moved us to a strange and barren land, where there was no mall, no Starbucks, no drive-thru anything. I was still mourning the loss of our father, and the life we had lived in Dallas. As much as I loved my mother—and you, too, Granny Bert and Aunt Genny—I hated it here. I tried everything in my power to get out of this god-forsaken, hillbilly backwoods and get back to the city. But thank goodness, the three most influential women in my life were smarter than me and knew this was exactly where we needed to be.

"Because then the strangest thing happened. It turned out this wasn't such a god-forsaken, barren land, after all. I met a really cool girl at school, and she was nice to me. Way nicer than my snobby friends in the city. And it turned out she was way cooler, too. She was a cheerleader, and a dancer, and she rode horses and liked to fish, and it just so happened her father was the chief of police. She quickly became the very best friend I have ever had, and she became the sister I have always wanted." Bethani paused to flash her brother a smile. "Sorry, bro. Having a twin brother is cool and all, but I always wanted a sister. And now I have one, because in a crazy twist of fate, our parents are getting married tomorrow."

The girl took a deep breath and looked directly at her mother, and at her soon-to-be stepfather. Flipping her long, blond hair over her shoulder, she continued.

"Mom, I know I judged you harshly when we first moved here. I blamed you for a lot of things that weren't your fault. I know you were trying to hold our little family together the only way you knew how. You tried to protect Blake and me from the truth, but you should have trusted us, Mom. You always sacrificed your own happiness for ours, and I want you to know how much we love you for that. But you gotta stop, Mom. You have to think about yourself every once and while. Because when you're happy, we're happy.

"And Mr.de. I tried so hard not to like you. You were like some bigger than life action hero, and you had my brother and my mother wrapped around your little finger, and I was determined not to follow suit. I thought that liking you would somehow be disloyal to my father, and I couldn't let that happen. But you just kept chipping away at the wall I built between us. You let me throw my fits and be a brat, and you were still so calm and nice and *good* to me. Way better than I deserved. But most of all, you were good to my mother. And you made her happy, something she definitely deserved. And then, before I even knew it, I found myself starting to wind around your finger, too. So now you have us all, right in the palm of your hand.

"But," she warned, flashing a cheeky grin, "don't think you're ever going to hear me admit that again. So, long story short. I thought my life was over when Mom dragged us here a little over a year ago. I had no way of knowing a new life was waiting for us. A new life with a new sister, a new set of grandparents, new friends, and, yes, a new father. So, I just want to say I'm happy for you both, and I couldn't be more excited about tomorrow. Here's to you, Mom, and to you, Daddy de."

Before the teen straightened from her deep bow, Madison had her wrapped in a tight hug, with Brash not far behind. Tears flowed freely around the room.

Megan took the stage next. With long, auburn hair and fashionable glasses resting upon a pert nose, Brash's daughter was the perfect counterbalance to the fair twins. She wasn't as tall and lanky as the other two, but her figure already held the promise of classical curves. With her vivacious personality and bright smile, Megan rarely met a stranger.

"After that tear-jerking speech, mine may sound a little lame," the teen confessed with a timid smile. "I haven't known the heartache and loss that Bethani, Blake, and their mom have known. I'm sorry they had to go through that, but it's what brought them back to The Sisters, and what led them into our lives.

"I don't have a sad story to tell. The truth is, I've always had a fairy-tale life. At least, that's how it's always felt to me. Even though they lived separately, my parents made me feel like a princess. I had two palaces, two sets of toys, two bedrooms, two Christmases, and *three* sets of grandparents." She wagged her eyebrows playfully, stirring a snicker amid the teary-eyed crowd. "That meant two kingdoms where I ruled as Princess Megan. How lucky could a girl get?" She flashed another charming smile, before she turned serious.

"You see, I've always thought of my dad as a king. His cowboy hat was his crown, and his police badge was his shining armor. And he was the smartest, and coolest, ruler in all the land. Would you believe this man taught me how to wear high-heels shoes? I know, I know. My mom does it with such grace, but I nearly broke my ankle every time I put on something taller than a flip-flop! But then my dad—the same man who showed me how to bait a hook and saddle a horse and shoot a gun—gave me a few pointers on shoes, of all things. It's all about balance, he said. Knowing where to put the pressure, and where to leave a little wiggle. He said it was the same way with raising kids. There were times he had to apply pressure, like curfews and rules about being alone with boys and going to church every Sunday, so he could allow me a little wiggle room on other things. And whatdaya know? I put on a pair of heels and strutted across the room like a runway model." She acted out the scene with exaggerated moves before continuing.

"My dad's sneaky like that. He's always sneaking in a life lesson when I least expect it. Like the time I was six, and my mom had just gotten remarried. I felt guilty, because Daddy overheard me say something about Momma Matt. Later that day, we went to the field house where he was coach, and he showed me some of the equipment the football players used. There was this thing that looked like a giant rubber band, and he showed me how stretchy it was. It pulled way out, two or three times its regular size, but when you turned it loose, it went back to its old size. Do you remember that day,

Daddy, and what you told me?"

His voice crackling just a bit, Brash's eyes gleamed with unshed tears as he nodded. "I remember, Princess."

"You told me that the heart was a lot like a rubber band. That it was stretchy. It could stretch to many times its normal size and have room to love many people and many things. But that, like the rubber band, it always came back to its true self. It never forgot its original shape or its original purpose. You explained that love was like that. Just because my heart stretched enough to let Momma Matt inside, it didn't mean it forgot to love you as much as ever.

"That was a good lesson to learn, because now my heart has stretched even more. Loving Momma Maddy takes nothing away from my own awesome mother. Loving a new brother and sister takes nothing away from the brat"—she threw a funny face and an affectionate smile toward her half-brother Trouper, who had curled up in their mother's lap and fallen asleep—"and loving a new set of grandparents doesn't change how I feel about my other grandparents. Everything is just multiplied. My heart has stretched enough to let everyone in.

"Best of all, my dad's heart has stretched. And believe me, the man already had a huge heart, even before it made room for the Reynolds clan! I can honestly say that my dad is the best person I know. By far the most generous. He's always giving of himself. His time, his talents, his protection. And his advice, I might add, whether we ask for it or not. So it's good to see him taking something for himself, for a change. He's taking a wife. A soul mate. A real chance at happiness and the ever after that he deserves. So, this is to my forever king, and his new queen. Long may you reign!"

After another round of hugs and tears, Blake took his turn to wish the couple well.

"I should have known better than to let my two sisters go first," the teen pretended to grumble. "They made all the good points first. Never two more deserving people. Check.

Hearts full of happiness. Check. New family circle. Check. More grandmothers to cook for us. Check. More Christmas dinners and Christmas presents. Check." He waggled his eyebrows for laughs.

"But here's a couple of things they didn't mention. They didn't mention what good examples our parents are setting for us. Mom, you're the strongest woman I know. When Dad died, our world turned upside down. Our life sort of fell apart, but you were the glue that held us together. Like Beth said, you tried to protect us, but we knew Dad left us without any money. We knew you didn't just suddenly decide you *liked* shopping at WalMart, or that McDonald's served better food than our favorite restaurants, or that you didn't need a big, fancy car after all. You cut corners where you could, made certain that Beth and I had everything we needed, and you cried into your pillow at night because you hated some of the jobs you took to make ends meet. But you were always smiling the next morning, and you never complained, and you never blamed Dad.

"We know you and Dad had some problems, but you never let that get in the way of reminding us how much he loved us, and how proud he was of us. You talk about Dad all the time, making sure Beth and I never forget him. You put your own differences aside, so Beth and I can remember the good parts of our old life. To me, that shows how strong you really are.

"You've shown us that making room for someone new doesn't mean we forget the someone old. Even Mr. de talks about Dad, asking how he did things and what he thought about this or that. I know it's his way of helping me honor my father's influence in my life, and letting me know it's okay to miss him, and to wish he was here with us, sharing new experiences."

Blake shifted his eyes to Brash, to address the man directly. "You've set a good example for me, showing me how to treat a woman with respect, and dignity, and as an equal. You let Mom make her own decisions, and you support her, even when you think she's wrong. You can cook and clean and wear a frilly apron—don't pretend we haven't all seen you, big guy—and still take down a criminal with a single look. Yeah, that one there. Just don't aim it at me. It's lethal. Anyway, you've been a good example for us all. You're brave and strong and reliable, and you'll give a person the shirt off your back if they need it. Everyone knows they can come to you for help. You know when to be tough, and you know when to be gentle. You're not afraid to let your feelings show, so that's a new lesson for me, and one I think I should learn. So, if Mom was the glue that held us together, you're the super glue that will make it stick, and you've bonded us into a new family unit. We're the Reynolds-deCordova family now. It's a mouthful, but best of all, it's a heart full." To hide the tears gathering in his blue eyes, Blake flashed a big smile and made a grand gesture with his arms. "Congratulations, you crazy kids."

There was little else to add to the heartfelt speeches, but the couple stood and accepted the applause from their loved ones.

"After those wonderful well wishes, there's not much we can say," Madison said, wiping away lingering tears.

"Just that Maddy and I have to be the luckiest couple on earth," Brash interjected, holding his fiancée by the waist. "We have each other, we have these three great young adults who continue to amaze us each and every day, and we have each of you. We can't get more blessed than that. Thank you for being a part of this tonight, and for being a part of our lives. We love you guys."

Beside him, Madison nodded vigorously through a veil of fresh tears. She was too emotional to speak. Too happy to express her feelings with mere words.

Tomorrow, she would have her wildflower wedding.

17

Her mind spinning with a thousand happy thoughts, Madison all but floated through her evening routine. Her feet were light as she waltzed around her luxurious bathroom, humming a favorite love song while she applied face cream.

When Nick Vilardi designed her suite of rooms during the renovation, she had thought them a bit over the top. Dominating one-half of the second floor, the rooms were all spacious and airy. Overkill for a single occupant, even if her closet was the envy of women everywhere. The decadent bathroom and the massive walk-in closet boasted double doors, matching those to the sitting room and adjoining library. Madison had considered it excessive extravagance, designed to impress the television audience more than to accommodate her needs.

But tonight, the extra space was appreciated. Caught up in the tune playing in her head and in her heart, Madison waltzed through the generous openings and spun like a ballerina, acting out the fantasy of being a queen.

Tonight, she felt like a queen. The queen of hearts.

Tomorrow, she would marry her king and bring him back here to their palace, where they would live happily ever after. And tomorrow night, she would no longer sleep alone in her custom-made bed. That thought, alone, was worth a double spin.

When her phone rang, Madison snatched it up mid-step. Without breaking tempo, she turned and glided gracefully into the sitting room, holding her nightgown aloft as if it were the finest ball gown.

"Speak to me, Your Highness," she said in her best haughty voice.

To her surprise, it wasn't Brash's voice that answered.

"Madison?" a woman's voice squeaked.

Her feet faltered, causing her to stumble. Disappointed to hear Collette's voice on the other end of the line instead of her fiancé's, Madison crashed into the cushions of the turret's settee.

"I'm sorry. I thought you were Brash."

"I know this isn't the best time to call, and I do apologize," Collette began. Madison couldn't determine if the slight whine in her voice was from alcohol or depression. Possibly both.

She didn't attempt to hide her weary sigh. There was nothing like a depressed friend to dampen the euphoria from just moments before. "What can I do for you, Collette?"

"I've been thinking about what you said."

"Mmm... which part?"

"About the autopsy and having peace of mind."

Thinking of her reaction last time it was mentioned, Madison defended herself, "I only wanted to help."

To her surprise, Collette replied, "I still don't like the idea of cutting him up, but I called the funeral home and asked them to wait on the cremation."

"Really? That's great. I think that was a very wise move, Collette. I think you'll find comfort in knowing what your husband died from."

"I called an hour too late," the other woman informed her. "They had just finished the cremation."

Madison felt a surge of disappointment. Now they might never know the truth behind Bobby Ray Erickson's death, and a murderer might get away with the crime.

On the other hand, she conceded, perhaps Bobby Ray had gone into anaphylactic shock and actually *did* die from natural causes. It wasn't the foul play Brash suspected, but also not the heart attack others so easily assumed.

Either way, an autopsy would have provided a definite answer.

"I'm sorry, Collette," Madison said with sincerity. "That's truly a shame."

"I shouldn't have been so stubborn. I should have listened to you and requested an autopsy. I just couldn't bear the thought of.... You know. Cutting up his body." A sniff worked its way into her words.

"I can't say I blame you, Collette. After the shock of unexpected death, it's an emotional and difficult time to make such an important decision."

"But you tried to tell me. I would at least know if it was a heart attack, allergic reaction, aneurysm... whatever. I knew it couldn't have been murder, not like you suggested the other day, but you were right about giving me peace of mind." Her voice fell to a new low. "Now I'll never know for sure."

It was the last thing she wanted to do on the eve of her wedding, but Madison spent the next half hour, coaxing Collette into better spirits. From the sound of things, reality had sunk in, and a delayed sense of grief had the other woman in its grip. Empathy for Collette's plight made it impossible to brush her off. In many ways, Madison was one of the few people who knew exactly what she was going through.

As the clock ticked closer to midnight, Collette's sniffles subsided. "I'm sorry, Madison," she apologized. "I don't know what's wrong with me, calling you tonight, of all nights! It's the night before your wedding, and the last thing you needed was to listen to me wallowing in my sorrow."

"I understand where you're coming from, Collette."

"I know, and I guess that's why I wanted to talk to you. You're the only one who understands. I may not have been happy in my marriage to Bobby Ray, but I still cared for him, on some level. I never thought he'd die so suddenly."

"We never expect these things."

"It just hit me, you know? The finality of it. The... stupidity of it."

Madison stifled a yawn, hoping the conversation was ending. "Death is difficult to understand," she agreed.

"It's only been two months since Jeanie died. We were still grieving her passing."

"Had she been ill?"

Collette's bark of laughter lacked humor. "She was probably healthier than you and I put together. She exercised, ate all the right foods, avoided alcohol and exposure to the sun. None of that mattered when she had a blow-out and ran into the back of an eighteen-wheeler."

"How sad."

"She kept telling Bobby Ray he needed to order her new tires, but he kept putting it off. He was too busy playing soldier." The bitterness in her voice was palatable. "But that's water under the bridge now. They're both gone, and none of it matters. I just wanted you to know that I did finally decide to have the autopsy done, even if I waited too long."

"I'm glad you let me know."

Collette's voice changed abruptly, taking on a bright and upbeat lilt. It was the conversation they should have had forty-five minutes ago. "So! Are you excited about tomorrow? I bet you can hardly wait!"

"To say I'm excited is an understatement."

"Tell me about your dress."

Madison could picture the other woman settling into a comfortable position, curling up like a teenager to hear the details of prom. She expected to hear her squeal at any moment, drooling over how *hot* Brash was.

"Collette, I don't mean to be rude, but I really need to go. As you pointed out, I have a big day tomorrow, and I'd like to be awake to enjoy it."

The apology took another three minutes, but at last, Collette hung up the phone.

Madison glanced at the text message that had come through a few moments earlier.

It's our wedding day, my love! Fourteen hours until our FOREVER begins.

18

Their wedding day dawned bright and sunny. How could it be anything less?

The bright sun was no match for Madison's smile. The silly thing wouldn't wipe off her face, even when she attempted to put on makeup. She settled for smile lines creased with foundation, and lipstick spread thin to stretch the breadth of her face.

"Oh, honey, you look absolutely stunning," her mother told her. Allie Cessna, known simply as Happy to her grandchildren, helped Madison dress for the wedding.

"Thank you, Mom."

"You're absolutely glowing. I don't think I've ever seen you so happy."

"I don't think I've ever been this happy," Madison confessed. "When the twins were born, I was ecstatic, but I was also scared and nervous. What did I know about being a mother, especially to *two* crying babies? And I was almost this happy when I married Gray, but I was also nervous. Yet oddly enough, today I'm not nervous at all. Today feels so absolutely *right*. All I feel is excited, and impatient, and completely and utterly content. *This* is what I've been waiting to feel my entire life."

Happy's eyes misted as she hugged her daughter. "That's because this was meant to be. You and Brash belong together."

"I love him so much, Mom. Every single day, I think I couldn't possibly love him more, and every single day, he proves me wrong."

"I know, honey. I feel the same way about your father. Even after forty-four years of marriage, I find something new about him to love every day. Here, I have something for you."

Madison looked down at the familiar piece of jewelry in her mother's hands. Allie had worn the braided silver bracelet for as long as Madison could remember. There were a dozen or so beaded charms sliding along the band, each holding a special memory for the older woman. Madison knew the story behind them all, having heard them numerous times over the years. And Madison had worn this very bracelet at her first wedding, as something borrowed.

"I want you to wear this," Happy said.

"I... do you think that's in good taste?" Madison worried. "I wore this to my first wedding."

"Honey, I know you and Gray had problems. I know he hurt you terribly, and he betrayed your trust. But don't forget that, once upon a time, you loved that man, and that he gave you the most precious gifts of your life. He'll always be a part of your life, because he's your children's father. And good or bad, he helped make you the woman you are today, and he prepared you for this day with Brash. Perhaps because of your heartache with Gray, you can embrace today with such confidence, and such certainty."

Happy circled the silver braid around Madison's slender wrist and fastened it. "My mother gave me this bracelet on my wedding day. I loaned it to you when you married Gray, but today, I'm giving it to you."

"But you love this bracelet! You always wear it."

"Yes, that's true. But I love you more." She stroked the individual charms, as if telling them goodbye. "I haven't always been the best mother to you, Maddy girl. I admit, there was a time in my life when I wasn't prepared to be a mother. You...You frightened me, if you must know. Even as a child, you seemed so much wiser than me. You were a solemn child, full of questions and quiet contemplation. You loved puzzles and figuring things out, and how things worked. And there I was, an adult, and I didn't even have my life figured out." She gave a nervous laugh, her eyes filled with tears as she fingered the bracelet. "You were so smart, and so inquisitive, and I was afraid I would stifle you. It seemed best to let your grandmother raise you. And she did a fine job. Your father and I are so proud of you, sweetheart."

Happy raised her eyes to her daughter's. They were both crying now and smiling through the tears. "And we couldn't be happier that you've found Brash. He's such a fine man. Maybe...maybe I knew, somewhere in my heart, that Gray wasn't your soul mate. Or maybe I was just selfish. I couldn't bring myself to give you this bracelet outright, not then, but it's different this time. It just feels right, just like you and Brash feel so right together. I want you to have this, Maddy dear, because I want you to be as happy with your soul mate as I have been with mine. I love you, sweetie."

"Thank you, Mom. That's such a beautiful thing to say, and such a beautiful gesture." She hugged her mother, clinging for a moment longer than necessary. "I love you, too. And I have no regrets about my childhood. It turned out just fine."

"We're both going to ruin our makeup if we keep this up," Happy cautioned. "Here, let me make sure your dress is straight before we hitch a ride to your wedding."

It was a simple sheath with an overlay of pale cream lace. Sashed at the waist with flutter sleeves just below the elbow, the ballerina-length dress revealed the graceful white sandals upon her feet. A simple diamond heart hung from a delicate chain around her neck, a gift from Brash last night at rehearsal. Along with her smile and the bracelet, it was the only adornment Madison needed.

They had dressed at Laura's house, as it was closest on the ranch to the wedding site. As the clock neared two, Madison made her way outside to the stagecoach. Flowers and ribbons adorned the refurbished antique vessel, which four white horses led. Ahead of her, the twins and Megan rode in an open carriage.

Two dozen wooden folding chairs were set up alongside the banks of the Brazos River, holding their nearest and dearest loved ones to share in the happy occasion.

A single guitarist strummed a sweet melody as the wedding party arrived. Madison and the kids arrived from the east, while Brash rode up from the west on his favorite horse. Madison's heart hitched in her chest when she saw her bridegroom. She didn't remember ever seeing him look so handsome, or so virile. Her knees were weak as she watched him and the preacher take their places beneath a simple wooden arch. Looking suspiciously like the one from Lydia's garden, its only disguise was a single spray of wildflowers on either side, held by a pale-yellow ribbon. The sprays bore a marked resemblance to the bouquet Madison held in her trembling fingers.

The song changed as Megan and Bethani stepped from their carriage. Madison had always been a huge fan of Bryan Adams, so a guitar rendition of *(Everything I Do) I Do It For You* played as the girls floated down the aisle and took their places across from the men.

When the *Wedding March* began, Madison forced herself not to run down the aisle toward her future husband. Smiling tenderly at her son, she allowed him to take her arm and escort her over the carpet of grass at a moderate pace. The guests stood as she approached, but after a brief scan and a welcoming smile, she only had eyes for Brash.

Her heart thudded wildly as Blake delivered her to the lawman's side. The teen brushed his mother's cheek with a kiss and firmly shook Brash's hand before taking his place as best man. With a dreamy sigh and a film of happiness in her eyes, Madison gazed up at her husband-to-be.

She barely heard the preacher's words. He admonished them to be faithful and true, and to put no one before God and the sanctity of marriage. Madison nodded when appropriate, but her mind and her heart raced ahead. She could already see their future, holding grandbabies and turning old together. She knew she would be every bit as happy then, as she was now.

They had written their own vows, which neither shared aloud until now. Turning toward one another and joining hands, Brash's rich baritone infused the afternoon sunshine with an extra layer of warmth.

"My beautiful bride," he began. Unable to resist, he touched her face with his fingertips. "There are no adequate words to describe how I feel about you. To say I love you sounds so ordinary, when you, my sweet Madison, are an extraordinary woman. I want to share my life with you, to know your sorrows and your joys, to walk this journey of a lifetime with you by my side. When you are troubled, I will help you find a solution. When you are sick, I will stay by your side and nurse you back to health. Even when we are apart, I will be with you, in mind and in spirit. I will be your soul mate, your lover, your helper, and your friend. We will be partners in this marriage, sharing the life we will make together. I promise to be your rock when you need added strength, to be your crutch when you get weary. I will be faithful and true, and I will never betray the trust or the love you bestow upon me. From this day forward, we are one. Everything I have, I give to you. My heart, my soul, my riches, my fears, my future. You complete me. Along with Megan, Blake, and Bethani, you are my everything, and I vow to love you until the day I die."

Madison recited her vows with misted eyes.

"You, Brash deCordova, are the missing piece of my heart. You complete me. I can think of no greater honor than to be allowed to share your life with you. You and Megan complete the broken circle of our family and make us whole again. I vow to share everything with you, to come to you when I have a problem, and to help ease whatever worries you are facing. Together, we will find a solution. I vow to be faithful and true, to nurse you back to health when you are ill, to cheer you on when you are weary, to share the good times and the bad, to give you a home and a place of refuge. I will be your partner in life, your lover, your confidante, your biggest admirer, your soul mate, and your friend. All that I have is yours, and I will love you and be true to you until the last breath I take."

"Do you have the rings?" the preacher asked.

Brash slid a simple white gold band onto her finger. It was slender and elegant, like the bride herself. "This ring is a reminder of my commitment to you, to my vow of fidelity and love, and of unconditional support. Like the circle of this ring, my love knows no end. From this day forward, sweetheart, we are one, until death do us part. Forever and always, and for keeps." He made certain the ring was snug. "I love you, Maddy."

A light breeze stirred the clouds above them, splashing a few drops of rain upon them. Madison laughed as she took a silver band and slid it onto Brash's long, tapered finger. "This ring is a symbol of my love and commitment to you. Like now, I can't promise that the skies will always be sunny and clear, but I can promise you that we'll face the clouds together. With this ring, I become your wife, and you become my husband. Forever and always, and until death do us part."

It seemed only fitting that their first kiss as husband and wife should take place here amid the wildflowers and fresh spring grasses blowing gently in the wind, here in the same spot along the Brazos where they had shared their very first kiss, ever. Brash didn't wait for the prompt. He pulled his bride into his arms and kissed her, his mouth hungry but carefully tempered for control.

"Well, ladies and gentlemen, it looks like I've been grandstanded," the preacher chuckled. "As soon as they find time to join us, I would like to pronounce these two fine people as husband and wife."

"Sorry, sir," Brash murmured, looking anything but remorseful. "I couldn't help myself."

"I understand. Now, by the powers vested in me by the State of Texas and our great and merciful Lord, I pronounce you husband and wife. What God has joined together, let no man put asunder. Ladies and gentleman, I present to you Mr. and Mrs. Brash deCordova. And family."

This kiss had a little more control, but only by a small margin. All too soon, they were interrupted by squeals from the girls and a hearty round of hugs from all three teenagers. The rest of their family wasn't far behind.

Another rustle of the clouds had everyone scurrying for cover, but Madison and Brash merely laughed. Nothing could put a damper on today's happiness. They even opted for an open-air carriage ride back to Laura's house, defying the heavens to rain in earnest.

As they drove away, Brash threw out a warning that he would arrest anyone who dared disturb them before six o'clock.

"That," Madison said dreamily as they left their guests behind, "was absolutely perfect. Simple, elegant, and uniquely ours."

"Best of all," Brash agreed, "it was legal." He pulled her closer with a sexy growl. "Come over here and kiss me, Mrs. deCordova."

As she well knew, her husband was a master at kissing. Brash had turned the technique into an art form, and his kisses never failed to delight her. As he cupped his large hand around her neck and held her face close, her skin tingled with anticipation. He gently rubbed his thumb back and forth, the rough texture a delicious contrast against the softness of her cheek. It was an enticing reminder of what was to come, when his hands would explore the rest of her body.

Slow to move in, he grazed his mouth along hers at first, barely touching her lips, making her want more. His breath was sweet with peppermint, warm with need.

He tortured her for an agonizingly long moment, trailing his lips over her cheek, her neck, that erotic spot just under her ear. While Madison melted beneath his touch—one quickened breath at a time, one thought evaporating upon another, one limb more languid than the next—he gathered her ever closer, still teasing, still refusing to give her the proper kiss she craved. She even whimpered, her mouth now watering for the taste of his. Brash refused to be rushed, tugging her closer, weaving his fingers into the fine hairs at the nape of her neck.

Then, and only then, did he touch his mouth to hers.

Long moments later, Brash raised his dark-auburn head and grumbled, "Why didn't we choose the stagecoach? At least it offered privacy."

Madison tucked her head into the crook of his neck, embarrassed by the intensity of their kisses. She had wound up sitting in his lap, completely lost to the pleasures of being in his arms. "Soon, my love," she whispered, laying her palm against his cheek.

"Not soon enough," he muttered thickly.

"Brash?" she ventured after a moment, suddenly shy.

"Yes, sweetheart?"

"It's... it's been awhile. Gray and I were all but separated those last two years. We slept in separate bedrooms. So I may not... I mean..."

"Shh. Let's not worry about that. It's been awhile for me,

too, love. I know I had a reputation as a player in high school, but I was never really like that, not even when I was young and stupid. I'd like to think I learned a few things as I got older, including how to control myself. I haven't been a monk all these years, but it's definitely been a while."

"I just don't want to disappoint you." She revealed her greatest fear in a shaky whisper.

"That's not possible, sweetheart. I love you. That's magical, all on its own."

Madison managed a laugh. "No pressure there. You just expect magic, is all."

"I promise you, sweetheart. You're worrying for nothing. And if it takes me all afternoon to prove it to you, I will."

It didn't take nearly that long. The first time was convincing enough, even though the magic was short and fast. They took their time after that, learning and exploring and practicing the miraculous art of love. Fully sated and replete with happiness, Madison dozed off in Brash's arms soon after.

It came as no surprise, but her husband was a master in the magic department, too.

19

Still steeped in the rosy glow of lovemaking, the couple was reluctant to leave their fantasy world and return among the living. But their guests awaited, and they knew the community had wanted this wedding almost as much as they had. Being loved and supported by so many people was too humbling to ignore.

Knowing they could pick up tonight where they left off now, the newlyweds changed into casual clothes and headed off to the party.

The old cotton gin was in rare form tonight, the cavernous space decorated with thousands of twinkling lights, tables covered in simple white cloths, and not a single yard of tulle. Each table sported a trail of wildflower bouquets, tied with raffia and presented in Mason jars for a simple but elegant country look. Two long buffet tables were laden with a feast befitting Southern royalty. From barbecued brisket and chicken to boiled crawfish and shrimp, there was plenty to choose from. Traditional sides included boiled potatoes and corn on the cob, coleslaw, pinto beans, sliced onions and pickles, and crusty slices of bread. More choices included a huge mixed greens salad, relishes, pickled okra and pickled peppers, a variety of cold salads, and several choices of pasta, with or without sauces. Another table offered fruits, cheeses, and crackers, amid cold meats and sausages. The dessert table, independent of the cake table itself, offered Lydia's peach cobbler, Granny Bert's pecan pie squares, cookies baked by the twins and Megan, and the delectable chocolate brownies that only Genny could perfect.

Brash and Madison moved among the crowd already gathered, thanking guests for coming and accepting their well wishes. As the party swelled and more people poured in, Madison suspected several slipped in without an invitation, but since there was plenty of food and drink, she saw no reason to monitor the door. As often in a small community—and particularly in their case, when so much of their lives had been publicized on national television—people assumed it was an event open to the public, and not a private celebration among family and close friends. As long as everyone remained cordial and well behaved, Madison was happy to share her special day with the entire town. She drew the line at radio audiences.

"Is that Nigel Barrett I see?" Brash murmured in her ear as they stood in the loosely formed receiving line, awaiting the next wave of well-wishers.

"I do believe it is. He cleans up quite nicely, doesn't he?"

"It's not like the old coot can't afford a new suit and a haircut. He just *chooses* to wear those worn-out overalls all the time."

"Because in his own words, why throw away a perfectly good pair of pants, when you can simply patch the knee and get another five years out of them?" She spoke through her teeth, smiling to an elderly couple that headed their way. "But is that Collette Erickson he's talking to?"

Brash extended his hand to the man who approached. "Good to see you, Merle, Verna. Thanks for coming."

By the time the Bishops wandered away, Nigel Barrett took their place.

"I'm glad you were able to come, Mr. Barrett. Have you gotten a plate yet?" Madison asked as they shook hands.

"Not yet. Wanted to stop by and give you my wedding present."

"I told you a gift wasn't necessary."

"I know. But I figured you'd both appreciate this *present* over my *presence.*" He made a point to emphasize the words. As he handed the envelope to Brash, he nodded toward the woman he was recently speaking with. "What's my nurse doing here?"

"Your nurse? Oh, you must mean Collette. I had no idea you knew her!"

"She works at the VA hospital in Waco. Does all my lab work. She's the only one who knows how to stick a fella without reaming out his veins."

Brash worked the certificate free from the envelope and read over it. With a stunned expression on his face, he quickly looked up to stare at the older gentleman.

"Mr. Barrett. I have no idea what to say. This—This is a very generous gift. Are you sure about this, sir?"

"I gave it to you, didn't I?" he asked gruffly. "I reckon I ain't lost my mind just yet, even if that fool on the other side of me thinks otherwise. I'll be damned if I give Sanchez a single percent of the rights before I kick the bucket, but you've always been fair to me, Brash. Treated my land with respect and took care of it better than I ever did. Even when the two of you were young, your daddies and granddaddies made sure the place was cleaned up after those dad-blamed pasture parties you kids favored. And don't think I ain't seen you down there recently, cleaning up behind the new crop of kids. I figure I can at least do right by you and give you the rest of the mineral rights."

Madison's eyes widened in surprise. "Are you serious? You're giving us full mineral rights to the land?"

"Don't get ahead of yourself, missy. I'm just giving you half for now. You'll have to wait on the other half till I keel over, just like the deed allows."

Brash extended his hand for a hearty handshake. "Thank you, sir. This is a very generous gift. We appreciate your generosity."

"Well, so far, your little bride ain't found any of my natural relatives, and I'm not about to leave it all to the government. I hear they're talking about leasing land again, so I figure you can start a little nest egg for your new family if they do."

"Are you sure you don't want to hang on to these until...well, until you release the other half?" Madison stumbled over a polite way to say, 'until you die.'

"Go ahead and say it. We're all thinking it, anyway. Yeah, I could hang on to the rights till I die and just award you the full one hundred percent upon my death, but what do I need with more money? You have teenagers. You can put it to better use than I can."

Overcome with the crotchety old man's generosity, Madison threw her arms around him and surprised him with a hug. "Thank you, Mr. Barrett! What a sweet and generous thing to do!"

He muttered blubbering noises about her foolishness and making too much of a simple gesture, but she knew he was pleased. After another round of handshakes—and some unsolicited advice from Nigel about how Brash should clear out the underbrush along the fence line between them—the older man shuffled off toward the buffet line.

"I can't believe that just happened," Brash murmured, tucking the envelope into his pocket for safekeeping.

"Full mineral rights on two hundred acres of land? That's good, right?" Madison asked, just to be certain.

"That's excellent. Almost unheard of these days."

"That was incredibly generous of him," Madison murmured. "And very surprising! To be honest, I wasn't sure he even liked me." She looked over her shoulder, pleased to see that Collette had joined the old man in line and was making small talk with him.

"What's not to like? I, for one, am crazy over you." Brash pulled her to him for a long, thorough kiss.

"Okay, you two, break it up." Blake appeared in front of them, carrying a heaping plate of crawfish.

"That's all you're eating? Just crawfish?" his mother asked. That hardly sounded like her son, the walking creature she lovingly called her bottomless pit.

"Oh, no," the lanky teen assured her. "My first two plates were a mix of everything, the third plate was all brisket, and this one is all crawfish. I'll base my fifth plate on whichever one I liked best."

"Please leave enough for our guests, son," Brash said, only half-kidding.

"And remember there's cake," Madison pitched in. "Genny made the wedding cake, so you know it's going to be delicious." Having studied under a pastry chef in Paris, Genny's cakes and pastries were her friend's most magnificent specialties.

"No offense, Mom, but I sure do miss Aunt Genny living with us and doing the cooking. Too bad she and Cutter didn't just move into the Big House with us. There's plenty of room." A slight sulk infused his words.

"No offense taken on my part, but you can't blame them for wanting their own home. Especially after Cutter went to all the trouble of remodeling his grandparents' old farmhouse."

"I guess. She could have at least left some of her recipes." The teen wasn't quite through pouting.

"We both know I would have butchered them," Madison pointed out. She was a fine cook herself, but no one quite compared to her best friend.

"Hey, let me polish off this plate, and then let's cut the cake. It will be a nice break before I go back for another round or two." The tall blond made a kissing sound in the air before ambling off. "Love you bunches, Mom. You too, old man."

Madison shook her head. It never ceased to amaze her how much her son could eat. It took a full moment for his parting words to sink in.

"Wait. Did he just tell you he loved you?"

Brash's eyes weren't completely dry as he smiled and said in a voice gruff with emotion, "Yeah. Yeah, he did."

Tears sprang to Maddy's eyes, as well. "The gifts just keep on coming, don't they?" she said in a soft voice.

"Sure do. And there go two more of the best presents I've ever received." He nodded toward Megan and Bethani as they scurried across the floor with some of their friends, headed toward the dessert table. "When, by the way, do we get to cut our cakes?"

He craned his head around to survey the bride's table. A five-tiered cake took center-stage, decorated with yellow candy roses and occasional sprigs of edible wildflowers. "Is it supposed to look like that?" he asked. He sounded skeptical.

"Like what?"

"Like a skinned cat. It looks like Genny ran out of frosting and spread it too thin."

Madison laughed aloud. "It's called a scraped cake, silly. And yes, it's supposed to look like that. Besides, think of it this way. We can eat two pieces instead of one, because it doesn't have all that frosting on it."

"Two things come to mind. One, I wonder if our son will leave enough for us to even have a second piece. And two, I may have to ask Genny for the leftover frosting. I can think of a better use for it than smearing it on cake." The timbre of his deep voice fell, along with his sensual gaze. "Like over your delectable body, for instance."

"I would burst into flames right about now," Madison whispered, "but I melted into a puddle when I heard you call Blake *our* son."

"For better or worse, sweetheart, and for keeps. We're one big family now."

Before he could work in another kiss, someone else came up to offer congratulations, and the moment was put on hold.

CRCRCRCR

After grabbing a quick plate of their own, the happy couple made their way to the bride's table for the formal cutting of the cake. Brash made a brief speech, thanking everyone for coming and sharing their special day with them, and Blake, Bethani, and Megan made a communal toast to their parents. After tears were sniffed away and pictures were taken, the five of them stacked one hand upon the other to clumsily slice through the first layer of cake.

Since it was crudely cut and over-sized, Blake offered to take that piece, and deftly handed his mother a smaller, neater slice. The teen used remarkable restraint, waiting until Madison and Brash fed each other their first bites before digging into his own piece with gusto.

As Madison encouraged guests to come up and have cake and punch, a ruckus broke out in the rear of the room. She glanced worriedly at Brash, wondering if a wedding crasher caused a scene. It was for that very reason they hadn't issued an open invitation in the newspaper, the way many couples did.

To her surprise, it wasn't a wedding crasher, but two of their invited guests. She watched as Nigel Barrett stood from his chair and all but crawled down Tony Sanchez's throat. The older man pulled the tablecloth when he moved, so Collette made a grab for his plate before it clattered to the floor. Tony stood with him, shadowing the curmudgeon with his bulky linebacker physique. The two men shouted at one another, anger slurring their words.

But there was no mistaking their final slung insults, before nearby guests pulled them apart.

"Over. My. Dead. Body." Nigel's words were clearly enunciated.

"Then do us all a favor and kick the bucket, old man!" Tony bellowed. He shook off a friend's restraining hold and bolted from the room, leaving an uncomfortable silence in his wake.

"And with that," Brash's deep voice boomed smoothly, "I think it's time to dance." He nodded to the bandleader, who quickly scrambled into place. As the bridegroom held out his hand for the first dance with his bride, the opening notes of a tender love ballad floated on the air.

They were halfway into their dance, slow and sexy and totally absorbed in one another, when another commotion broke into their private little world.

The sounds vaguely registered in Madison's love-hazed mind. Coughing. A stifled gag. Rustling. A dull thud. Followed, now, by gasps and a startled cry.

Each sound broke her slowly out of the fog, until her eyes were wide and frantically searching the room, making certain the sounds hadn't come from her children. When she located all three of them, laughing in a far corner with friends, her next thought was of her grandmother. Granny Bert and Sticker awaited their turn on the dance floor, their feet impatiently tapping out time with the song.

As Madison continued to scan the crowd, more people became aware of the strange noises near the dance floor. Reining her focus in, Madison noticed movement at the far table behind them, in the very place the last commotion had taken place. Her first worry was that Tony had returned and taken the argument back up, but she soon saw that wasn't the case.

A black coat draped across the table, and Collette stood over it, pumping its lumpy form. "Help!" she squeaked. Her voice gradually increased in volume. "This—This man needs help! I think he's choking!"

Allen Wynn turned the coat over, revealing the crumpled form of Nigel Barrett. "He's not choking," Allen corrected, his deep voice carrying across the crowded room. "I think he's dead!"

୧୪୧୫୧୫୧

For a single moment, time stood still. The band stopped playing mid-note. A hush fell over the huge room. A sole spurt of laughter from the far corner—where the kids hung out, ignorant of what had happened beyond them—twinkled in the air and echoed in the empty chambers of the tall, metal-clad ceiling. Someone sniffed.

And then everything happened at once, as people leapt over chairs to rush to Nigel's aid, and as a nervous chatter moved in a wave through the crowd, much like the childhood game of *Gossip.* Someone whispered the ugly truth to their neighbor, who turned and shared the shocking news with their neighbor, who gasped the words to the person next to them, and so on. Brash spurred into action, leaving his bride alone on the dance floor as, for the second time in less than three weeks, he rushed to the aid of a fallen man.

Once again, he was too late.

Asking guests to step back, Madison approached the table with dread. Even without Allen's blurted words, one look at Nigel's gray face spoke volumes. The old man was gone.

She looked around for Collette but saw she had retreated to the shadows of a darkened corner. The all-too-familiar sequence of events had to bring back ugly memories for the new widow.

Brash and some of the other men worked to lay Nigel's

prone body upon the table. Madison quickly snatched away plates, clearing the space for its solemn load.

As she pulled away the plate the older man had fallen upon, she was surprised to see a half-eaten shrimp buried within a pile of chopped brisket and folded into a slice of bread. Judging from the shape of the remaining bread, she guessed that the man had taken a large bite of the shrimp-tainted meat. But that didn't make sense. Nigel himself had told her he was allergic to shellfish.

While everyone around her worked to lay out his lifeless body, Madison grabbed a napkin and carefully wrapped up the half-eaten fold over. She wasn't sure of its significance, but a sixth sense told her something wasn't right.

No pun intended, but something here was fishy.

20

"What a day."

It was late by the time they fell into bed. It was hardly the romantic return they had anticipated.

Up until the very moment they saw Nigel Barrett's body slumped over the table, Madison could think of nothing but returning to their bedchambers and familiarizing herself with the fine specimen of her husband's body. She craved to feel his fingers on her skin again, to feel his quickened breath in her ear once more as they moved as one, finding the wholeness she had never known until him.

But one look into the lifeless face of their unlikely benefactor, and thoughts such as those had frozen in time. She still felt cold, all these hours later.

"Come here, Mrs. deCordova," Brash said, pulling her into his arms and tucking her safely against his chest. "Not exactly what I had planned for tonight, but you're beside me, and that's all that matters."

"I still can't believe it, Brash," she murmured. A single fat tear slid from her cheek and landed on his bare skin. "After that wonderful gesture, gifting us the mineral rights..." She shook her head, trying to arrange the scrambled thoughts in her head. "I just can't believe it. He was searching for his family, so he wouldn't die alone. So he could leave behind the legacy of his family's land. And now he's gone, just like that."

"It's sad, that's for certain."

"And at our wedding reception, of all places."

"I can't tell you how sorry I am, inviting Tony to the wedding. I never imagined... I thought for one day, the two of them could act like cordial adults."

"I can't believe you may have to arrest your friend for murder," Madison whispered in a sad voice.

It held no more regret than his. "I have to at least bring him in for questioning."

"You've known Tony for how long?"

"Almost twenty years. We were both drafted to play for the pros, right out of college. When I came home to marry Shannon and turned to coaching, I told him he had a job, if he ever gave up the game himself. Two years later, he was out. I brought him to A&M with me, and later to Baylor." His fingers trailed absently over her arm, tracing an abstract pattern of anguish and self-imposed guilt. "I'm the one who introduced him to Nigel. I talked him into buying a hundred acres. At the time, it seemed the perfect solution for them both. I never dreamed they would work their way into this ferocious argument of theirs. Or that Nigel would end up dead because of it."

"You can't blame yourself, honey. That was between the two of them and had nothing to do with you. Nigel's gift tonight proves he never blamed you for any of this."

"I know that. And as the third wheel, I tried hard to remain neutral. The fact is, I could see where both of them were coming from. But as the chief of police, I should have put an end to this, long ago."

"There's no law against arguing, Brash. From what I understand, until tonight, that's all it ever was. A very long-running, heated, emotional argument. Nothing you could put a stop to."

"That's the part I can't wrap my head around," he admitted. "Tony is my friend. Why would he wait until tonight of all nights, our wedding night, *at our reception*, to finally act on their decade-old feud? It just doesn't make sense."

"I don't think it was something he planned. I'm guessing Tony found out about Nigel's gift to us, and it made him so angry that he acted irrationally."

"A crime of passion?"

"I'd much rather believe that," Maddy whispered, snuggling closer against him, "than to believe we invited a cold-blooded killer to our reception."

C3CRCQCR

"Is there anything else I can get for you, husband of mine?" Madison bent to press a kiss onto his lips the next morning, tasting of maple syrup and apple-cured bacon.

"I could pretend to be asleep, and you could use your special wake-up technique on me again."

"But we're both already dressed, and the goal of the wake-up technique is to get us completely naked and in the shower."

"I'm glad you went with the oversized option when you remodeled the bathroom."

"I never knew how handy all that space would become," she agreed, matching the wicked twinkle in his eyes with a glimmer of her own.

"I will take more coffee, if you don't mind."

She moved to get the coffee pot. "I'm sure you have a rough day ahead of you."

"Tony agreed to voluntarily come down to the station. I advised him to bring his attorney with him, but he insisted it wasn't necessary."

"Could we have it wrong? Is it possible Tony didn't kill Nigel?"

"Of course it's possible. Nigel could have accidentally ingested that shrimp, but it seems highly unlikely. The seafood was on one table, the barbecue on the other. Any mix-up had to happen at the table. And we all know Tony had means, opportunity, and motive."

"But we're assuming he knew Nigel was allergic to shellfish, when that might not be the case. I get the feeling the men weren't ever close and personal friends, and that's not something that comes up in casual conversation."

"It could," Brash argued. "They've known each other for over ten years. Who knows what conversations they've had during that time? And for all we know, it was something Tony discovered last night. It may have given him the perfect opportunity, especially if it was a crime of passion, like you suggested."

"But how would Tony have gotten the shrimp into Nigel's fold over? He couldn't very well say 'excuse me, while I bury my shrimp in your brisket.'"

"Call me a lovesick fool on his honeymoon, but that has a dirty ring to it," Brash grinned.

Madison swatted him on the shoulder. "I'm serious. How would Tony meddle with Nigel's plate, especially without someone seeing him?"

"I don't know. That's what I plan to ask my old friend. Under oath."

"I wish I could come with you, sweetheart."

"You shouldn't have to spend your first full day as a newlywed at the police station."

"Neither should you," she pointed out.

"I know, and I'm sorry. I know I'm off duty, but I feel I need to be there for this. I'm sorry to run out on you."

"I understand, Brash. I hate it for your sake, not mine. Tony is your friend."

"As was Nigel. I owe it to him to do a thorough investigation into his death, no matter where the leads take me."

21

Even though her client was no longer alive, Madison felt compelled to continue her investigation into the old man's next of kin. If nothing else, any newly discovered family could attend his funeral.

Madison had papers scattered over her desk as she waded through the life and times of Nigel Barrett. With the old Barrett family Bible as her road map and copies of records found at the county clerk's office, Madison was knee deep in piecing together his family tree.

The reading was interesting. Madison always enjoyed learning about history, and the Barrett family was steeped in it. The old Bible traced bloodlines back to the 1700s, when the first Nigel Barrett left Ireland to settle in the southern portion of North America. The trail led through Virginia, Alabama, and into Texas. Samuel Earl Barrett and his brother Eugene were among the original Old Three Hundred to receive a land grant from Stephen F. Austin. According to the Bible, the land along the Brazos had been in the Barrett family since 1827, when the brothers laid claim to a sitio (four thousand, four hundred plus acres) for ranching purposes. In the midst of settling and clearing the wild land, the Barretts were caught up in the Runaway Scrape and were forced to temporarily leave their new home when Santa Anna invaded Texas. By the time they returned, their log cabins had been ravaged, by either the Mexican Army or the Indians. The Bible bore the record of starting over, and of all the marriages, births, and deaths since that time. There were interesting notes written in the margins, noting memorable moments in time. Several old papers and certificates were stuffed among the yellowing pages, none of which Madison disturbed.

The shrinking of the Barrett dynasty made Madison sad.

Through the years, those four thousand acres had shrunk to four hundred. According to the old Bible, some ten or so years after the Republic of Texas was admitted into the Union, the Barretts sold most of their sitio to Bertram Randolph. The planter took advantage of the rich river-bottom soil and soon built a cotton empire along the Brazos. Madison knew that before his death in the early 1900s, Randolph gave each of his quarrelsome daughters, Naomi and Juliet, sufficient land to start their own towns but left the bulk of his estate to his most trusted employee, Andrew deCordova.

Fast forward a hundred plus years later, and the deCordova and Barrett families still owned the land.

But the saddest fact of all was that the Barrett clan, once so large and robust, had shrunk to a single soul, and now even he was gone. Madison understood now why the old man had been so eager to find his unknown family. A collateral descendant was better than no descendant at all. With him gone, the Barrett legacy was extinguished, for all intents and purposes. It wasn't just about the land; who would inherit the family Bible? Would anyone ever know the history of their family, as recorded in the thick old tome?

The thought was depressing. If only to herself, Madison pledged to find Nigel's long-lost family.

According to Collette, the most likely close relative was RR78, whoever that might be. The cryptic profile identified the person only as a male living in Texas. Until he replied to her request to connect, she was at a dead end.

At least she had the name of Nigel's niece now. Madison typed it into her database searches. As she feared with a given name such as Laura Jean—not to mention the almost generic surname of Thomas—there were dozens of hits. Searching for Laura Jean Huddleston, Laura Jean Ruiz, and Laura Jean Winston only compounded the results. She confined her search to people in Central Texas, specifically the Waco/Temple/Killeen/Marlin area, trimming the list down to eighteen. By the time Madison threw in the parameters of an estimated age and the assumption of race, the list dwindled to seven.

She paired the name Eric with each of the last names and searched again, but the two resulting leads were doubtful. Abandoning that angle for now, she concentrated on the seven women on her list.

Most of the hits came from obituaries, which didn't bode well for finding Nigel's surviving relatives. Tracking down the families of the deceased women meant even more searches and a serious investment of her time. For now, Madison put copies of the obituaries into a file for later perusal.

By mid-afternoon, Madison's back ached, and her eyes were crossed. This was hardly how she had envisioned her first day as a newlywed. She knew for her dear husband, it must be ten times worse. He was still at the police station, interrogating one of his oldest friends on possible murder charges.

Taking a break, Madison made a glass of iced tea and carried it to the front porch swing. It was another lovely spring day and, being a Sunday, the street out front was quiet.

She settled in and replayed the joyful events of yesterday in her head. Despite the leaky clouds and the disastrous

ending to the reception, it had been a wonderful day. She
allowed her mind to stroll through the happy moments that
joined her life with that of the man she loved.

All too soon, the remembered timeline brought her to
the reception, and her thoughts stumbled into that fateful
moment when Tony and Nigel got into an argument. She
tried to recall exactly what she had seen, exactly what she
had overheard.

Nigel and Tony were seated across from one another,
and Nigel was already on his feet, towering over Tony. She
vaguely remembered Allen tugging on Nigel's arm, trying to
settle him down, and Collette grabbing for the tablecloth.
The white cloth bunched in Nigel's hand, right along with
his napkin.

For a man of such considerable bulk, Tony had moved
quickly, coming to his feet and meeting Nigel nose to nose
over the wildflower centerpiece. A former linebacker and
still in his prime, Tony was bigger and stronger than the
older gentleman, but old Nigel hadn't backed down. He had
yelled at the other man, something about over his dead
body.

Tony hadn't been opposed to the suggestion. Hadn't he
said something to that order? Something about Nigel doing
everyone a favor and kicking the bucket? The guest seated
next to Tony—another former NFL player, though his name
escaped her now—pulled him away and tried to reason with
him, but she recalled how Tony jerked his arm free and
stalked off, his face dark with anger.

The question was, had Tony been angry enough to do
something to harm the older man? And when would he
have done it? Even if Nigel left his plate unattended, there
were people all around them. Surely, someone would have
noticed him meddling with the other man's food. And given
their frequent animosity toward one another, Madison
couldn't image a scenario where Tony had offered to fetch
seconds for his cantankerous neighbor.

So how, she wondered, would Tony have managed to taint Nigel's fold-over with the deadly shrimp?

Before she could ponder the question further, a familiar truck pulled up. With his ever-present welding rig and faithful dog perched upon the flatbed, Cutter Montgomery drove straight into the driveway. Because he was like family, he was one of the few people to have access to the gate's code.

"Morning, Mrs. deCordova!" he called jovially as he climbed from the truck.

Madison returned the greeting with a wave and a happy smile. "Good morning to you, Mr. Montgomery."

She watched as the younger man approached. To the dismay of women throughout the county, from the ages of two to ninety-two, Cutter Montgomery was off the market. The man was totally and utterly in love with his wife.

Married life agreed well with the handsome firefighter. The laugh lines around his blue eyes and sensual mouth appeared deeper now. His broad, bony shoulders still punched from the cotton of his western-styled shirt, but they seemed more relaxed, as if they had finally found the skin that fit. Just six weeks in, but Madison thought marriage had already thickened his flat belly, ever so slightly.

"I hate to come calling at the honeymoon cottage so soon, but I'm looking for your new husband." Only Cutter would call the three-story mansion a cottage. He had an easy sense of humor about him, a special knack of putting people at ease and bringing a smile to their faces.

One touched hers now. "I'll forgive you, especially since I'm alone here at the cottage." The amusement fell from her face. "Brash is still down at the police station."

A slight frown puckered his brow. "I didn't see his truck. Guess I missed it."

"Would you like some tea?" She moved aside, making room for him there on the swing.

He pulled the cowboy hat from his head as the swing

danced beneath his weight.

"Thanks, but Genny's expecting me back soon. If I play my cards right, she'll be taking a batch of apple turnovers out of the oven about the time I walk through the door." He winked mischievously.

"You're going to turn *into* an apple turnover one of these days!" Madison predicted with a sharp burst of laughter.

"Can I help it if my wife is the best cook in the state?"

"I know Blake is certainly missing her and her culinary talents these days. The poor kid is stuck with having his mother cook for him."

"You can send him over to the house once in a while for a mercy meal. No offense," Cutter added quickly. "You're a fine cook, yourself."

She laughed again. "No offense taken. I'll be the first to agree that my friend is a better cook than I am."

A comfortable moment lingered between them, until Cutter shifted upon the swing. Madison sensed it correlated with a shift in his mood.

"What is it, Cutter?" she asked in a resigned voice.

"Why do you think something's up?"

"Because I know you. And I also know you wouldn't come over to the 'honeymoon cottage' unless there was something serious afoot. Spill it."

He didn't answer immediately. "So Brash is down at the police station, questioning his old friend about murder?"

"Unfortunately, yes."

"Motive?"

Madison's shrug was graceful, despite the mood it reflected. "Anger issues? An argument that got out of hand? Money? Upon Nigel's death, Tony will get fifty percent of the mineral rights to the land he bought from him. I suppose that could be a motive."

Cutter fingered the straw hat in his lap, not quite meeting her eyes. "I was in town earlier and heard some rumbling. I thought I should give Brash a heads up."

She nodded. "With Tony being his friend, I know Brash will come under extra scrutiny."

"It's not just the Tony angle."

"What is it, then?"

"Word of Nigel's wedding gift has made it through the grapevine."

"That didn't take long, even by The Sisters' standards!" There was no humor in her snort. A full moment passed before she angled her head and thought to ask, "But what does that have to do with anything?"

"There's a few—and by a few, I mean one. Joel Werner— who thinks that complicates matters and offers a new motive to killing ol' Nigel."

"I get the Joel Werner thing. The man is after Brash's job and makes no bones about it. But, again, what does our wedding gift have to do with anything?"

"Is it true that Nigel gave you fifty percent of the mineral rights on your land as a wedding present?"

"Yes, that's correct."

"So when Nigel dies, Brash and you would own the full rights."

"Right. But I still don't see—" She broke off abruptly, as a sick feeling wormed its way into her stomach. "Wait. You can't be suggesting... That—That's ludicrous!"

"Of course it is. And *I'm* not suggesting it. But Joel Werner wasted no time in making the suggestion."

Madison stared at her friend in horror. "That man's actually accusing Brash of—of murdering Nigel?"

"Not yet, he's not. But I have no doubt it's coming. Right now, he's just planting the seeds of doubt. Suggesting that Brash and Tony may have been in on this together. But I'm sure it won't be long, and he'll start talk about Brash being the one to benefit the most from Nigel's death."

"That is utterly insane."

"I know. And I hate to lay this at your feet—on your honeymoon, of all times—but I thought you two needed to know. It's better to snip these things off in the bud, before they burst out in full bloom."

"Absolutely," Madison agreed, but her voice sounded dazed. She had obvious trouble absorbing the farcical rumblings. "Thank you. Thank you for bringing this to our attention."

Cutter laid a comforting hand on her arm. "You do know that very few people will even listen to the man. He's a fanatic, and most folks see him for the sleek politician he is, spouting lies about other people to make himself look better."

"But there will be a few..."

"There's always a few, Maddy. The important thing is that anyone with any sense knows Brash would never be part of something like this, no matter how much money was at stake. For every person who gives Joel Werner the time of day, there will be ten others who have Brash's back. And I'll be at the head of that line."

"I know that, Cutter. And thank you. You and Genny are always there for us when we need you." She hugged his neck and felt the kiss he brushed against her hair.

It wasn't until Cutter said goodbye and started for the front steps that Madison thought to ask, "Hey, Cutter. You said something about money being at stake. What are mineral rights worth, anyway?"

"It all depends, but right now, a decent price would be a thousand dollars an acre. That's just the bonus consideration, mind you, for allowing the company rights to exploration. If they should drill a well and hit a vein, then you would get royalties. Some of those could be quite hefty."

"I didn't realize mineral rights were such a big deal."

"That's why a lot of people sell the land but retain the mineral rights. These days, it's rare to own a full one hundred per cent of the rights to any piece of property. Even fifty percent is good."

"I see." Her tone was distracted, as she digested the

information he had just told her. Lifting her hand in a wan farewell, she said something about his turnovers getting cold, but her mind was already moving ahead.

Maybe I should be asking if Tony's decade-old feud with Nigel over the mineral rights was worth murder, she mused. She paused to do the math in her head.

If the bonus on leasing was worth a thousand dollars an acre, even fifty percent of the mineral rights on Tony's hundred acres would amount to $50,000. Not a fortune, but maybe the former player had fallen on hard times and was desperate. According to the news, people committed murder for far less. Just the other day, she read about a woman who stabbed a co-worker to death because she stole her fifty-cent ink pen. She even used the stolen ballpoint to do the deed.

Tony Sanchez hardly seemed like one of them, however. From what she could see, he was a polite, personable man. True, he had a temper, but that didn't qualify him as a murderer.

While she was doing math, Madison added up some other numbers in her head. Even after selling to Brash and Tony, Nigel Barrett retained four hundred acres of land. Leasing rights on that could amount to as much as $400,000, plus the retained rights on Tony's land. Add the income from the two existing wells, the actual value of the land itself, the cattle and the crops, and his estate was worth a fortune. The house wouldn't amount to much, Madison conceded, but the electronics inside might.

The old man's net worth added a new dimension to his death. It wasn't hard to imagine someone might kill him to get access to his millions, but without an heir apparent, who would benefit the most from his death?

The sick feeling plagued her stomach again, making her queasy.

Joel Werner would ask that very question, and Madison didn't like the answer he would undoubtedly supply.

She did the math again, gasping when she realized that the bonus consideration on Brash's two hundred acres could amount to as much as $200,000, and that every penny would be his. Theirs.

To some, particularly Joel Werner, that could be construed as reason enough to commit murder.

෫෬෫෬

Brash returned home an hour later. In the space of a single day, her handsome husband seemed to have aged five years. His face looked haggard and drawn, and his color was slightly off. His knee popped as he lowered himself into the welcoming cushions of the couch.

When he tugged on her hand, she landed in a heap beside him, sinking into the butter-soft leather and the indention beside his two-hundred plus pounds of solid muscle. The feel of his warm, hard body next to hers momentarily distracted her.

"You aren't really going to arrest Tony, are you?" she asked, searching his dark eyes in concern. She couldn't remember him ever looking so weary.

"I don't want to. But I'm already getting pressure to do so."

"From where?" she demanded. Who dared pressure her husband, thinking they could do his job better than he could?

"Both mayors. The Juliet city council. There's a call on my phone from Billy Blackburn that I haven't answered, so I'm guessing the Naomi city council feels the same. And now the media is involved, so you can imagine what's to come."

"Why is the media involved?"

His sigh was heavy. Head tilted back to rest against the sofa cushion, Brash opened one eye to consult his new bride. "You really have to ask that question? You're still HOME TV's little darling, you know. Even if I didn't come with my own small claim to fame, there's Tony's time in the spotlight to consider. Pro-Ball Hall of Famer, former Super Bowl Champion, that gig on the prime-time dance show. We may not have invited the cameras to the wedding, but they were set up outside at the reception, and they caught plenty on tape. I'm guessing you haven't had the television on today?"

"No."

"They keep showing a clip of Tony storming out of the party, just after he and Nigel had words. They like to point out that less than fifteen minutes later, paramedics arrived on the scene to try to resuscitate one of our guests, the very man Tony was reported to have had a heated argument with. For added punch, they remind people of who you and I are, and why Tony was on the guest list." He rubbed his hand over his face, as if trying to smooth out some of the fatigue.

"I'm sorry, sweetheart. I know how hard this must be on you."

"To his credit, Tony came in voluntarily today and answered every question I had. Despite the circumstantial evidence against him, I really don't peg him for the crime. I've known Tony for almost twenty years. I just don't think he's capable of murder. But if not him, then who?"

"I've been asking myself the same thing. The only people who could possibly gain anything from his death were Tony, any relatives Nigel may or may not have, and... and you."

Instead of looking perturbed, Brash looked amused. "You mean *us*," he reminded her, winding his arm around her shoulders. "In case you've forgotten, we're married now. Everything I own is half yours. If I gain from his death, so do you."

"Believe me, I haven't forgotten. Even though I spent the day elbow-deep in research, the thought was never far from my mind. I am now Mrs. Brash Andrew deCordova." She curled into his side, her voice a soft sigh. "Loosely translated, that means the luckiest—and happiest—woman on the face of the earth."

"It's been a rough day, Mrs. deCordova. Show me just how happy you are."

Several kisses later, Madison laid her head upon his chest and snuggled in for a good hug.

"There're two things I need to tell you," she said after a while.

She felt him heave a deep sigh. "From the sound of your voice, neither is good."

"I haven't had a chance to tell you about it, but Friday night after the rehearsal dinner, Collette called me and talked for forty-five minutes. She told me she finally decided to have an autopsy performed on Bobby Ray's body."

His voice lifted. "I stand corrected. That's good news."

"Not really. She was too late. They had just completed cremating his body."

His chest deflated beneath her once again.

"But," she said, interjecting a hint of optimism into her voice, "as it turns out, perhaps his death was natural, after all. Collette confirmed something his friends told me. Like Nigel, Bobby Ray was allergic to seafood, particularly shrimp. Someone said they saw him eating a shrimp earlier in the day, and Collette claimed he was known to sneak a bite every now and then. Even though no one was aware of him ever having a severe reaction in the past, it doesn't mean it couldn't have happened this time."

"I suppose he had many of the symptoms." She glanced up to catch the thoughtful expression on Brash's face. "Blotchy skin, difficulty breathing, disoriented. The way he staggered away from the cannon suggested he was confused and a bit dizzy. Anaphylactic shock can cause a sudden drop in blood pressure, dizziness, and lightheadedness."

"I've heard that a person's sensitivity to shellfish can worsen over time, and that each episode can be worse than the previous one. It's possible that this episode was *the big one*, so to speak."

"Maybe."

"So, in a way, you were still right," Madison pointed out. "He didn't die of the heart attack everyone assumed."

"There's another possibility, you know."

"What's that?"

"I could have been flat-out wrong."

Madison pretended to consider the possibility before discarding it. "Nah," she decided. "That couldn't be it." She turned her face up to accept his dropped kiss.

"So that was one thing you wanted to tell me. You said you had two."

When Maddy extricated herself from his arms and twisted to look at him, he braced himself for the worst. She soon delivered.

"Cutter dropped by earlier. He said he was in town and heard rumblings. To begin with, word of Nigel's wedding gift to us has already climbed its way through the grapevine." Seeing his infamous smirk, she nodded. "I agree. Fast, even for our grapevine. But it gets worse. Knowing you would own full mineral rights on the two hundred acres, Joel Werner has pointed out that it could be to your advantage if Nigel died."

Brash stared at her in surprise, blinking as if to better comprehend her moving lips. His voice was deceptively calm as her words sank it. "He's accusing me of murdering Nigel?"

"Not yet," she was quick to point out, "but Cutter thinks he's planting the seeds. Right now, he's merely pointing out how you and Tony are old and personal friends, and how you could be in cahoots to fatten your pocketbooks."

"That's assuming, of course, that the oil company leases the land," Brash pointed out.

"I heard one already made an offer. However, that didn't come from Nigel. But yes," she agreed, "assuming."

"So how did this supposedly work? Tony and I teamed up to get our hands on a lease that, so far, doesn't even exist, and we thought my wedding reception would the perfect place to commit murder?" Brash shook his head in disbelief. "If Joel Werner can sell that one, he's even slicker than I give him credit for."

"We already know the man is gunning for you. This just gives him more ammunition."

"He's firing blanks," Brash said flatly. "Look. I'm sure he'll try to make a mountain out of a molehill, but when it's all said and done, it's still a molehill." He tried gathering her back into his arms. "Let's forget about Nigel, and Tony, and especially Werner, and concentrate on the two newlyweds in the room."

Madison resisted, but only slightly. "I don't think you're taking this seriously enough. I hate to point this out, but you just spent the entire afternoon questioning Tony over a molehill."

"A molehill with fire ants," he corrected. "This wasn't the first time Tony and Nigel argued over the rights. And enough people heard Tony's comment about 'do us all a favor and kick the bucket' to have it construed as a threat."

"Still..." Her protests weakened as Brash nibbled her earlobe.

"Still, I feel you are seriously neglecting your husband," he murmured. His words were a low rumble against the delicate column of her neck.

Her reply came out husky. "I—I am?"

"Absolutely." His mouth left a trail of moist heat down the side of her neck, over her collarbone and worked its way beneath the collar of her shirt. His fingers deftly dispensed of the buttons, exposing more skin to his wandering ministrations. "We've been married for over twenty-four hours, and you haven't made love to me half as many times." He pushed aside the troublesome blouse. "Definitely neglect."

"Hmm. Tell me, officer, is that a criminal offense?" She tried for a playful tone, but her words were breathless.

"Oh, yes. Punishable," he informed her in a deliciously low voice, "by a *fine* twenty-four hours in bed." He deliberately omitted the word 'and.'

As his mouth wandered lower, Madison knew it would be a fine punishment, in deed.

22

She knew hoping for twenty-four hours was being greedy.

At best, they managed eight. The phone started ringing early the next morning. After the third call, they gave up and crawled from the tangled covers.

"I guess you're getting off early for good behavior," Brash told her. A sexy twinkle appeared in his dark eyes as they trailed over her body. "Very good, as a matter of fact."

After accepting his kiss, Maddy made an observation of her own. "Reality is no fun."

Brash cupped a hand around her neck, and his expression turned sober. "You're sure you don't mind delaying our honeymoon? Because we can still go to Maryland."

"Of course, I *mind*. But I understand. Now is too crucial of a time for us to leave." When he would have spoken, she placed a finger to his lips. "Not only do you need to be here for the case, and for Tony, but we can't afford to turn our backs on Joel Werner. The man will twist our absence to his advantage, making it seem that you're running away."

"I know. But this was the perfect time for you and me to

get away. The kids are gone all week, skiing in Aspen with Charles and Annette."

Madison slid her arms around his neck. "So we'll still have a kid-free week and this big ole house, all to ourselves. We can honeymoon at home, and then later, when things have settled down, we'll go to Maryland like we planned."

"I was looking forward to seeing that Spy House you talked so much about."

"Why?" she teased, initiating a seductive kiss. "We might not make it out of the bedroom."

"Speaking of such... I notice the phone stopped ringing," he murmured, edging her back toward the bed.

"And technically, you have the day scheduled off..."

Brash paused long enough to set the ringer to silent. "Your sentence just got reinstated, Mrs. deCordova."

"The charge this time?"

"Skipping out on your honeymoon."

By the time they made it downstairs for coffee and a late breakfast, they had a dozen missed calls on both their phones, and several messages on the home phone. They spent the next fifteen minutes, sorting through which were important, which were noisy neighbors, and which were reporters.

While Brash canceled their plane tickets, Madison called *The Columbia Inn at Peralynna* and explained their situation. She, Genny, and Granny Bert had visited the stately mansion-turned-boutique-hotel (so like the Big House, in many ways) last month as part of Genny's bachelorette trip. The trip had turned out much more adventuresome—and dangerous—than anticipated, but it had also made them new friends and snagged them a free return visit. The innkeeper quickly assured her the offer was still good, redeemable at their convenience.

"All done," Madison reported. "Sophie was very gracious and understood completely. Given her close association with the CIA, FBI, and all those other alphabet organizations, she understands the need to be flexible. I promised to call as soon as this is all straightened out."

"I promise, we will go," Brash said, brushing a kiss into her hair. "Hey, I left something I need in the squad car. I'll run get it and be back to help you with breakfast."

"Don't be long," she warned. "I'm about to start the toast."

Brash quickly realized the difference between living in his previous modest-sized home and living here in the Big House. When he came downstairs earlier wearing just his jeans, he gave no thought to the rest of his wardrobe. Now, only half-dressed, he needed to run to the car, which, oddly enough, was closer in proximity than the master bedroom. The sheer size of his new home would take some getting used to.

Stuffing his bare feet into the cowboy boots he had abandoned last night at the front door, he reasoned that by the time he went upstairs and found a shirt, the toast would be ready. Or, he could slip outside—shirtless—and be back in time to help his bride in the kitchen.

He threw open the door and started onto the front porch. When an insect landed on the back of his neck, he crooked his elbow and slapped it.

"Chief deCordova!"

Hearing his name called, Brash looked up in time to see the flash. A half dozen or more reporters stood lined up along the fence, cameras flashing and television film rolling. After a full moment of shock, caught in broad day like a deer in the headlights, Brash retreated into the house and slammed the door.

"Maddy!" he bellowed. "You won't believe what's outside!"

⊗⊘⊗⊘

The pictures quickly made the rounds of all the news outlets.

If the name Brash deCordova made for a good headline, the photo of a shirtless Brash deCordova made for an excellent one. The shot caught him with sexy bed-head hair, dark stubble on his jaw, and half-zipped, low-slung jeans. With his elbow up and his hand behind his neck, he could have easily been posing for a pin-up calendar. Add the exposed tops of his rugged cowboy boots, the broad expanse of bare chest, the satisfied look of a man in love, and the photo went viral by nightfall.

"I didn't realize I was married to a sex symbol," Maddy teased.

Brash tossed the remote control onto the couch in disgust. "That's the third network to run that stupid picture," he complained. "I didn't get this much attention when I was in the NFL!"

"Should've put a shirt on before you went outside," she teased.

"Don't worry, I've learned my lesson. Leave a spare shirt in the foyer closet." He paused for a moment in reflection. "Is there a foyer closet?"

"Under the stairway."

"Got it. Leave a spare shirt and a pair of shoes handy, so I don't have to hike all the way back upstairs to the bedroom."

"A house this size does take some getting used to," Madison admitted.

"The problem with that silly picture," he continued, picking up the thread of his complaint as if it had never been broken, "is that, without it, no one would pay attention to this story yet. I'd have time to conduct more interviews, talk to the DA about possible charges, and make a rational, conscientious decision. But with it, and with all the attention it's bringing, the brass is breathing down my neck to charge Tony with murder."

"Not everyone reads the newsprint, you know. Most get hung up on the photo. Oh, and the sensational headlines, like my personal favorite." She panned her hand across an invisible billboard. "*Role Model, or Model Role?*"

Brash growled at his wife's antics. "This isn't funny, Madison."

Schooling her face into a solemn expression, she managed a contrite nod. More or less.

"I'm serious," he insisted.

Madison vigorously nodded in agreement, biting her inner lip to keep from grinning.

"If I knew which one of those reporters took the picture, I'd sue!"

"I've seen about five versions of the same basic shot, so I think they all took one. And why not? You make an excellent subject. Very handsome, and oh, so sexy." She couldn't help but waggle her eyebrows.

"I'm glad you find my humiliation so amusing."

"I'm sorry, sweetheart," she said sincerely, slipping her arms around his waist. "I'm just trying to make the best of a bad situation."

Before Brash could make a comeback, Maddy's phone rang. Seeing her grandmother's name pop up on the screen, she answered.

"Are you watching the news?"

"No, we turned it off."

"Turn it back on! That fool Joel Werner is talking. Channel 50."

As her grandmother disconnected without as much as a goodbye, Maddy grabbed the remote and turned the television back on. She waved away Brash's look of confusion, motioning toward the screen.

A news reporter held the microphone to Joel Werner's carefully poised face. Madison had no doubt he had practiced the pose, achieving just the right mix of vulnerable citizen and seasoned leadership. He was dressed in a button-down shirt and tie, not a single hair out of place, as he crooned into the mic.

"...said, I've heard it all over town. Folks are saying we don't want a playboy chief of police. We want strong, dependable leadership. Someone who shows no favoritism and who has the tenacity and integrity to go after criminals, no matter who they are. Someone who doesn't take a vacation in the middle of a big case."

"Isn't it true that Chief deCordova recently broke up an illegal narcotics and gambling network that had been operating not only here, but all over the county? And that many of those involved were highly esteemed members of the community, including a local banker?" the reporter asked.

"Yes, but that was after he and his fiancée had been kidnapped by members of the organization. What does that say for his competency if the man, himself, can be kidnapped?"

"I imagine his supporters would say the fact that he came out of the situation alive and put the perpetrators behind bars speaks well for his competency," the reported pointed out. "Speaking of his fiancée, Madison Reynolds of HOME TV fame, isn't it true that Chief deCordova was married two days ago? A honeymoon typically follows. Is that the vacation you referred to?"

"Yes, yes, he did get married on Saturday," Werner confirmed, nodding as if that proved his very point. "Poor Nigel Barrett was murdered there, *at the reception.* A reception where his alleged killer was an invited guest! That's the point the townspeople are making. Chief deCordova is a close friend of the accused—"

"Excuse me, but I must point out that the official cause of death has not been released, and there is currently no evidence to support the fact Nigel Barrett was murdered," the reporter inserted. "Therefore, there are no charges of murder, and no accused."

Werner kept talking, ignoring the interruption. "—and, in fact, had a guest list full of famous and elite at his wedding reception. That fact alone, in addition to the way he posed for the cameras this morning, proves Brash deCordova feels he is above the law and can conduct this sham of an investigation in any manner he pleases."

The moment he referenced the photo, the newsroom wasted no time in pasting a thumbnail of the image into the corner of the screen.

"To clarify, Mr. Werner, did you attend the reception?"

"I did not."

"But as you understand it, several in attendance were, indeed, high-profile guests?"

"No doubt. Tony Sanchez, for instance, and Mick Malchy. Both of them played pro ball with deCordova. Chuck Norris lives in the area, you know, and is rumored to be a close friend of the chief. And of course Trevor Washington was there, who was the official at the center of the referee scandal that rocked college ball while deCordova was head coach at Baylor. I—"

"Surely, you aren't suggesting that Chief deCordova was involved in the college referee scandal! RefGate happened years ago, and from what I can recall, all involved were fully exonerated."

"There were unanswered questions in that case, just as there are questions here. It seems odd that in both situations—RefGate and now Barrett's death—Brash deCordova had a great deal to gain financially."

"Are you suggesting that Chief deCordova—at that time Coach deCordova—was involved in the RefGate scandal and is now somehow involved in the death of a wealthy local land owner?"

"*I'm* not saying anything," Werner denied, an innocent smile spreading across his face. "I'm merely expressing some of the many, many concerns I've heard throughout the twin cities of Naomi and Juliet. Twice the citizens, twice the worries of collusion. Worries that perhaps the chief is allowing personal relationships and personal gain to cloud his judgment and make him unfit to hold the revered title of chief of police."

The reporter turned back to face the camera. "And there you have it, Scott. Reporting live from the streets of Naomi and Juliet, Texas, better known as The Sisters, this is Cameron Colson for EYE50 News."

As the screen segued to the weather forecast, Maddy hit the mute button. Irate energy bounced her off the couch and onto her feet.

"Can you believe the gall of that man!" she raged. "How dare him! Who does he think he is, making those kinds of accusations against you? And they're all false, every one of them!"

"Not all of them," Brash said wearily. "We did get married Saturday. Technically, I am off work, whether you call it a honeymoon or a vacation. We did have several high-profile guests at the wedding, including the ones he named. And, unfortunately, that is where Nigel died. All those things were true."

"And that's where the truth ended. For starters, there's no proof Nigel was murdered. It could have been an accident."

Where her voice was high pitched and irate, his was calm and even. "It could have."

"And no one has been arrested yet or charged with murder. Tony is not the alleged killer, or the accused, or whatever insinuating term he used."

"You and I both know that."

"And practically accusing *you* of that college scandal! How dare him!"

"He claimed those weren't *his* words," Brash pointed out, his voice even but slightly sardonic. "He was just a vessel for the people."

"The people, my eye!" Madison huffed. "You'd be hard pressed to find even *two* people who said any of those things about you, much less *"twice"* the citizens! Maybe Sharona Werner and Myrna Lewis, but no one else! He made it sound as if half the population had suddenly turned on you."

"I think her name is Sharese. And for all we know, half the town *may* have turned on me by now."

"You know that's not true, Brash. People here adore you. They know you're the best chief of police we've ever had."

"People can be easily influenced, Maddy. Stir up their emotions, play on their insecurities, fans their doubts, and even the staunchest supporter can suddenly turn against you."

"How can you sound so calm and rational about this? Doesn't that man infuriate you the way he does me?"

"Absolutely."

"Then how can you just sit here and take it?" she demanded.

"As opposed to what?" he reasoned. "Ranting and raving, which will accomplish exactly nothing? Rushing out and demanding the cameras give me equal air time? That would be playing into his hand. For now, I won't give him the satisfaction of a reply." His strong jawline settled into what Madison recognized as stubborn determination.

She was still irate enough for them both. "Then you're a better person than me! Just who does that man think he is!" She balled up her hands and rammed them onto her hips.

"We know exactly who he is," Brash said quietly. "He's the man out to get my job."

23

Madison avoided her phone as much as possible the next day, even though it rang excessively. By noon, she had turned it off, but not before taking some of the more important calls.

The kids called, having caught sight of Brash on the Colorado news feeds. Megan's first inclination was to catch the first flight home, but Maddy assured the teen that her father was handling things fine and preferred she stay and have a good time. In truth, none of the teenagers should be exposed to the circus now camped out on the sidewalk. It reminded Madison too much of their time in the spotlight with *Home Again*, and the invasion of privacy they all suffered through.

Genny called to say she was bringing supper that night; now wasn't the time for Madison to be concerned with cooking. Madison reminded her friend that no one had died (other than Nigel), but Genny said it was the least she could do, and that cooking for others was how she expressed her love.

Her parents called and offered to prolong their visit.

They could stay at the house and ward off unwanted guests, they said, but Madison gently reminded them that this was her honeymoon, of sorts. As long as everyone stayed off the front porch, and Brash remained fully clothed, they were good for now.

Granny Bert vocalized her disdain for both Joel and Sharese Werner and offered to "get the dirt" on them. Her sources were already abuzz with speculation. She claimed the sordid facts might come in handy in case the cameras interviewed other concerned citizens, namely herself. She gave examples of how she could innocently slip a slanderous comment into any given conversation without arousing suspicion or sounding biased. Her age, she claimed, gave her undeniable leeway in thinly veiled insults and accusations. Madison thanked Granny Bert for her support and refrained from mentioning that the insults were not nearly as veiled as her grandmother liked to imagine.

There were calls from Shannon, Laura, and Derron, all of which Madison returned. Encouraging messages left by George Gail Burton and other *In A Pinch* clients both past and present, a 'friend' in Dallas who hadn't called since the last time Madison and family made national news, and some from cousins and aunts. There was a not-so-encouraging message from Myrna Lewis, spouting some of her continued differences with the newly married couple. A smattering of hang-ups and what she considered junk calls, even though most referenced the incident in question. And there was a rather disturbing call from Collette that Madison chose not to return. In truth, she had no idea how to respond.

"Hey, girl, this is Collette. First of all, I just want to say WOW. I knew your man was hot, but I had no idea he was *that* hot! If you're ever up for a threesome... No, seriously, I just wanted to call and tell you I have your back. I know what it's like to have people talk about you. Everyone thinks I'm such an evil witch for not having a big funeral for Bobby Ray, but I just didn't see the point. I'm not going to pretend

I'm devastated, just so his friends can play soldier. They've even started calling me and harassing me about it. Oh, and someone mentioned you came to Waco and talked with them? What's that about?

"I was sorry about your friend. Well, both your friends, actually. The one who got killed and the one who did the killing. What a shame, on both accounts. I guess you lost a client, too, huh? Remember to look into that RR78 person. I'm positive he's a good match.

"Okay, that's all for now, I guess. Just calling to send my love. Call me if you need to talk. You've been such a help to me, and I'd like to return the favor. Oh. And remember. Happiness comes in three. *Ciao.*"

Madison dropped the phone with a grimace, as if handling it could somehow stain her hands. How, exactly, had Collette meant that parting comment about happiness coming in three? Was it a play on the old superstition of death coming in threes? Bobby Ray and Nigel were deaths one and two; she hoped there wasn't a third. Or was it a hint that her previous suggestion of a threesome hadn't been a joke, after all?

Either way, the call left her feeling unsettled. Madison didn't take death lightly, and she certainly didn't compare it to happiness.

Most of all, Madison didn't share. Not when it came to her husband.

She found it easiest to simply turn her phone off and ignore any future calls for the day.

❦❦❦❦

"I told you, Joel Werner is a weasel," Cutter reiterated.

When he and Genny came to drop off dinner, they brought enough to feed even Blake, had he been there. Pointing out there was more than enough to share, Brash and Madison insisted the couple stay and eat.

After the meal, they settled into the family/media room for a visit.

"I cannot believe he's spouting all those lies. And on national television, no less!" Genny added.

"We've had the television off most of the day," Madison admitted. "I don't dare get on social media."

"Wise choice," her friend muttered dryly, hiding behind her wine glass.

"That bad?"

"Not if you like seeing pictures of your husband. Which I'm sure you do, just not in this context. And not linked with other women."

"Hold on. What are talking about?"

"Oh, they've dragged up some old photos from somewhere," Genny said. "Some go all the way back to high school and show a different girl on his arm after every football game. Someone even found one of him hauling hay without his shirt on. There are pictures from college parties and from some toga party he went to, where the sheet barely covered the most crucial places. That one has been particularly popular, by the way." Genny flashed a cheesy dimpled smile at Brash, who actually blushed.

"Geesh, where do they come up with these?" he wondered aloud.

"You forget, my love," Madison answered. "Back before Facebook, we had a thing called scrapbooks. Every teenage girl had one."

"And apparently, the ones who knew you can't wait to share their favorite photos," Genny agreed.

"There are pictures from your days in the NFL, especially ones from the locker rooms and anything that shows you without a shirt. I sense a theme going on," Cutter pitched in.

"I thought you didn't do social media," Madison remembered.

"I don't. But I know how to stalk someone on it, all the same." He grinned and pumped his eyebrows a time or two.

"I'm sure Werner is behind this somehow," Brash said. "Even if he didn't start it, you can bet he's promoting it and taking full advantage of the fallout."

"So, you happen to have a great body. We could all see that, even through the clothes," Madison reasoned. "How does that make you an ineffective chief of police? If anything, it should prove you're in prime physical condition and able-bodied enough to do the job."

"Yeah," Cutter agreed. "Maybe you could work that into your next campaign." He stood and struck a pose, similar to the one of Brash floating around the universe. "*Let my body protect your body.*"

"Cut it out," Brash complained. "And that's part of the problem, you know. I don't have a next campaign. I'm not an elected official, voted in—or out—by the public. I'm at the mercy of my higher ups, and if they're not happy with me, they can cut me loose at any time."

"You know they would never do that, Brash," Genny protested.

"I don't know that," he argued. "With all this nonsense floating around, and with so much attention focused not just on me, but on this case, they could decide I'm a liability, more than an asset. Right now, Werner is harping on my friendship with Tony and on my notoriety, which he fans every chance he gets."

"And the more attention this case gets, the more pressure they're putting on you to arrest your friend," Cutter surmised.

"Exactly. We can't even prove there *is* a case, because we can't prove that Nigel's death wasn't simply an accident, but the media attention will push them into forcing my hand. The good news is, I don't think there's enough to make the case against Tony stick. The bad news is, Werner will eventually turn the focus to me, claiming I had the most to gain."

"I don't get it," Genny admitted. "Why you? How would you benefit from his death?"

"The same way Tony would benefit. Upon Nigel's death, fifty percent of the mineral rights on the land we purchased would revert to us. Since his wedding gift to us was the other fifty percent, Maddy and I now own a full one hundred percent. If we signed with an oil and gas company for a thousand dollars an acre, our bonus consideration would be about $200,000."

Genny's eyes widened, and Cutter let out a low whistle of appreciation.

"You can bet Werner will play it for all it's worth. If you think people like the headlines now, just wait until they suggest I actually murdered someone. They won't need a bunch of shirtless pictures then. They'll prefer the ones of me with cuffs on my wrists and chains around my feet."

"It won't come to that, sweetheart," his new bride insisted. "And so far, we don't know if anyone is even listening to all this nonsense Joel Werner is spouting. No one local, at any rate."

"What can we do to help?" Genny wanted to know.

"Assuming Nigel was indeed murdered by way of ingesting that shrimp, and assuming my friend Tony did not do it," Brash answered, "I'd say the next step is to find out who really *did* kill Nigel."

"But how do we do that?"

"Maddy has a theory that the person most likely to benefit from Nigel's death is his next of kin, and I tend to agree. So, the obvious answer is to find his next of kin."

Madison grimaced. "Yes, but easier said than done. I've been working on Nigel's family tree project for weeks now, and still haven't found a definite connection. The closest thing I have is RR78, a male living in Texas."

"That's vague." Cutter frowned.

"Yep. I've reached out and asked for him to contact me,

but who knows when, or if, he will?"

Genny still frowned, failing to follow their train of thought. "Let me get this straight. You're saying if someone knew they were Nigel's next of kin, they might kill him for the inheritance, right? But Nigel lost track of his family years ago. So how does that give you a suspect?"

"Nigel may have lost track of his brother and sister, but that doesn't mean *they* didn't keep up with *him*. Granny Bert, for instance, has known all along where his sister was. Even though she ran away from home at an early age and cut ties with her family, she kept in touch with someone back here at home."

"So if her children knew—"

"She only had one daughter."

Genny nodded, continuing with her hypothesis. "So if her daughter knew she was related to the Barretts of River County, she could presumably make the connection. Assuming she knew Nigel was loaded, and assuming she has homicidal tendencies, I suppose that theory could work." She cocked her head at an angle. "But, how would this niece have gotten into the reception?"

"You saw how crowded it was. I saw several people there who weren't invited."

"Good point. Still, isn't this theory making a lot of assumptions?"

"Unless we find another plausible suspect," Madison admitted, "I'm afraid Joel Werner will make the assumption Brash was the person most likely to benefit from Nigel's death. It would never stick, but if a little thing like a photograph can wreak so much havoc, can you imagine the damage a murder charge would do?"

"What can we do? There has to be something we can do to speed this along."

Madison hesitated, slightly uncomfortable with what she was about to say. "I suppose I could enlist Collette to help," she finally suggested. She still hadn't told Brash about the message, nor was she certain she ever would. It was weird enough, her having heard it.

"Hey, that's not a bad idea!" Genny said, with an enthusiasm Madison didn't share.

Sharing.

That was the reason for her discomfort.

24

Somewhat reluctantly, Madison arranged to meet Collette the next day. Brash had appointments with his 'higher ups' and the River County ADA, so the timing was good for another trip to Waco. With the afternoon off, Collette offered to help Madison in her search. They agreed to meet at the McLennan County Courthouse.

Now, faced with the seemingly endless volumes of public records around her, Madison felt a bit overwhelmed. Her visit to the local courthouse had been much less stressful, especially given the fact her research there was straightforward. There, she had been armed with the names of both Nigel's parents and had faced few variables. None of his eight siblings had marriages or subsequent births recorded in the county tomes to complicate her research. Their births, and in most cases, their deaths, were their only mention in the records of time. Plus, River County had only a fraction of the residents McLennan County had.

"You said your mother-in-law was doing some research for her family tree, right? Do you know where she looked? How she got started?" Madison asked.

"You'll need a name, at the very least, and a year. Guesstimates may have to do. Who are we looking for?"

Madison turned toward the other woman. "I never told you, but Nigel Barrett was the client whose family I was searching for. Even though he's gone now, I thought if I could locate his relatives, they could at least attend his memorial services."

She didn't mention she was trying to clear Tony's name and, in doing so, clear Brash's, as well. The less they mentioned Brash, the better.

"Of nine children, only Nigel and two siblings survived to adulthood," she explained, glancing down at her notes. "Earl Wayne Barrett and Betty Jean Barrett Thomas. Earl had two sons and a daughter. One of the sons passed away as a child, the other may or may not still be living, so the daughter, Barbara, is the most viable candidate. Betty Jean had one daughter, Laura Jean, born in '56 and married multiple times, from what I understand."

"Give me the dates of their births, and I'll check out Earl and his children," Collette volunteered. "You look for Laura."

After two hours of digging through old records, they took a break at the coffee shop across the street.

"I'm afraid Earl and his descendants are a dead end," Collette sighed. She stirred cream into her coffee and took a cautious sip. "James Earl died in prison, and I found a death record for a Barbara Barrett Morse that appears to fit our girl. So, it appears that any legitimate heirs, or relatives, will have to come from Betty Jean's descendants. Any luck on your end?"

Madison sipped her coffee with a nod. "A little. At any rate, it's more than I had. I already knew her daughter had a connection to the Ruiz family in Chilton, but when I reached out to them, they denied knowing her."

"The ones that own the big furniture store? I see their commercial on TV."

"Yes. Today I found proof she married their son, Garmin Ruiz, in '82. Since she married a Sammy Huddleston just a few years later, I'm assuming they divorced, and the Ruiz family banished her from their family tree."

"Did she have children?"

"I haven't found any so far. But I did learn something else of use."

"Oh?" Collette asked with interest. "What's that?"

"I had her name wrong, which may account for not finding her online. Her name is Lorie Jean, not Laura Jean."

"Hmm, that could be it. That means this Lorie Jean and her children would be the only relatives for poor Mr. Barrett, huh?"

"It appears that way. You know, in all the craziness that's happened since the wedding, I never got to ask you about Nigel Barrett. I was surprised to see that the two of you knew one another."

"Yes, I did know him," the other woman confirmed. "I suppose it won't be violating any privacy laws to say he was one of our patients at the clinic. Very sweet old man. He always struck me as lonely, too. He told me once that he had no family."

Madison sipped on her coffee, making no comment on Nigel's personality. Perhaps he conducted himself differently at the doctor's office than he did at home. "He told me you were the only technician who knew how to draw blood."

Collette smiled with what looked like genuine affection. "He always said that. I don't normally draw blood, but when they had trouble hitting his vein that very first time he came in, I gave it a try. After that, he would specifically request me, claiming I was the only one who could do it without it hurting. I didn't mind helping out. We'll certainly miss him at the clinic."

"Sitting beside him as you were, I suppose you heard the argument between him and Tony Sanchez?"

"How could I not? I was worried about Mr. Barrett's blood pressure. He was so angry!"

"Did you happen to see Nigel eat seafood that night?"

"Oh, no, absolutely not. He was highly allergic. Just like Bobby Ray was. Worse, actually."

This surprised Madison. "You were aware of his allergies?"

"I did the man's blood work and studied his genetic makeup," Collette reminded her. "I knew everything about his health condition."

"Do you recall if he mentioned his allergies that night at the table?"

"I don't remember."

"What about the conversation that led up to the argument? Do you remember what was said?"

"I already gave my statement to the police. Ask that hot husband of yours."

"This is for my own curiosity." Madison was quick to steer the conversation away from Brash.

Collette swirled her coffee before answering. "Something about mineral rights. Mr. Barrett had them, the other man wanted them. It went back and forth for several minutes, before Mr. Barrett got to his feet and started yelling, which everyone heard."

"And Tony didn't return to the table after that, correct?"

"No. Even his friend left."

"Tony didn't by chance bring Nigel a plate of food, did he? A refill, maybe, when he went after seconds for himself?"

"Why would he? That sounds like something a friend would do, and they didn't seem too friendly, in my opinion."

"It was just a thought."

Collette set her coffee down and looked Madison square in the face. "I have a few questions for you, too."

Madison braced herself. *Please, please, please! Don't let it be about a threesome!*

"They kept talking about mineral rights. Apparently, the football player thought he should have them, instead of leaving them to Mr. Barrett's estate. Now that Mr. Barrett has passed, what becomes of them?"

"Good question. Presumably, they will pass to his estate."

"Is that the real reason you're looking for his next of kin?"

"In part," Madison admitted. "Like I said, I also think it would nice if a relative could attend his services."

Plus, she said to herself, *I'm trying to prove that person could be responsible for his death, so that no one accuses my husband.*

Collette couldn't hear the thoughts running through Madison's head, especially as she herself was speaking. "Then I suggest you find this Lorie Jean woman. Oh, and RR78."

"Speaking of RR78... I wonder who he might be. We haven't found any record of Earl or Betty Jean's grandchildren."

"We'll keep looking. Because if I understood what Mr. Barrett and the football player were saying, someone could inherit a sizable estate. I don't really understand how mineral rights work, but they must be important, if the player was willing to kill over them."

"Keep in mind, there's no proof Nigel was murdered."

"I saw the look in that other man's eye," Collette argued. "It wasn't an accident."

"We don't know that."

Collette shook her head in disagreement. "Bobby Ray's death was an accident. He couldn't resist taking a bite of his favorite food now and then, because I refused to cook it for him. I even gave up eating it myself when we got married, even though his allergies were never that pronounced. But Mr. Barrett was known to have severe allergic reactions to seafood. His entire family had a history of respiratory issues and sensitivity to allergens, whether they were seasonal, airborne, or food allergies. Mr. Barrett would never have deliberately eaten that shrimp," she concluded.

She leaned in a bit, changing subjects. "Speaking of Bobby Ray, that brings me to my next question. Pete Vansant tells me you met with some of the troops last week. Why?" Her gaze was direct.

"Like I told you, Collette, Brash felt that something wasn't quite right when your husband died. I wanted an opportunity to speak with his peers and hear their impressions from the day."

Collette pulled in a deep breath, clearly upset. "Look, Madison—" she began, her voice filled with irritation.

Madison held up a hand to stop the tirade she sensed was coming. "Please. You don't have to say anything. After talking to his friends and after the conversation you and I had the other night, Brash and I have concluded that your husband died of natural causes. I'm sorry if we caused you any undue stress during an already difficult time. Please understand that we only had the best intentions at heart." She didn't bother adding that, with his body already cremated, foul play couldn't be proved or disproved now, even if they continued to pursue the issue.

"I understand. And I do appreciate that." Collette nodded demurely and tucked her hands into her lap, accepting the apology with grace.

Madison drained her cup and collected their trash.

"Well, hello, Mrs. Erickson," a man said, approaching their table with a cup of java in hand. "What are you doing over on this side of town?"

Collette's smile was polite, if not a bit stiff. "Just having coffee with a friend."

"You know who I am, right? Frank Fuller, from the clinic."

Her expression warmed only marginally. The smile on her lips never quite reached her eyes. "Yes, of course, Mr. Fuller."

"I've just been over at the courthouse," he explained, even though she didn't ask. He rattled on, not appearing to notice her lukewarm reception to his presence. "I told you about my work as a landman. Or a petroleum land agent, as they call us these days. I guess they think that sounds more impressive." He reached into his front shirt pocket and pulled out a handful of business cards. "See? Says it right there on the card. I'll leave these two here with you ladies, in case you ever have need of my services."

"I doubt it, but thanks," Collette said. "My friend isn't local."

"Oh, well, sure. I work all over Central Texas. Went out to West Texas once, but it's too flat out there for my tastes. Good oil country, but dry and dusty. And East Texas has too many pine trees. Messes with my allergies. North Texas' not too bad, but I prefer it here in the middle of the state, thank you very much." He rocked back on his heels, sloshing a bit of coffee on the floor as he did so. He looked down in disgust. "Look at me. Such a klutz."

As he swooped down to wipe up his mess, Collette rolled her eyes.

"Say," Frank Fuller said as he straightened, sending only a bit more dribble over the side of his cup, "did you hear about Nigel Barrett? The poor man died over the weekend. He told me he was in a bad way, but I never realized he was that close to the end."

"Yes, I heard. It's a real shame," Collette agreed. She made a show of gathering her purse, signaling they were about to leave.

The man either missed the subtle clue or chose to overlook it. "From what I hear," he continued, "it wasn't the cancer that got him. I heard on the news that he may have been murdered."

"Very sad," Collette murmured.

"He was a big landowner, you know. Oh, well, sure. Of course you knew. Nigel told everybody about his land." He made a motion with his hand, as if waving away a pesky fly. "With the industry cranking back up, and him being in the hotbed of activity, he could have stood to make a small fortune, just on his bonus consideration."

Madison would have introduced herself, but Collette stood and stuffed her chair back under the table.

"It was really great seeing you, Mr. Fuller, but we have to go. My friend has a long drive in front of her."

"Oh, well, sure. You be careful out there, Missy. Gotta drive for all the other fools on the road, not just yourself."

"Absolutely," Madison murmured, confused by Collette's sudden rush to leave. The other woman wheeled about and started for the door, expecting Madison to follow.

As they stepped onto the sidewalk, Collette huffed out an exasperated breath. "I'm sorry, but that man would talk our ears off if we gave him half a chance! Believe me, in thirty minutes, you would be begging me to intervene."

"I would have been interested to hear what he had to say about Nigel, though," Madison admitted.

"Oh, well, sure," Collette mimicked the man. She rolled her eyes again. "I swear! It takes him an hour to explain a chance meeting in an elevator. Save yourself the bother," Collette advised.

Inside her purse, Collette's telephone rang. "If you don't mind," Collette said, ignoring the ring tone playing in her purse, "I think I won't go in with you. I have some errands to run."

"Absolutely. I know you have the afternoon off and have better things to do than help me. I do appreciate everything you've done for me. You've been a true help."

"It's the least I can do."

They crossed the street and parted near the steps of the courthouse, where Collette offered a final word of encouragement.

"You and that hot husband of yours keep your chins up. Whatever is going on will be over soon, and everything will work out. I promise."

"Thank you, Collette," Madison smiled. "I appreciate it."

CRCRCRCR

Madison returned to the archives for more research on Lorie Jean Thomas. With the added surnames of Ruiz and Huddleston, she spent another forty-five minutes looking for the third marriage certificate Granny Bert had alluded to, and for a death certificate. She found neither.

As she started for the exit, she noticed Frank Fuller sitting at a large table, surrounded by several opened volumes of the thick tomes. She hesitated for only a moment before approaching.

"Hello. Frank, isn't that right?" she asked with a smile.

"Oh, well, sure. That's right. Frank Fuller." He stood and thrust out his hand.

"We weren't properly introduced before. I'm Madison Reynolds." Realizing the slip, she started to correct herself, but stopped. If Frank Fuller were following the story of Nigel's death, he would no doubt recognize the name deCordova. Just this once, she would let the slip go.

He peered over her shoulder. "Where's my favorite lab tech?"

"You mean Collette? She had to leave."

"She works in the lab over at the VA hospital," he needlessly explained. "Runs some high-tech piece of machinery, but drew blood for Nigel as a special favor." He waved his hands again, a gesture Madison already recognized.

"Is that how you knew Nigel Barrett? He and I are from the same town."

"Oh, well, sure. I met him at the VA hospital. Struck up a conversation while we waited our turn to have the blood sucked from our veins." He said the words almost cheerfully, as if he were describing a sporting event instead of a procedure most people dreaded. "Ran into him a time or two after that, mostly in the waiting room or the elevator. Sure hated to hear of his passing."

"Yes, we all did."

"Wonder what's going to happen with his land, now that he's gone?"

Madison's hesitation was the only encouragement he needed to continue. "When he found out what I did for a living, being a landman and all, he asked me what happened in a situation where there was no heir apparent. I could tell he was worried about passing on without having someone to leave his estate to."

"Yes, he was. I was working with Mr. Barrett at the time of his death," Madison explained, "helping him find his heirs. That's actually why I'm here today, searching records. I'm sorry I couldn't find his relatives before he passed away, but I'm doing my best to find them now."

"Oh, well, sure. That's good of you. Not to mention you could be making someone very rich. Another oil boom could have made Nigel an easy million, many times over."

"On seven hundred acres of land? That's more than I would have imagined."

"Oh, well, sure. That and more. Nigel held a small percentage of the royalty deed to most of the Barretts' original land grant. They were part of Stephen F.'s Old Three Hundred, you see. Nigel told me all about it, too, sitting in that waiting room." Frank rocked back on his heels again, bumping into the chair behind him.

Madison blinked at him in surprise. "Are you sure about that?"

"Absolutely. I'd never encountered such a thing, and I thought I'd heard it all! But Nigel explained how it was written into the original deed, and how a judge had interpreted it to mean the Barrett estate would always have a stake in the royalty rights for that chunk of the Brazos

Valley. Just goes to prove," Frank said with a pleased smile, "you never know what you'll learn at the doctor's office."

"You called them royalty rights," Madison noted, "not mineral rights."

"Oh, well, sure. As opposed to executive rights." He nodded, even though the explanation went over her head. "Generally speaking, owning executive rights to the minerals allows a person to enter into a lease agreement and receive leasing bonuses, shut-in payments and royalties, and the like. The person who owns royalty rights has no say in leasing the minerals but earns money off them whenever oil or gas is produced." He shifted his stance and started a more detailed explanation. "You see—"

Sensing he geared up for a lengthy conversation, Madison saw her chance for a hasty exit. "You've been quite a help, and it's been great talking with you. But I can see you're busy, and I know how important your work is, so I'll leave you to it. It was nice meeting you, Mr. Fuller. Have a great day."

"Oh, well, sure. Safe travels to you. Did you get a card earlier?" He held another out, which Madison took and stuffed into her purse.

"And remember," he called after her. "You gotta drive for all the other fools on the road, not just yourself."

25

Rolling back into The Sisters at a quarter past five, Madison was surprised to see the clinic was still open. Glancing at the insurance papers still in the backseat, the ones she kept forgetting to drop off with Doc Menger, Madison whipped into the parking lot and ran them inside.

"Hi, Rachel. I'm glad you're still here," she told the receptionist. "Here're those papers I promised."

"Great. Give me a minute, and I'll just make a copy."

To Madison's relief, the waiting room was empty, so there was no one to point and whisper behind her back. She hadn't been out since the wedding, and certainly not since Brash's sudden burst of stardom.

Today's trip to Waco didn't count; strangers couldn't be nearly as critical as the locals could.

While she waited for Rachel to finish, Madison glanced idly toward the television in the corner. A cable news channel shared images of a flood in western Nebraska and the destruction left behind. Then another image flashed onto the screen, causing her to do a double take.

Her eyes widened as she watched her husband tuck Tony

Sanchez into the backseat of his police cruiser, the cuffs clearly visible on Tony's hands. The voice was off, but the ticker-tape caption said that NFL Hall of Famer Tony Sanchez had been arrested in Texas on charges of manslaughter.

Madison didn't bother reading the rest. Her eyes homed in on Brash. He carried himself stiffly, his rigid posture a silent testimony to his displeasure. She didn't need to see the hard lines bracketing his mouth, or his brooding eyes—hidden now by dark glasses—to know he performed a duty forced upon him, one he clearly did not agree with. She noted he wore his official uniform, complete with service weapon, instead of the jeans and western shirt he left home in this morning.

"Isn't that crazy?" Rachel said, returning to the window and seeing Madison absorbed in the television. "The news crews have been all around town, just like when they were filming your show!"

"Brash arrested Tony Sanchez?" The needless question ripped from Madison.

Rachel eyed her suspiciously. "He's *your* husband," she pointed out. "I figured you, of all people, would know what the chief was doing."

With a weak shake of her head, she mentioned being out of town all day. She didn't add that they hadn't spoken today, both busy with their own tasks, and had exchanged only the briefest of texts. Obviously, Brash's meetings this morning hadn't gone as he had hoped.

"About two hours ago," Rachel went on, "two cruisers came zooming through town, lights and sirens full blast. A big black SUV was behind them, and then another cruiser. The news vans were close behind, and a half dozen Nosy Nellies. According to the news, they arrested your husband's friend and took him to the River County Jail. That's just a replay," she said, nodding to the screen. When a sly smile slid across the younger woman's face, Madison glanced back to see the infamous shot of Brash now filling the screen.

"I wish they would stop showing that picture!" Madison said, stomping her foot in irritation.

"Why?" Rachel asked with a leer. "You may see it every day, but the rest of America isn't so lucky. We love it!"

Madison did her best not to snatch the papers from the other woman's hands.

"I'm sorry they're giving Chief deCordova so much trouble," Rachel said. "He's been a really good chief, and I hate hearing the rumors people are saying about him. I wanted to give that Joel Werner a piece of my mind when he was saying all that in here the other day, but it wasn't my place. I'm sorry, though, that anyone is listening to him. He's just out to get the chief's job."

Her words made Madison feel better. It even helped settle her nerves, knowing not everyone had taken loss of their senses. "Thank you, Rachel. I'll pass your message along to the chief. I know he'll appreciate it."

"If he's really wants to show his appreciation," she joked, "he can sign a copy of that picture and drop it by."

Madison had a quick comeback. "Not if he wants to stay married."

ζεζε

Madison drove directly to the police station, where there was an unusual amount of activity. Too late, she remembered the television cameras. As she stepped from her car, two microphones thrust into her face.

"Mrs. deCordova! Is it true that you and your new husband received a generous gift from the deceased man, just moments before Tony Sanchez slipped poison into his food?"

"Mrs. deCordova! First of all, congratulations on your recent marriage! How does it feel to be married to America's newest sex symbol? Is it true your husband just signed deals with *Nike* and *Victor's Fantasy?*"

As ridiculous as both questions were, Madison used a trick she had learned last year, when the media wouldn't give her a moment's peace. She lifted her head and looked expectantly in the distance, as if seeing something of particular interest. Out of natural curiosity, the reporters turned in the direction she looked, giving her the perfect opportunity to slip away.

It took little time for them to catch up with her, circling around her like sharks closing in on their prey.

"What is your response to claims your husband colluded with Tony Sanchez to not only get Nigel Barrett out of the picture, but to gain control of his alleged fortune?"

"Is it true you and your husband are beneficiaries of the reclusive millionaire's estate?"

"There's new talk of reopening the RefGate investigation. Are you at all concerned that your husband could be implicated in wrongdoing?"

"Mrs. deCordova! Is it true the Texas Rangers have been called in to take over, in light of Chief deCordova's alleged involvement in the case?"

Overwhelmed with the swarming reporters, Madison batted at them like they were flies. She was grateful to see the officer rushing forward to take her arm. Together, they pushed through the offending crowd.

"Give the woman some room, for Heaven's sake!" the officer barked.

Hearing the decidedly feminine voice, Madison jerked her gaze to the woman beside her. Even in khaki uniform, severe ponytail, and no makeup, Misty Abraham was a stunning woman. The officer wasn't as tall as she but had curves in places Maddy could only envy.

"Sorry about that. Chief asked us to keep a lookout for you and prevent that from happening." The blonde officer swept Madison into the police station before pausing for a proper greeting. "I'm Misty Abraham. It's a pleasure to meet you, Mrs. deCordova."

Madison searched the deputy's face for the slightest trace of a smirk. She seemed completely sincere, affording Madison due reverence as the chief's wife. If she harbored any resentment or jealousy toward her, the officer kept the emotions well hidden behind an impenetrable layer of professionalism and respect.

Madison offered her hand for a welcoming shake, trusting that the woman was sincere. "It's a pleasure to meet you, too. And please. Call me Madison."

Misty took her hand but challenged the offer. "Do the other deputies call you that?"

"Well... no," she admitted.

"It's hard enough, being the only female on an all-male roster," Misty said, doing a half-roll of the eyes. "Don't get me in trouble with the guys my very first day!"

In spite of herself, Madison felt a surge of relief. She hated thinking Brash had kept this from her. "I wondered about that. I didn't realize you were starting so soon."

"I wasn't scheduled to start for another two weeks, but given the recent buzz of activity," she hesitated slightly over the word buzz, "they thought the team might need an extra hand."

"I hope Brash warned you. It's not always this crazy around here."

Inside the station, it was relatively quiet, especially in comparison to the media circus outside. Someone bumped around in a back room, making an occasional noise loud enough to override the clatter of the police scanner. Vina was gone for the day, but Wayne Arrington took her place behind the front counter, clicking away on his computer while fielding a steady flow of phone calls. Madison glimpsed someone in the hallway and heard another voice coming from the deputy's den, the name given to the communal office shared by both deputies. With the arrival of Misty Abraham, that number was now three.

"He hasn't had time to do anything more than swear me in and show me to my desk," Misty confessed. "It's been that kind of day."

"Speaking of my husband... is he here?"

"He isn't back from Riverton yet, but he called in and said he's on his way. I'll let him know you're in his office, if you decide to wait." To her credit, the officer didn't pretend to have control of whether Madison stayed or not. "By the way, congratulations on your wedding. I hear it was lovely."

"Thank you. We thought so!" Madison beamed. "Well," she backtracked, the smile faltering, "up until one of our guests died."

Misty's eyes twinkled with mischief. "Sort of gives new meaning to a *killer party*, huh?"

Madison couldn't help but snicker. After an emotional week, a stressful day, dismay over Tony's arrest, and now the unexpected arrival of Brash's ex-girlfriend, she needed an outlet for her frayed nerves. The comment struck her as funny, deepening the snicker into a giggle. Misty responded with a snort of amusement that sounded more like a braying mule, and not at all feminine. That such a beautiful woman had such an ugly laugh was even more amusing. (And somehow gratifying, if she were being completely honest with herself.) Madison's giggle turned to a chuckle. Soon, even that turned into all-out laughter.

By the time Brash entered the station via the back entrance, the two women were in full hilarity. Tears streaked down Maddy's face, and Misty tried holding her coarse guffaw back with her hand, to no avail. The sound howled through her fingers like a strong wind.

"This is a surprise," Brash remarked dryly. He wasn't sure the women had even heard him come in, and he certainly hadn't expected them to be waiting here together, laughing like two old friends. He was tired and hungry, and angered by the day's turn of events. And, to be honest, he was now a bit unsettled to come in and see the easy camaraderie between his new wife and his old girlfriend.

Not that he and Misty Abraham had ever been seriously involved. Finding Misty easy to be with, they had gone out several times over the course of a year. She understood the demands of the job, and the two of them had quite a bit in common, but when working around both their schedules became challenging, Brash decided the relationship simply wasn't worth the effort.

At the sound of his voice, both women turned toward him in surprise.

They were quite the contrast. Maddy was tall and slender, a study in understated curves and elegant sophistication. Her dark-chestnut hair was cut in a fashionable bob that accentuated her long, graceful neck and brought out the deep set of her hazel eyes. Dressed in tasteful but modest attire, she not only demanded a man's attention, she demanded his respect.

Misty wasn't quite as tall, but where Maddy was lean and lithe, the blonde had generous curves. Those curves molded into her uniform, swelling in all the best places. With her fresh, pert face, her long blonde hair, and her big, brooding eyes—blue, he thought he remembered—she demanded not only a man's attention, but also a healthy portion of his libido.

But one look at Maddy's smiling face, one hint of her sweet laughter floating on the air, and the day's burdens lifted from Brash's shoulders. The second woman all but faded from his vision. All he saw was his wife.

"Maddy." The low murmur was somewhere between a command and a plea. His eyes held hers as she crossed the room and allowed him to fold her into his arms.

For a long moment, Brash simply held her, rocking her gently in his embrace. It was the balm they both needed, the soothing antidote to a prickly day. The warmth they sought from a cold, bitter world. Snippets of their vows echoed through both their minds.

As an afterthought, Brash remembered there were other people in the room, namely his new deputy. Without relinquishing his hold on his wife, he opened his eyes and nodded to the other woman.

"Officer Abraham," he acknowledged. He thought he saw a flash of regret in her eyes as she studied their embrace, but it made no difference. Brash had no regrets.

Madison pulled away to politely include her, their arms still linked. "Misty and I were getting better acquainted," she explained to her husband. "Apparently, she picked a fine day to join the force."

"Yeah, I'm sorry about that," he apologized, his voice weary. "It's been a heck of a day. Sweetheart, will you excuse us for just a minute while I give Officer Abraham her orders for the evening? I won't be long."

"Will you be able to leave soon?" she asked hopefully.

Brash looked around the station, noting the relative calm. "Yeah, one way or another."

"Then I'll go on home and start dinner. You do what you need to do here."

"Are you sure?"

"You look like you could use a nice, warm meal."

He dipped his head to murmur against her cheek. "Never mind the meal. All I need is my wife."

"I'll fix us a bite anyway," she promised, her hand lingering on his chest. She was new to this wife of the chief gig, unsure of protocol when it came to public displays of affection.

Brash had no such qualms. He scooped her face into his hands and gave her a very thorough kiss, unconcerned with what anyone else thought. "I'll see you at home, Mrs. de."

Releasing her, he stepped back and called into the hallway. "Schimanski! Walk my wife to the car. You have my permission to shoot any reporter who intrudes in her personal space."

The younger officer appeared with a grin on his face. "Yes, sir!" he said.

"On second thought, I want you to follow her home. Make sure no one harasses her before she gets safely inside."

"I'll be fine, Brash. Unfortunately, this isn't my first brush with reporters."

"All the same, let Schimanski clear the way for you. I'll be home as soon as I can."

Madison smiled at the female officer who stood waiting patiently for her orders. "It was nice to meet you, Officer Abraham."

"You, too, Mrs. de." Her blue eyes twinkled, letting Madison know she had heard the deep rumble of Brash's words.

If she heard those, she had probably heard the ones before them, too. Like a blushing new bride, Madison couldn't help the flush that lightly stained her cheeks.

26

"Girl, what kind of mess did you get yourself tangled up in this time?" Granny Bert demanded, plopping down without ceremony at Madison's breakfast table.

Madison delivered coffee to her grandmother, served with a frown. "You make it sound like I go looking for all this trouble," she sulked as she slid into her own seat.

"You either look for it, or it looks for you," the older woman reasoned. "What in tarnation is all this hoopla about this time? There are reporters camped out by your gate again. Danged near ran over one of them with the Buick when he tried slipping in alongside me. Of course," she added, hiding her smirk behind the coffee cup, "I *was* trying to teach him a lesson."

"Seems like last year, doesn't it?" Madison's sigh was resigned. "But with all the *Home Again* hoopla, the mood was different. Sure, any story was a good story, but at least, they seemed to be rooting *for* us, not against us. This time, it's all so... so vindictive. They're looking for dirt, and the muddier, the better." She propped her elbows upon the table and cradled her cheeks with her hands. "Some honeymoon this has turned out to be."

Granny Bert leaned in with a worried look on her face. "All the stress hasn't affected Brash's performance, has it?" she asked in a confidential tone.

When she realized her grandmother's meaning, Madison was mortified. "Of course not!" she snapped. *Not* that she wanted to discuss her sex life with her grandmother!

"Good. That's good." The older woman sat back in obvious relief, reaching out to pat her granddaughter's arm. "Wanda won't be so glad to hear it," she admitted, "but Sybil will be."

Madison stared at her grandmother in horror. "Your friends are *betting* on our sex life?"

"Just a friendly little wager." Her shrug said it was of no importance. "The loser buys margaritas the next time we go to *Montelongo's.* Wanda figured all the stress of being a sudden sex symbol and accused of colluding with a murderer might be too much for a man to handle, but you'll be happy to know, Sybil had full confidence in him."

"No, I am not *happy* about any of this!" She enunciated her displeasure. "Please tell me that *you* did not engage in this... this degrading and humiliating farce of a bet!"

"No, child. That would just be crass." Her grandmother's look was reproachful.

"And it's not crass for your friends?" Madison challenged. "Two old women, speculating on how successful my honeymoon will be?"

"Watch who you're calling old," Granny Bert warned. "And before you climb too high up on your soap box, remember that both are single and lonely, and sometimes, the only thrills they get are the vicarious ones. You may have found your handsome prince to live out forever with, but spare a little mercy for those less fortunate, mind you."

Refusing to feel guilty, Madison brushed off the rebuke. She glared at her grandmother over the cup's rim as she took a big gulp of coffee. The sting of hot liquid didn't burn nearly as badly as did her grandmother and her shenanigans.

"That's another thing," Madison grumbled, still on a roll. "You used to hear the words 'plotted' and 'in cahoots.' Now the buzzword is 'colluded.'"

"Folks do seem to get good mileage out of the word."

"The thing is, there's no definitive proof Nigel was killed. For all we know, it was a needless accident. They've charged Tony on nothing but circumstantial evidence."

"Then it will be up to the prosecutor to prove he's guilty."

"I know that's the way our forefathers designed it, but that's not the new reality." Madison's observation was jaded and sad. "These days, people rush to judgment. There's no such thing these days as innocent until proven guilty. There's only guilty because someone else said so. Usually on social media."

"Sad, but true," her grandmother agreed. "When I took Sybil to the Tuesday/Thursday Clinic for a refill on her blood pressure medicine, I overheard the office staff talking. They already had poor Tony behind bars and had thrown away the key. One of the receptionists is a friend of Sharese Werner's, and she was repeating the lies Joel keeps spouting. She started in on Brash, saying how he would make more money than anyone would on Nigel's death. Said she wouldn't be surprised if they didn't arrest him next."

"They were saying this in front of the entire waiting room?" Madison asked in dismay.

"They were talking among themselves, but their voices carried. Especially once Sybil and I moved to that little cubicle where they take your blood pressure. Good thing the doc didn't take mine that day; it would have been sky-high! But don't worry," her grandmother added with a satisfied sniff. "I got even with that nosy Rosemary."

"The neighbor?" Madison guessed. When her grandmother nodded, Maddy gave her a stern look. "Granny Bert, what did you do?"

"As we were leaving, I caught her in the hallway, texting on her phone. So I pretended I didn't know how to use one, and asked her to send me a text so I could see how it's done."

Madison looked skeptical. Her grandmother was a quiz on the smart phone. "And she believed you?"

"Why not? I'm just a poor eighty-one-year old woman who grew up with one of those phones shaped like a candlestick. We had to ask the operator to connect us every time we wanted to talk. We didn't have these newfangled gadgets with all the confusing buttons and those smiley yellow faces and a choice of beeps or whistles." She laid it on thick, looking every bit the part of the overwhelmed senior citizen, confused with modern technology. "We thought we were something, getting our rotary dial phones. Made listening in on the party line so much easier. Why, the only running water we had was when we threw the wash water out the back door and watched it run downhill. We shared electricity with the folks next door, so we could only use it on Mondays, Wednesdays, and Fridays. Neither of us used it on Sundays, as it was the Lord's Day. We—"

"Okay, okay." Madison waved her hands as if they were white flags. She called a truce, putting an end to the wild exaggerations. "I get it. You convinced her not only that you couldn't use the modern cell phone, but that you grew up a hillbilly. Neither could be further from the truth, but she obviously doesn't know you're a skilled actress, not to mention borderline con artist. What I don't get is how you got even with her."

Instead of looking insulted by the description, Granny Bert looked as pleased as if she had won an Emmy. "It's nice to know my skills are appreciated. I do work on them, you know. And as for getting even, by having her text me, I now have her telephone number. Which I promptly shared with every telemarketer that has called the house in the past two days. I then called a half dozen vehicle warranty places, timeshare resorts, and health insurance companies to request information, leaving her number as a callback." She thumped the table with a satisfied smirk. "That ought to keep her busybody-self occupied for a while!"

It would only encourage her grandmother, but Madison couldn't keep from laughing. "Oh, Granny, what are we going to do with you!"

"There is no wrath like a grandmother scorned."

Madison laughed again, pleased that her grandmother already considered Brash a member of her family. For Bertha Cessna, family ties meant everything. "Mess with one, you mess with all," she often claimed.

"People should watch what they say and where they say it," Granny Bert continued. "Now. Tell me what the plan is. How are we going to stage our counterattack?"

"Counterattack?"

"We all know Joel Werner was the one to sic the press on this story. He's gunning for Brash's job and will do whatever it takes to get him out of the picture. I told you I could dig up some dirt on him, so yesterday I made a few other calls. Your fifth cousin Ray Cessna is retired from the Pasadena police force. It just so happens Wormy Werner was under his command, and it turns out our boy spent a good deal of time on probation. Ray couldn't go into the details, but there was an incident where Werner was suspected of tampering with evidence. It must have been something big, because he cut some sort of deal with Werner. He wasn't kicked out of law enforcement entirely, just out of Harris County."

"So he came north to Huntsville," Madison murmured. "And now to The Sisters."

"We have family in Walker County, too," Granny Bert continued. "Your great uncle Travis was a professor at Sam Houston and his granddaughter Lacey is on the Huntsville police force. She didn't have much nice to say about Wormy Werner. Neither did your cousin George, who was a Walker

County sheriff's deputy, or my friend Bentley, who was assistant DA for many years. All say that Werner was known for using excessive force, turning in shoddy evidence and shoddy reports, and was somehow tangled up in a suspicious death of a local landowner. There was never enough evidence to make a case, so it was eventually ruled a suicide. But I could tell they all still had their doubts, and they all suspected that Wormy Werner was somehow involved."

Madison gave her grandmother a sharp look. "What are you saying? That Joel Werner had something to do with Nigel's death?"

"I'm saying Wormy Werner is a sleaze ball with a shady past. He brags about being a Walker County deputy, but he didn't mention that he was low man on the totem pole and relegated to duties no one else wanted. I'm saying he can't rely on his resume to get him a new job in law enforcement, so he'll find another way in." She rapped her knuckles on the table. "Mark my words. Joel Werner is not to be trusted."

"Still..." Madison's expression was skeptical. "To suggest he would stoop to murder, just to frame Brash..."

Granny Bert held up her hands. "Mind you, I'm not accusing the man. I'm just saying it's worth looking into."

"Maybe," Madison said, still doubtful. "I do agree that, even if he didn't have anything to do with the crime itself, he is definitely using it to his advantage. And I agree that Werner was probably the one to 'sic the press' on this story, as you say.

"But," Madison added, and it was a big, heavy 'but,' pushed out on a resigned sigh, "it's taken on a life of its own. The press has sunk their teeth in, and they aren't letting go, anytime soon."

"Not," her grandmother agreed, "until they get a better story."

Madison frowned. "What's that supposed to mean?"

"I mean it's time to buckle down and get them a better story."

27

"I hate to bother you, dollface, but I need to come in today."

Even though he couldn't see her, Madison frowned at her employee through the phone. "Why would that bother me? That's what I pay you for."

"But this *is* your honeymoon," Derron pointed out. "Staycation or not, you'd probably like a little privacy."

"You're absolutely right, I would. But the reporters camped out on my lawn and the cable news channels make that impossible. You may as well come on down and join the circus."

"Do you need to clear it with the hubby first?"

"I'm not sure. Maybe you should call down to the police station and ask him."

"Ouch. No need to get snarky, girlfriend."

Madison's reply was weary. "Just be careful turning in the gate. Granny Bert nearly ran over a reporter earlier."

"Was she trying to?"

"Well, yes, but let's not give them something else to find fault with. And for Heaven's sake, don't talk to any of them!"

"Not unless it's that yummy Gavin from Channel 22. He's just too cute to ignore."

"Solidarity, Derron," she reminded him. "We need to put up a united front. No one talks to the press."

"Okay, okay," he sulked. "But I can still preen for them, can't I?"

"As long as your lips remain sealed."

"You're no fun. But you can't stop me from wearing my favorite shirt."

"Both the peacock shirt and the red silk are a bit much, don't you think? Wear the blue. It brings out the color of your eyes and looks much more like spring."

"Good idea, girlfriend. See you in a few."

With Derron coming in to the office, Madison decided to join him. No use rattling around in the big old house when she could be working.

Her office had been Phase One of the remodel. Madison was still awestruck each time she entered the room, knowing this gorgeous space was hers. Originally the home's formal library, built-in cabinetry and exquisite burled-walnut paneling wrapped the room in timeless tradition. The extensive woodwork could have felt dark and drab, but Kiki Paretta was a genius at decorating. HOME TV's style guru brightened the room with a variety of light sources: subtle track lighting, sconces, lamps, multiple chandeliers, and natural light streaming through gauzy white curtains. She used cream-colored upholstery and accents to contrast against the wood, giving the room a fresh, inviting look. A tufted leather executive chair sat behind the antique desk, coordinating with two groupings of chairs; one clustered around the fireplace, the other within the nook of the turret. The cream color paired with dusky blue to continue in the decadent piled rugs, afghans, and artwork.

The true wonder of the room was the state-of-the-art computer center, concealed within a custom-built cabinet. Like everything else new in the room, it came compliments of the show's sponsors, and was ground zero for the impressive alarm system installed on the property.

Derron's desk, a wonderfully done smaller version of hers, sat near the French doors off the east porch. *In a Pinch* clients used this door to access the business, bypassing the heart of the home. Madison stopped at his desk before proceeding to hers, firing up both computers.

She skimmed through her email messages, quickly determining which needed answering, which could wait, and which could be deleted. The majority fell in the latter category.

One message in particular caught her eye. She wasn't familiar with the sender's address, but the subject referenced MyFam.com and RR78. Clicking on the message, she read:

Got your note. Yeah, looks like we're kin. Would be willing to meet and talk.

Madison sent back a reply, asking RR78 his location. She hoped he wasn't in far West Texas or down in South Texas; she didn't relish a seven-plus hour drive to meet in person. Depending on his answer, a virtual meeting might have to suffice.

She knew she shouldn't, but Madison gave in to the temptation and clicked on her social media account. Pictures of Tony and Brash filled the page. The most popular was the one of Brash ushering a handcuffed Tony into the backseat of the cruiser. There were photos of the men in their football jerseys, side by side at fundraising events and sports galas, and a particular favorite of the men and their dates at some black-tie event. Two beautiful women clung to their sides, dressed in evening gowns that were tasteful but skimpy. Their hairstyles were the only timestamp the photos needed. The images served as a reminder that the two men—the accused and his arresting offer—had a long history of friendship.

There were more photos of Brash. While most were of his now infamous bare chest, many included other people in the shot. All were beautiful women, famous people, or both. The theme was easy to detect. Brash deCordova was depicted as a womanizing playboy with connections. He was comfortable being in the spotlight and had many rich and powerful friends. A heavily "liked" photo was one of him and a handful of state lawmakers on a pheasant hunt, the governor of Texas among them. The men posed with their shotguns and a bag of the day's harvest. Madison knew the significance of the photo was to exploit his friendship and accessibility to influential decision makers. One rendition of the photo came with the caption *'Mockery of the justice system. With friends like these, jury's in the bag!'*

Never mind that Brash hadn't been accused of any wrongdoing. Not officially. But that didn't stop the reporters and the social media jury from jumping to conclusions.

"Trial and jury by social media," she muttered aloud. Her scowl was like thunder.

"Talking to yourself?"

The sound of Derron's voice startled her. She had been so engrossed in the nonsense on the computer, she hadn't heard the alarm's beep and him coming in.

"Better than yelling at the computer, unlike someone I know," she replied.

"It's a proven fact that yelling at the computer screen releases endorphins and lowers stress levels." The blond-headed man leaned over and air-kissed her cheeks.

"Another of your highly *un*scientific studies?" she guessed.

He shrugged his sculpted but petite shoulders. "Perhaps. But I stand by the results."

"What urgent business required you to fight your way through the mob outside?" Madison asked, as Derron settled at his desk. Even though he left everything in impeccable order at the end of each day, it always took him a good five minutes to arrange things to his liking the next time he sat down.

"Besides the fact that I lost Gorgeous Gavin's number and hoped to see him again? I needed to consult the calendar. *New Again Upholstery* in Navasota called and wanted us to fill in during paternity leave for one of the webbers."

"How long is that?"

"Two weeks." At her raised eyebrows, he explained, "It's one of the dads."

"Do you know anything about upholstery?"

"I was hoping you did."

A two-week gig was always good for the bottom line. Pursing her lips, Madison admitted, "Depending on how many other jobs we have scheduled, one of us may have to learn."

Derron pulled up the schedule so they could review upcoming projects. They spent the next ten minutes plotting potential conflicts, holes in the calendar and therefore holes in the budget, and possible upcoming projects.

"Before we accept, you'd better make a few calls. Dean Lewis mentioned needing me again next month when they attend a conference in Florida, and Jolly Dewberry wanted you to build his wife a closet." For all his flamboyant ways and his finesse as an executive assistant—not to mention a fashion stylist—the man was an exceptional carpenter. Like everything else he did, Derron managed it in style, most often wearing a frilly work apron and using decorated tools.

With Derron on the phone, Madison returned to her computer. Before she closed the window for social media, she saw someone had sent a private message.

I'm sorry to bother you. My name is Barbara Barrett Motte. The local funeral home suggested I contact you concerning services for my uncle, Nigel Barrett. Are you the person in charge of arrangements?

The question hit her hard. In truth, Madison had given no thought to Nigel's service. She supposed that if anyone organized such an event, it would most likely be her and

Brash. *I bet Joel Werner will love that, milking it for all it's worth!*

The moment the thought ran through her mind, she felt guilty. The man deserved a decent burial, no matter how the critics chose to construe it. Overseeing Nigel's final farewell didn't prove she and Brash had close ties to the man; it proved he had no one else to take care of the matter for him. The thought was sobering, making Madison's heart bleed for him.

The significance of the message slowly sunk in. At least now, perhaps Nigel would have family at his side as his body was lowered into the earth.

Of course, given all the attention his death garnered, this could be a fortune-seeker posing as his niece in order to claim his estate. The news hadn't yet revealed the fact he had no heirs, but they repeatedly mentioned his assumed fortune. It was the only tenuous tie they had to Tony and would become even more important if—when—they tried implicating Brash in Nigel's murder. It was surprising that more people hadn't already lined up, claiming a stake in the Barrett fortune.

Or, perhaps this was Earl's daughter, the Barbara she had been looking for. Again, given all the attention his death garnered, it was entirely possible the woman had heard about it on the news and wanted to say a proper goodbye to the uncle she had never known.

A third possibility occurred to her, and she couldn't type her reply fast enough. Obviously, this Barbara person had known all along that Nigel Barrett was her uncle. Madison had no idea how she could have managed it—had she paid someone to put the shrimp on his plate? Poisoned him before the reception? Crashed the party and slipped the shrimp into the sandwich herself?—but this could be the person most likely to benefit from Nigel's death and, therefore, be the person most likely to have killed him.

Arrangements are pending. Do you live nearby? Perhaps

you could help plan his memorial.

She saw the dancing bubbles, telling her the other person was typing.

I live at Lake Whitney. I would be honored to help. My father and uncle parted on bad terms, but I always wanted to know more about my family. This will be a start. Are you his daughter? My cousin?

Madison could almost hear the hope in the woman's response.

I'm sorry, but I was just a friend. Let me check with the funeral home and see when we can meet with them. Is tomorrow afternoon good for you?

When Barbara agreed that it was, Madison promised to be in touch.

She immediately called the funeral home, where she was put on hold. As she listened to the solemn music on the line, her phone beeped with an incoming call. She ignored the first two calls from Collette and one from her grandmother, but when the funeral director put her on hold to check his schedule, she finally answered the beep. This time, it was Collette again.

"I'm sorry, Collette. I can't talk. I'm on the phone with the funeral home."

"Okay, I'll make this really quick. I think I found something on your RR78."

"Can you send it to me in a text? Believe it or not, I also found Nigel's niece Barbara."

"Really? Where?" She couldn't have sounded more surprised.

"She lives in Whitney, and she's helping me make arrangements. I'm setting up our appointment with the funeral home now, so I really need to go."

"I understand. Call me later. Bye."

When the director came back on the line, he set up a two o'clock appointment the next day to meet with her and Barbara Barrett Motte. She was sending the information via direct message to the other woman when her phone rang. Again.

She cradled the device on her shoulder as she typed. "Hello, Granny. Sorry I couldn't answer earlier."

Without preamble, her grandmother launched into the reason for the call. "The Juliet City Council has called a special meeting for tonight, and has invited the Naomi Council to sit in. This can't be good."

The news rattled Madison. "What can we do?"

"I'm calling in the troops. We need as much support present tonight as possible. Get on the phone and call everyone you know and tell them to be at the meeting at seven o'clock sharp."

"Do we know for a fact this meeting is about Brash?"

"Do we know for a fact Joel Werner is a weasel out to get your husband's job?" her grandmother countered.

"Without a doubt."

"I hear he's encouraged the media outlets to be there tonight, too. It can only mean one thing. He's planning to make his big push to get Brash suspended. He thinks with Brash down, he can move right in, but we're going to show Weasel Werner he has another think coming! Get on the horn and call everyone you know. I'll be at your house at 6:15 to discuss strategy."

"Wait! Does Brash know?"

"I'm not sure. Better call him and give him a heads-up. I don't want him blindsided when the mayor calls."

As she called her husband's number, Madison spoke to her employee. "Drop whatever you're doing and change gears. We need a support team for tonight's city council meeting. Weasel Werner is trying to unseat Brash. Seven o'clock sharp and bring support posters... Sweetheart?" she said, when she heard his deep voice answer. She put effort into keeping hers cheerful. "How's your day going?"

"Not so bad that I need support posters," he teased. "Not yet, anyway. What gives?"

"Granny Bert just got word there's a special session joint city council meeting tonight. Has anyone called you yet?"

"Not yet. But we all know your grandmother hears things first, long before the rest of us. Even those of us whose jobs are hanging in the balance."

"I'm sure it won't come down to that, sweetheart. But we both know Weasel Werner will try his best."

Brash was able to keep his sense of humor, even during dark moments like these. "What happened to Wormy Werner?" he asked, having heard that moniker at last count.

"Weasels are even worse than worms," Madison informed him. "The man is definitely a weasel. But don't worry. Granny Bert has a plan."

"That, sweetheart, is a true oxymoron. 'Don't worry' and 'a plan by Granny Bert' should never be used in the same sentence. They simply don't jive."

Her warning was stern. "Never underestimate my grandmother."

"I wouldn't dream of it."

28

Word of the special meeting spread faster than wildfire through the sistering cities; it spread at the breakneck speed of juicy gossip. Long before the scheduled seven o'clock start time, the venue had changed to the high school gymnasium to accommodate the expected crowd.

Someone wisely appointed Vina Jones as doorman. She assigned seats as people came through the doors, and no one dared argue with the stern enforcer. She instructed Brash's supporters to have a seat on the much larger *Home* side of the court. Those backing Werner were relegated to the *Visitors* section.

There were, no doubt, some who came undecided or with the intentions of siding with Joel Werner, but a stare-down from Vina had them scurrying over to Brash's side. The nearby trashcan soon filled with their hastily abandoned 'Werner for Police Chief' pennants. Myrna Lewis handed out the professionally printed paraphernalia in the parking lot, proof that this was no spur-of-the-moment attack. Madison noted that very few of the paper fans were thrown away, but she understood why. No one wanted to part with his or her very own copy of the now infamous bare-chested photo. Even though one side disparaged Brash deCordova for his playboy ways and his lack of professionalism, the other side openly exploited his sex appeal.

The opposite side of the parking lot was Camp deCordova, where tables were set up with handmade posters and an assortment of cookies and refreshments. If Granny Bert's friends knew anything, it was how to impress the locals and ply them with home-baked goods.

Megan and the twins couldn't make it back from Colorado in time for the meeting, but they gathered the troops from afar and asked friends to stand in for them. A smattering of high school students still in town during Spring Break and four uniformed cheerleaders led chants and kept spirits high as the townspeople poured into the gymnasium.

New Beginnings closed early, as well as a few other businesses that were still open after five. A sign at the café urged all citizens to attend the meeting and support their esteemed chief of police.

By the time Brash, Madison, and Granny Bert arrived, the obvious support and outpouring of love was humbling. The *Home* bleachers were full and supporters stood in the aisles and along the floor, refusing to take a seat on the opposing side, even if it promised to be a long night.

A half dozen or more news crews recorded it all as it happened.

The meeting was called to order and a brief agenda given. After both mayors spoke, touting having the community's best interests at heart and the need for transparency and justice, they opened the floor to speakers already on the agenda.

Joel Werner was first. He gave a long-winded speech about the lack of professionalism in the current department. He was quick to point out the recent uptick in crime across the community, ignoring the correlating national trend and focusing only on The Sisters. In case anyone had been living under a rock during the past few days, he rehashed Nigel Barrett's death and the arrest of Tony Sanchez. He played up Brash's friendship with the accused and reminded people of his other famous friends, painting Chief deCordova as believing himself above the law. He used the recent media frenzy as 'proof' that the current chief of police was distracted by his love for attention and his need to be in the headlines.

After pointing out Nigel's generous gift to the newlyweds, he fell short of accusing Brash of outright murder, but he planted the seeds of doubt. He pointed out how easy it would be for the chief of police and his good friend to conspire against a helpless old man and slip a deadly shrimp into his food. Doing so, he claimed, would ensure a sudden windfall for both men. He alluded to a secret reason Brash might need the money, which he claimed would be revealed in time. Joel Werner concluded his carefully rehearsed speech with a glowing recap of his own accomplishments as a police officer.

Just before taking a seat, he reminded the joint councils of what was at stake and urged them to consider asking Chief of Police deCordova to step down. As a concerned citizen and a qualified peace officer—and knowing how long it took to find good, honest leadership and protection—he volunteered his services in the interim.

Brash's response wasn't nearly as long. Or as pompous.

He told the crowd he was honored to have served as their chief for the past six years, and with the continued support of the community and both city councils, he planned to serve them for many years to come. He didn't quote his past victories or point out the discrepancies in Werner's skewed report. He said his record spoke for itself. He gave credit to his deputies and his staff for the exceptional work they did, and to the community for making their jobs easier and more pleasurable. He spoke only briefly about Nigel and Tony, claiming friendship and affection for both men, and sincere regret over the current situation. He refused to comment on Werner's thinly veiled accusations, saying he trusted the criminal justice system to sort out the particulars of this case and mete out the correct punishment. His only reference to the notorious photo was to remind the crowd of his recent nuptials and to state that the media frenzy had intruded upon their honeymoon and what should have been a sacred and private moment between him and his bride. He closed by thanking the city councils, the outpouring of support from the towns, his family, his staff, and, last but not least, the love of his life who now wore his ring and who had been pulled into this circus by association.

The home crowd gave him a standing ovation, as well as a few crossovers from the other side.

Myrna Lewis was the next scheduled speaker.

Myrna did not have the skills or the voice to be a public speaker. Her voice was high pitched and squeaky, and always reminded Madison of nails scraped across a chalkboard. Her abrasive personality was a perfect match for the audio.

When her name was called as the next speaker, people shifted uncomfortably in their seats. They knew from experience that Myrna's report would be scathing and bitter, a reflection of the woman herself. No one wanted to hear Myrna Lewis speak, and for once, she seemed attuned to what others were feeling. For that reason, she came prepared with a video.

The first few shots were reruns of the week's headlines. Brash without his shirt, Brash arresting Tony, Brash with a series of famous athletes, actors, and politicians, followed by several pictures of Brash with beautiful women at his side, none of which were his new wife. She paused the video on a shot of him and an actress known for her sexy roles and skimpy outfits.

"I ask you. Is this the role model we want for our town? Is this playboy a man we trust with our homes, our families, our very lives?" She screeched out the words in her grating voice.

Someone in the crowd yelled out, "Seems he's done a jam-up job so far!"

"Can't think of a better role model, myself!" someone else said.

"Look at all the good he's down for the town!" came another call. "Sit down, Myrna, and quit making a spectacle of yourself!"

The round little woman glared up into the stands, looking for the culprits who dared interrupt her. Myrna had the misfortune to have a body almost as wide as it was tall, and the appearance of having no neck. Instead of wearing clothes that made the best of her attributes, she was completely oblivious to fashion. Tonight, she wore a shapeless dress that draped over her body like a tent and came just below her knees. The bright orange was reminiscent of the jumpsuits worn in jail and did nothing to flatter her figure or her complexion. She wore white tube socks that sported a red band at the top, and a pair of serviceable black rubber-soled shoes. With her ever-present fanny pack strapped around the widest part of her girth, she looked like an overly bright, plump pumpkin banded in half.

She hit the play button, showing another series of photos, these of her beloved yard being trampled by a runaway goat. The caption under the pictures berated the local police department for making light of the destruction and for siding with the local 'derelict youth' of the community. It then segued to a series of pictures featuring some of the area's young people, partying near the river in what the caption claimed was 'with the support and blessing' of their esteemed chief of police. There was the question of 'can we trust his judgment?' as it showed him on a morning after, picking up the discarded beer cans and tossing them into the back of his personal truck. Mention of 'divided loyalties' as it flashed between a photo of him and Tony with their famous professional sports team, and him and the local small-town football team. A panned shot of the sprawling river-bottom ranch his family owned and a close-up of a working pump jack. The words 'Opportunity,' 'Means,' and a picture of their wedding reception, taken at a distance. The single word 'Motive?' and the picture of a bag of money, followed by a picture Madison had seen before on Facebook. It was the photo of Brash and his new deputy, Misty Abraham, at some sort of carnival. They were obviously there as a couple, their arms wrapped around each other and wearing silly grins on their faces while holding over-sized alcoholic beverage souvenir cups.

The photo was only there for a moment, but it was enough to stir an audible gasp among the crowd. The picture immediately merged into one of Brash working at his summer camp for underprivileged youth. Madison thought it was an odd picture for Myrna to use to depict Brash's poor character. If anything, the photo showcased his generous and giving nature.

She thought it even stranger that the woman should use the second photo. This was of him working a wreck in pouring rain mixed with a generous amount of sleet. Rivulets of water streamed off his hat and down the front of his poncho, while beads of ice crusted on his shirt collar. By the time the words 'Community service? Neighborhood beautification projects?' flashed on the screen, she heard her grandmother's pleased chuckle beside her. Next came a photo of Myrna Lewis herself.

Myrna was well known around town for her 'special technique' of gardening. To get her lawn precisely the way she wanted it, she could often be found on her hands and knees, hand-cutting her grass with a pair of shears. To save wear on her knees, she sometimes lay down and rolled on the grass from one area to another. In this picture, she wore one of her more colorful outfits and was caught mid-roll, so that she appeared to be writhing in pain. The photo was no doubt snapped as she yelled obscenities to the photographer, freezing her features in an open-mouth grimace.

The crowd couldn't help but laugh.

Myrna had been watching the crowd, feeding off the expressions of surprise she read in their faces. When they laughed, the satisfied smirk fell from Myrna's face, and she jerked her attention back to the screen. She gasped as she saw the photo they were laughing over.

She punched a button on the remote, and the next photo came up. This one was of Brash helping an elderly woman out of her car. Myrna jabbed the button again, and a photo of Sharese and Joel Werner appeared. They were both glassy-eyed and rosy cheeked, surrounded by discarded cocktail glasses and empty wine bottles. Myrna waved the remote in the air frantically, trying to get it to stop. Each photo was more incriminating than the last.

Joel Werner as a young man, being booked into the Bexar County Jail. A more recent photo of him sitting in the defendant's seat during a trial. A picture of him making an obscene gesture while posing beside a wax replica of Madonna. More pictures of him and his wife partying, always with plenty of alcohol in hand. Another picture of Myrna on the lawn, this one with her broad backside turned up in the air. A close-up of a newspaper showing Werner's photograph and a headline reading 'Local Deputy Detained for Questioning.'

While Myrna could think to do nothing but stomp her foot and click needlessly on the remote, Joel Werner stood and demanded that someone put a stop to 'this mockery of a meeting.' All the while, the crowd roared with laughter, particularly when the final picture came up. It was of the Werners from several years ago, presumably at a Halloween party. Sharese wore a tiny little cheerleader outfit that barely contained her generous bosom, and Joel was dressed as a bulked-up football player. Oddly enough, he wore a jersey that touted Brash's name and number.

Joel Werner had dressed as Brash for Halloween. The irony and hypocrisy wasn't lost upon the crowd.

In typical fashion, Brash came to the rescue. He pulled the plug on the projector and then shut the laptop computer playing the slideshow, effectively putting an end to the compromised presentation.

Granny Bert stood up amid Myrna's sputtering and took control of the mic.

She reminded the crowd that she needed no introduction. She had been mayor of Juliet for many years, an elected county official before that, and she and her family were institutions in the sister cities. Along with the deCordova family, they were the backbone of the community. She reminded the city councils of how proud everyone had been when their hometown hero had gone on to national stardom, and of how Brash had returned to his roots to serve, protect, and nurture his own. She reminded them of his many good deeds within the community and referred to specific times when he had come to the rescue of those judging him.

"I'm just going to say one thing about all these ridiculous pictures floating around tonight, and on the news, and on the internet," Bertha Cessna told the crowd. "Bull feathers! In all the years Brash has been back in town, has anyone seen evidence of him being a playboy? The single women of this community—and plenty of those who weren't!—have chased after that poor man until they were blue in the face, and for the most part, he hasn't given them the time of day! He's been too busy being a devoted father and lawman to have much of a social life. The fact that his so-called 'playboy lifestyle' hasn't surfaced until now, just as he marries, is laughable. I don't know about you folks, but I resent the fact that an outsider comes into our close-knit community and assumes we are too stupid to see through his antics."

She turned directly toward Joel Werner, pinning him

with her intense gaze. "Sir, we are not a bunch of backwoods hillbillies, too ignorant to see what you're up to. You want Brash deCordova's job. If that last picture is to be believed, you want to *be* Brash deCordova! And you'll stoop to whatever means it takes to worm your way in."

She could have said so much more. She could have referenced the disparaging photos of Werner and his wife or pointed out that all pictures shown were in the public domain and readily available on the internet. She could have gone on about taking things out of context and making mountains out of molehills. It was, in fact, what the crowd expected of the older woman, who was well known for her outspoken opinions.

Instead, Granny Bert turned back to the city council seated on the floor, and to the crowd in the stands. "And that, my friends," she said, effectively dismissing the farce by giving it no further comment, "is enough about that."

When the cheers from the crowd quieted, someone on the floor made a hasty motion to table further discussion concerning the chief's status. The motion unanimously carried and within minutes, the meeting adjourned.

Madison grabbed her grandmother's arm before they were swept away in the crowd. Already, people were filing out of the bleachers to come down and congratulate Brash and to offer their support.

"Granny!" she hissed. "What did you do to that video?"

"I didn't do a thing," she assured her granddaughter. "Wanda Shank's grandson lives next door to Myrna and just happens to be a whiz on the computer. Somehow, their internet connections often get all tangled up, and he was able to tap into her presentation. Honestly, I had nothing to do with it, but I couldn't have been prouder of the results if I had."

"Thank you for what you said up there. And for organizing this whole, amazing response. Your 'sources' really came through."

"Let's just hope that wormy weasel crawls back under the rock he came from."

But something told Madison it wouldn't be that easy. As rewarding and vindicating as the evening had been, she couldn't help but worry.

Joel Werner wasn't the type to take public humiliation lightly. The look in his eyes was nothing short of chilling, and a shiver worked its way through her shoulders as she imagined what lengths he might go to seek his revenge.

Not to mention the lengths he had gone in setting up this evening—this entire campaign, in fact. His attack had been well planned and well executed, from the slow building of public distrust to garnering Myrna Lewis' help, from the printed promotional items to getting the press involved. This had taken many hours of thought and preparation.

A nagging question haunted her mind.

Was the man capable of murder? Had killing Nigel been a small part of his overall scheme?

If so, what might he do next?

29

Tony Sanchez's arraignment was Friday. He was released from jail on his own recognizance and a token bail. The reporters followed the story closely, but oddly enough, made very few references to his arresting officer or their long-standing friendship. When Brash's name was mentioned, it was in reference to last evening's outpouring of love and support by his hometown community.

Snippets from the night ran on the national news, heralding it as 'how a small town in Texas supports its hometown hero.' The focus shifted from Brash's playboy 'sans shirt' lifestyle to his good ol' boy appeal, depicted by the handmade posters, homemade baked goods, and heartfelt community support. The latter angle wasn't nearly as exciting as the first, and interest in the story took a steep tumble.

Somewhere in the Midwest, another politician was accused of sexual misconduct, and just like that, the press had a better story. If Madison didn't know better, she would have suspected her grandmother had something to do with the shift in attention, but even Granny Bert wouldn't stoop so low. That was definitely more Joel Werner's style.

It had been a stressful week, but the weekend was on its way. The teens would be in from their ski trip late that evening. Having missed them terribly, Madison freshened all three rooms and planned a big weekend brunch to celebrate their homecoming.

With an hour to spare before her two o'clock meeting with Barbara Motte, Madison joined Derron in the office.

There was no way to verify the woman's relationship to Nigel before the meeting, but it didn't matter. What mattered was that a lonely old man would be laid to rest with mourners standing over him, at least one of whom had possible familial ties. The courts would decide who controlled his fortune, but it had fallen upon Madison and Brash to control his last rites. For this, any claim of kinship was better than no claim at all.

Madison leafed through the old Barrett family Bible once more, deciding she would ultimately give it to the person who inherited his estate. It was too early to assume Barbara from Lake Whitney was that person, but Madison hoped she was. Finding just one confirmed relative was enough to make her feel as if she hadn't let Nigel down completely.

Belatedly remembering Frank Fuller's reference to notes in the old Bible, she wondered where she might find them. Supposedly, they established a legal claim to land sold a hundred years ago.

"Dollface?" Derron called from his desk, interrupting her perusal of the thick tome. "Can I delete these photos in the folder marked Erickson Death? These are just duplicates, right?"

"Right." In lieu of an official photographer on the day of Bobby Ray's death, Brash had asked her to take photos on her phone while he interviewed the ensemble cast. She had forwarded the photos to the police department but kept an online copy, just in case.

With his death officially ruled natural causes and the case

now closed, there was no need to keep the pictures. "Yeah, go ahead," she said, waving her hand in dismissal. She closed the Bible and set it aside, thinking she would come back to it later. "You know what?" she said, changing her mind. "Wait on deleting those. Let me take one more look at them, and then I'll do it myself."

"Whatever, boss lady. Just trying to clear up some space in the cloud. The internet is like molasses today."

"I'll go through them now."

She pulled up the file on her computer and clicked on the first photograph. It was of the fallen man, a much closer shot than she felt comfortable taking, but one she knew was necessary for proper documentation. Against the pallor of death, his cheeks were still blotched and ruddy. She detected welts against his neck and along the side of his face. She had seen similar marks on Nigel's skin, reinforcing the assumption that both men had died of a severe allergic reaction.

There were more photos of Bobby Ray, but it seemed somehow sacrilegious to study them too closely. She clicked off them, moving on to images of the crowd. She had snapped photos at random that day, catching expressions of shock and surprise, even boredom, in the faces of the crowd.

Brash sometimes coached her in the art of surveillance, particularly when she worked a case for private detective Murray Archer. He had once told her that you never knew when you might catch someone unawares, capturing their innermost thoughts on camera with a random shot. More than one case, he claimed, had been solved in such a happenchance manner. Taking that advice to heart, Madison had panned through the crowd that day, forcing time to a standstill, one frame at a time.

Glancing through the pictures again, she saw nothing amiss this time, either. She and Brash had studied the photos many times over the last few weeks, hoping to catch a gleam in someone's eye, or a smirk of satisfaction upon a vengeful face. There was nothing.

Derron paused behind her as he dropped a file onto her desk. "The file on all things upholstery," he explained, glancing at her computer. "Ooh, love that shade of chartreuse." He tapped the screen, pointing to the arm of someone in the crowd. "Wonder how it would look on me?"

"Don't you already have a shirt that color?"

"No."

Madison scrunched her face in contemplation. "I know I've seen that color somewhere."

"Not on me. But you may soon," he added with a saucy grin. "I feel another shopping excursion coming on."

"Hmm. Oh, well, doesn't matter." She closed the folder and would have hit the delete button, but noticed she had a new message. Eager to see what RR78 had to say, she abandoned the folder in favor of reading his reply message.

I'm in Central Texas. Little podunk town called Marlin, just south of Waco. Can meet today at 5. Leave town tomorrow for a job, be gone a month or so.

Madison knew she couldn't meet Barbara at two, plan Nigel's memorial, drive north to Marlin, and be there by five. However, if he was leaving town for an extended time, it sounded as if today was the best opportunity to meet with him. And his location certainly fit the general area of Nigel's family, making him an even more likely candidate as a relative.

She was contemplating her choices when the telephone rang. Not recognizing the number, she answered with caution. The media had miraculously stopped calling, but she never knew when a stubborn reporter might linger around, looking for a mop-up story.

"Hello?"

"Hello, this is Detective Donald Peters with the Whitney Police Department. Is this Madison Reynolds?"

"Yes, this is she." Madison was too stunned to correct him with her married name. Why was someone from the Whitney Police Department calling her? Was he calling to warn her that Barbara Motte was a fraud? A known con artist?

"I think you may have had plans to meet with one of our local residents this afternoon, if the circled notation in her address book is to be believed. Are you acquainted with Barbara Motte of 1379 Morning Glory Circle?"

"I have an appointment with her this afternoon," Madison confirmed.

"I'm afraid you'll have to change your plans, ma'am. I'm calling to inform you that Mrs. Motte was attacked in her home last night and is currently undergoing surgery at a nearby hospital."

"What?" The word left her mouth with a gasp. "Is she—is she all right?"

"From what I understand, she's in serious condition. That's all I'm at liberty to say. How well do you know Mrs. Motte?"

"Not at all. I was meeting her for the first time."

"So, you have no clue as to why someone would brutally attack her in her home?"

"N—No," Madison said. The officer told her little else, other than the fact that the scene was quite violent. He gave her the name of the hospital and advised her to call there for further updates, even though they weren't likely to release any information without written consent from the patient.

But as Madison hung up the phone, she suspected she *did* know why Barbara had been attacked. Somehow, someway, this was related to Nigel Barrett.

"Are you okay?" Derron asked, noting her pale color.

"Not really. The lead I had on Nigel's next of kin was brutally attacked in her home last night and is in surgery as we speak."

"That's horrible!"

"I can't help but think it has something to do with Nigel and her connection to his estate."

Derron nibbled his lower lip in worry. "What are you going to do about it?"

"The first thing I'm going to do," she decided, turning back to her computer, "is reply to my other lead, RR78. How do you feel about a quick trip to Marlin?"

ೞೞೞೞ

RR78 agreed to meet but only if she came to him. He cited a busy evening, preparing for his departure the next day.

"I'm still not sure this is a good idea," Derron whined as they neared their destination.

"Maybe not, but it's too late to turn back now."

"Weren't you somewhere near here when that car ran you off the road last week?"

"Yes, but that had nothing to do with the man I'm meeting today."

"You're sure about that?"

"Absolutely. Ninety-five percent," she assured him. "I'm sure that was a random incident. At any rate, if it was aimed at me personally, it was most likely a man name Petey Vansant. PV. This guy today is RR."

"As in Road Rage?" Derron suggested dryly.

Madison wrinkled her nose, trying to hide the fact his assessment rattled her nerves. "What's the 78 for?" she taunted.

"The number of people he's run off the road?"

"Okay, so I'm ninety percent sure the two aren't connected." She pursed her lips as she took the exit. "Definitely eighty percent."

"You aren't making me feel any better, dollface," he

243

pointed out.

"Look, I owe it to Nigel to find his next of kin. The thought of burying him all alone, with no one to mourn his passing, just breaks my heart. If I can find at least one person related to him, I'll feel like I didn't let him down completely. He may never have gotten to meet his family while he was alive, but perhaps some of them can at least attend his funeral."

"Aren't you forgetting the part where you suspect one of his relatives may have been responsible for his death? For all you know, you're walking into a trap."

"If this RR78 killed Nigel," she reasoned, "he would hardly plan to meet with him today, would he? He thinks he's been corresponding with the man. Plus, he didn't answer my message until *after* Nigel died."

"So, if the Barbara woman isn't responsible for his death and neither is RR78, then who do you think is?"

"I'm working two different theories at the moment. If it's a family member, I'm hoping RR78 can tell me about some of his other relatives. One of them may have been aware of their connection to Nigel and decided to cash in on it."

"And the other theory?"

"It may sound crazy, but I haven't ruled out the possibility that Joel Werner may have done it, simply to frame Brash." She snuck a glance at her passenger. "Does that sound absolutely insane?"

"Honestly, no. After seeing Werner's face last night at that meeting, I wouldn't put much past that man." Peering through the windshield to read street signs, Derron pointed to their left. "The directions say to turn here."

Two minutes later, they pulled up in front of a well-kept modular home at the end of a quiet street. The lawn was immaculate, but Madison had the distinct impression that several things had been recently removed from the yard. A lonely flagpole stood amid a stand of bluebonnets, its ropes conspicuously bare. A large patch of trampled brown grass suggested something large and heavy once sat upon it. Near the front door, a few springs of taller grass edged a round, barren spot on the ground. Perhaps a flowerpot once resided there, she thought.

Something else had been removed from near the gable of the house. At first glance, the vinyl siding didn't appear faded, but there was a distinct Texas-shaped image on the side of the house, its color a few shades darker and more vibrant in relief.

The entire setting gave off a forlorn vibe, one just short of abandonment. Madison wondered if this RR78 weren't moving altogether, rather than leaving for only a month. She glanced at the car in the driveway and saw that it was completely packed, crammed with boxes and suitcases and an assortment of odds and ends. She spotted a lampshade stuffed into the back window, with a winter coat crammed in beside it.

She couldn't explain it, but she felt apprehensive about going inside. The doublewide home was nice enough, and certainly well kept, but she couldn't shake the feeling that something was off.

Turning to her assistant, she faked a bright smile. "Ready?"

"As ready as I'll ever be, I suppose." With a sigh, he stepped gingerly from the car and shut the door behind him. "The place looks almost empty," he noted. "I feel like I should be tiptoeing."

"You, too, huh?"

They exchanged shrugs as they climbed the steps to the small porch.

"Oh, look. Someone's a fan," Derron pointed out. The entire porch was a mosaic of the infamous Texas 'Come and Take It' flag. Madison knew the skirmish at Gonzales was a precursor to the Texas Revolution, when Mexican forces tried taking a cannon from the Texians and met unexpected resistance. In light of recent gun law debates, the historic flag enjoyed new popularity today.

Madison knocked on the door and waited for a response. On the second try, she heard the safety chain rattle and a woman's voice float through the narrow opening. "Yes? May I— Madison! What are you doing here?"

"Collette?" She stared at her friend in surprise. "What— What are you doing here?"

The other woman laughed and opened the door more fully. "That's supposed to be my question. I live here. What are *you* doing here?"

"I'm supposed to meet someone here." Her brow wrinkled and she looked around, clearly confused. "Is this 1835 Milam?"

"Oh, yes. Bobby Ray insisted we buy this exact lot because his hero, Ben Milam, was killed in the Siege of Bexar in 1835. He claimed it was kismet, or some such nonsense." She rolled her eyes before motioning them forward. "Come on in."

Madison felt as if she had stepped into the twilight zone. Nothing made sense. Even as she allowed Collette to tug her by the arm, her mind protested that something wasn't right. Why had RR78 instructed her to meet him here, of all places?

"But..." She sputtered the protest, even as she stepped through the door.

"Hello, Derron," Collette said. Like the time she greeted Frank Fuller, the smile never quite reached her eyes. "Now tell me," she continued, once they were both inside. "Who were you meeting here?"

"Actually, RR78 reached out to me today. He asked that we meet here." Even as she heard herself say the words, they made no sense.

"RR78? Isn't that Nigel Barrett's next of kin?"

"There's a good possibility he's kin," Madison agreed.

"I told you," Collette said, her voice suddenly sharp. "He was the only positive match on there. The others were very distant, if at all."

"But... why would he ask me to meet him here?"

Collette flipped her hair over her shoulder. "How should I know? But while you're here, would you like to see what's left of Bobby Ray's collection? I've sold most of it already, but there's still plenty of junk left."

She turned without waiting for an answer, expecting Madison and Derron to follow. Madison threw a skeptical look toward her friend, who answered with a curious expression on his face. He twirled his finger near his temple and pointed at Collette's back, indicating he thought she was crazy. Madison couldn't help but think he might be right, as she reluctantly followed the other woman further into the house.

"Are you moving?" Madison asked, noting barren spaces on the walls. It wasn't just the walls, however. There were items obviously missing from all the rooms, including anything personal. The rooms appeared to have been picked over, and she wondered how much of that was loaded into the car outside.

"I told you, I sold most of Bobby Ray's junk," Collette answered. "He had it scattered all over the house. Insisted we decorate with it, even though it was never my style."

"He must have had some of it outside, too. I noticed dead spots in your yard."

"Oh no, that was where we buried the neighbors," she quipped. She laughed when she saw Derron's face turn white. "I'm kidding. Come on in. This is one of his rooms."

As she said, there wasn't a great deal left. Nothing, Madison imagined, compared to what once filled the room. An empty display case stood against one wall. Another wall had a few random pieces scattered along a bookshelf and three pedestal bases, now bare of their treasures. A few pieces of framed artwork hung on the walls, mostly photographs and certificates. Most likely, things that were important only to her late husband and had no value on the open market.

Derron stepped further into the room to examine some of the framed pieces, while Madison feigned interest in a leather scabbard.

"You see what I mean," Colette said, motioning about the room. "Nothing but junk."

"To each his own, they say," Madison murmured.

Derron caught her eye and discreetly motioned her over.

Her assistant was acting strange, even for him. As nonchalantly as possible, Madison crossed the room. Colette concentrated on a small canvas bag she held.

Derron cocked his head toward the photograph behind him. Madison recognized Bobby Ray and several other members of the militia group, all dressed in their period costumes. Only Colette and one other woman wore normal clothing. Judging from the proud smile on Bobby Ray's face as he accepted some sort of white looped rope, Madison imagined it was the promotion ceremony when he became captain.

"So?" she mouthed to Derron.

He tugged on his shirt, earning a deep scowl from his boss. His efforts grew more exaggerated, as he threw his eyes toward the picture on the wall. Finally understanding, Madison focused on Colette's outfit in the photograph.

Bright chartreuse.

It doesn't mean a thing, she told herself.

Still, a sense of unease crawled up Madison's back. She cleared her throat and eased over to inspect one of the framed documents. It was a certificate of promotion awarded to the dedicated and honorable Captain Robert Raymond Erickson.

Bobby Ray.

Robert Raymond.

RR.

Madison drew in a deep, unsteady breath. Her eyes flew to Derron's, and she gave the tiniest shake of her head, willing him not to ask questions. The two of them had been in tight situations before and managed just fine. This would be no different. They would make an excuse, followed by a hasty exit, and when they were far, far down the road, they would determine what it all meant.

She already knew what part of it meant. It meant that Collette had been in the crowd that day during the cannon demonstration, far longer than she originally admitted. That was the same chartreuse jacket in both photographs. And if Collette was there when her husband fell, why did she wait a good ten minutes to come rushing forward, pretending to have been across the park at the time of his death?

It meant something else, as well. Even though it could be a coincidence (there were hundreds of thousands of people with the initials RR), it meant that meeting RR78 here, at this address, was no accident. No misunderstanding. Most likely, her late husband—or Collette herself—was the person known as RR78.

But what either of those facts meant, Madison had no idea.

She willed her voice to sound normal when she said, "It looks like you've done a good job at selling most of his collection."

"I suppose," Collette agreed, still occupied with the bag. It was fat and round, like a small white pumpkin. Madison wondered what the fascination was. "I didn't get nearly what he paid for all this junk in the first place, but I made a decent amount. Enough to help me start over before Jeannie's inheritance kicks in."

"That's good. We're really happy for you, aren't we, Derron?" She threw a cautionary glance toward him and he nodded in silence. Wide-eyed and pale, her assistant was clearly as confused and uncomfortable as she was. "But there's not a lot left to see, and obviously my meeting's been canceled, so I think we'll go now."

"I still have so much to show you," Collette insisted.

"Let's go in the other room."

"Honestly, I need to get back. I didn't realize it was so late."

"Geez," Derron played along. "Would you look at the time?"

"You have time. After all, you were planning to meet RR78, weren't you?" Collette moved into the hallway ahead of them, pointing the way with the canvas bag still in hand. "This way for the rest of the tour, please." Her voice was playful as she acted the part of a tour guide.

Madison knew they should insist on leaving. Ask Collette to move aside so they could make their way to the door and out to the car. None of this made sense, particularly this gnawing sense of unease in her stomach.

She needed time to think. If she could put some distance between herself and the situation, she could rationalize that Collette was her friend (of sorts) and posed no danger to her, no matter what the hairs on the back of her neck claimed. She could come up with some explanation as to why Collette hadn't come forward the moment her husband fell—shock, most likely—and why a stranger would give this address as a meeting place. She could convince herself it was a simple mistake. Spellcheck, perhaps (she, if anyone, knew the havoc wreaked by that malady!) or a mistyped street address.

If she only had the time and the space to think it through, she could rationalize that, while Collette was a strange person, prone to mood swings, she was in no way dangerous.

Look at her now. She was smiling, inviting them to see the rest of her late husband's collection. Never mind that she almost seemed proud, despite having repeatedly professed to hate Bobby Ray's hobby. Madison could chalk it up to another mood swing, or to the conflicting feelings of grief and resentment of a recent widow. Feelings she knew herself, all too well.

Continuing the tour wouldn't give her time and distance,

but maybe it would give her answers.

Resigned, Madison turned into the room on the right.

30

The room was dark, having some sort of stationary cover over the window. The air inside was stale and dry, and held a distinct acrid tang. Madison's first thought was sulfur, reminding her of the black powder rifles fired at Washington-on-the-Brazos. The ones that so fascinated her son.

"This was his ammunition room," Collette explained. "You'll have to excuse the smell, but this is what I had to put up with. Bobby Ray and his toys!" Her voice turned irate as she glared at the items still in the room.

Wooden crates stacked against one wall, all labeled with "Explosive" and "Caution! Handle with Care" stamps. A table with a set of scales and several antique instruments sat against another, and in the very center of the room was a long, narrow table. A three-foot cannon sat upon it, looking quite authentic despite its scaled-down size. Madison noticed that all the air vents were closed in the room, adding to the musky odor and the stifling stillness.

"Is—is that a real cannon?" Derron asked cautiously.

"Oh, yes. Bobby Ray made it himself. It was one of his

most treasured pieces. The buyer offered a nice price for it, but let's just say... I have different plans for this."

"Very interesting," was Madison's only reply, as she hung near the door.

"Go on in. Take a look around," Collette encouraged.

"Oh, that's okay. We really do need to get back."

"I insist."

Madison had two choices. Refuse and make a scene, thereby exposing the crazy thoughts racing through her head and trampling through the hairs on the back of her neck. Or, she could go along with the request—the one spoken with just enough edge to make it more of a command than a request—and use it as an opportunity to ask questions.

When given a choice, Madison always preferred conversation to confrontation. She stepped forward toward the cannon.

"Are you familiar with how cannons work?" Collette wanted to know.

"Not really."

"Neither was I. But when you're married to a weaponry enthusiast, you learn. Here, let me show you some of the things I've picked up through the years."

Madison made a last-ditch effort to leave. "That's really not necessary," she began. "We need—"

"But what if RR78 arrives? I'll show you how this works while we wait for him to show up." She motioned for them to gather around the table. "Come on, this will be fun. You can both help me."

Derron threw Madison a sharp look, but he followed her lead and edged toward the narrow table.

"This bag," she held up the canvas pouch as she spoke, "holds the black powder. It's what makes the cannon go *boom!*" She said the word with such unexpected force, both of her guests jumped. She laughed gaily at their reaction. "Sorry. Bobby Ray loved to do that to unsuspecting bystanders. The blast was always his favorite part of the demonstration. Of course, he wasn't too thrilled with that last explosion."

Okay, Madison reasoned to herself. *A bit crass when speaking of your late husband, but it gives me an opening.*

She tried for a conversational tone. "I was thinking about that earlier. You weren't there for the actual demonstration, isn't that what you said?"

"That's what I said." Collette busied herself gathering items stored on the lower shelf of the table.

"So, if someone thought they saw you in the crowd that day by the cannons, they would be mistaken?"

"That's right."

Derron pitched in so that it sounded less like an inquisition. "I don't blame you," he commiserated with Collette. "I wouldn't want to be that close to all the noise, either. Or all that smoke."

"From what I understand," Collette agreed, "that smoke can be *deadly.*"

Did Madison imagine it, or was there a coy smile playing around the edges of the woman's mouth? Even though their marriage was all but over, surely she didn't find humor in her husband's death!

Continuing with the demonstration, Collette explained that swabbing the barrel with a wet sponge was the first step to firing the weapon. "Being that we've started with a cold cannon, we can skip that part today. But you can still be our vent man, Madison. Keep your thumb over this hole, so no draft can come in and spark an unwanted flame. This is how you load it. You put the charge all the way to the back, and gently tap it in. Here, Derron. You can do the honors." She handed him a thick wooden dowel as she carefully placed the canvas bag into the barrel of the tabletop cannon. "Easy, now. You don't want it to *blow up* in your face."

"What's in the bag?" Madison asked, still uneasy with Collette's almost jovial attitude.

"The conventional answer is black powder, but Bobby

Ray liked to experiment. If he was shooting the cannon at night, he would sometimes add things like salt or metal filings to add color and spark."

It crossed Madison's mind that the charge that day could have contained metal shavings. Had they somehow penetrated his skin and caused his death? But, no. There had been no blood.

But something set off Brash's radar, she reasoned.

"Bobby Ray wasn't allergic to black powder, was he?" she asked. Until now, the thought hadn't occurred to her, but given his high sensitivity to so many other things, it seemed likely. "That day at Washington-on-the-Brazos, Bobby Ray was standing near the blast point," she said. "If he was allergic to what was in the charge..."

"He wasn't allergic to the *black powder* that was in the charge." Collette emphasized the words 'black powder' as she waved her hand around the room. "Which is good, since this room is full of it. So, whatever you do, don't light a match." Her voice took on a teasing quality.

Derron's face lost a bit more color. "Is that why the vents are closed and the window is sealed?"

"Yes. He harped on the importance of keeping the atmosphere as stable as possible when loading. He made all his own ammunition. Like everything else about his hobby, he was obsessed with authenticity." She laughed, but the coarse rendition lacked humor. "If he were here, he would scold me for skipping the crucial step of swabbing the barrel. A five-minute lecture would follow on the importance of firing a clean, dry cannon."

"Someone from the cannon crew that day recalled an odd odor," Madison said, still grasping for a reasonable explanation as to why he had died. "He said it reminded him of crab legs. Do you have any idea what it could have been?"

"Long John Silver's Crab Cake of the Day Special?" she quipped. Her voice had that cheerful, teasing quality again.

"Shrimp shavings? A bit of seafood surprise, mixed in with the gunpowder?" Her lilting tone turned dramatic, and she clutched a hand to her chest. "Can you imagine how that might have affected someone increasingly allergic to seafood, like Bobby Ray? Coming out compressed and under pressure, so close to him? The air would have been saturated with all those allergens, right there in his face. He might not have been able to breathe!"

After that long and dramatic hypothesis, Collette did a complete turnabout. With a nonchalant shrug, she answered, "How would I know what was in the bag?"

Madison was certain her gulp echoed around the room. Edging closer to Derron, she struggled to stay calm. Surely, Collette hadn't meant to suggest... The concept was too ludicrous to even entertain.

"His allergies were getting worse?" she questioned instead, impressed with how even her voice sounded. Not at all like her thudding heart, or her hitched breath.

"Yes. I had him on a strict diet, formulated for optimum results." A contemplative expression crossed her face, but she shook it off. "I guess I miscalculated somehow. His sensitivity increased more rapidly than expected."

Derron threw his boss a look of utter confusion, not understanding the other woman's ramblings.

The sickening feeling in Madison's stomach suggested she understood all too well.

Collette worked in medical sciences. She had knowledge of allergens. Of severe sensitivities that often proved fatal. Theoretically, she would know how to manipulate exposure for a specific result. That result, presumably, would be to keep the patient healthy and away from known irritants.

But what if, Madison's sick stomach wondered, *a person was trapped in a bad marriage and wanted a way out?* Granny Bert told a story about a woman she knew who, over the course of several months, gradually poisoned her abusive husband. The individual dosage was too small to detect on its own but had debilitating results when compounded. Eventually, the man died but, according to her grandmother, the wife's suspected involvement was never proved.

What if Collette tried something similar? What if she had exposed Bobby Ray to allergens in small but ever-increasing quantities? It could have been to build his resistance.

Not with that look in her eye, her queasy stomach argued. *She was building him up for 'the big one.'*

"Bobby Ray ate shrimp that day," Madison blurted out. "He snitched a piece off Petey Vansant's plate."

Collette stopped what she was doing and stared at Madison in surprise. Her eyes batted once or twice as she digested the news. "Where did you hear that?" she snapped.

"His friends told me."

The other woman nodded slowly. "It makes sense," she rationalized in a clinical voice. "The blotchy skin and wheezing. Two tainted blasts, in close succession and in such close proximity to the subject, could have done it. Could have been the shrimp that broke the fisherman's net, so to speak." She used the modified analogy with a sly smile. With another shrug, she turned her attention back to the cannon. "Like I said, he died too soon."

With another complete turnabout, her voice took on an instructional tone. "With the charge packed in tightly, and your thumb still on that vent hole, we put in our wad." She held up the wad of rags before stuffing them down the barrel. "Derron, use the rammer to pack them in, nice and tight. Back in the day, the cannonballs weren't a precise fit for the bore, and you want maximum velocity when they discharge."

"To hate his hobby so much," Derron observed, tapping the wad in with the charge, "you certainly know a lot about it."

"Knowledge is freedom."

With that cryptic comment, Collette dropped a crude black ball into the barrel. It looked old and rough, and slightly lumpy.

"What—What was that?" Derron asked.

Her tone was matter of fact. "The cannonball, obviously. What else would it be?"

"I–I assumed you would use a blank," he stuttered. "There's not really any black powder in that charge bag, is there? Just a little something for show?"

The way her eyes twinkled with laughter, it was difficult to take her seriously when she said, "Now, where's the fun in that?" She retrieved something from the shelf below as she continued, "Derron, I need you to grab the barrel with both hands. Down on this end, near Madison. Yes, like that. Keep your thumb there in place, girlfriend. And use your other hand to cup around it, so that no draft gets in. You're both doing great."

The woman's ramblings made no sense, and her mood swings were concerning. Madison had gone along so far, but now Collette wanted both her hands over the vent hole. "What are we doing, Collette?" she practically snapped. "I don't understand why—"

"We're almost done. Derron, if you could just slip your hands a bit further... yes, like that. I'll use this rope to secure everything in place."

Madison couldn't see what was happening. Neither could Derron, with his hands beneath the cannon as they were. He felt her drape a rope gently against his hands, the fibers tickling the tender skin along his wrists.

"Give me just a minute, and I'll be done." Collette did something with the thin length of rope, chattering as she worked. "This is a crucial step in the process. I suppose all steps are crucial, even the ones that seem so mundane. Without changing your positions, can either of you read the label on that top box? Can you tell what powder strength we're using?"

Madison had to twist a bit to read the label. She didn't see anything about powder strength, just a warning about being *Highly Flammable.* As she squinted to read the words beneath *Extreme Danger,* she felt something cold touch her wrists. Madison heard a double snap, followed closely by Derron's exclamation.

When Derron attempted to move, the loose ropes against his wrists immediately tightened into a constrictor knot. "What the—!"

"Now, now," Collette chided in a playful voice. "Watch your mouth. There are ladies present."

Madison stared in horror at the handcuffs around both her wrists. Even as she jerked, Collette snapped another lock in place. A chain circled the circumference of the barrel and hooked onto the handcuffs, effectively binding her to the cannon.

"Collette! What are you doing?" Madison cried.

"I'm tying up a few loose ends before I collect on Jeannie's inheritance. I mentioned that earlier, didn't I? With Bobby Ray dying so suddenly, I become the sole beneficiary."

Derron was aghast as he put the pieces together. "You killed your husband so you could collect on his mother's insurance policy?" His voice rose on the last words.

"Not an insurance policy, you imbecile. Inheritance. There's a difference." Her sniff sounded truly offended.

Madison tried reasoning with her. "Collette, think this through. You can't seriously intend—"

"Believe me. I've thought of nothing else for the last six months. It started out so simple—get the mother-in-law out of the picture, inherit the millions, then have the hubby go into anaphylactic shock and kick the bucket—but, I swear, it's just been one complication after another." She shook her head like a person vexed with bad luck. She could have been naming off minor complications in her day, not reasons she had committed murder.

"First, Bobby Ray did that stupid DNA test behind my back and stirred up a whole string of potential relatives. I had to speed things up and get rid of Jeannie before she hosted a family reunion. Can you imagine how that would have diluted our inheritance, sharing with all those people?

"Then, Bobby Ray up and died. I should have expected as much. The fool never could hold his liquor. Or his pee. Or his performance in the bedroom. Why should his allergies be any different? Total wimp."

While Collette shook her head in disgust, Madison and Derron tugged in vain to get free.

"Then," Collette continued, "Nigel went and did a DNA test, too! That really complicated things."

"Nigel?" Madison's cry was one of total surprise.

Collette laughed at her stunned expression. "You really didn't know? And you fancy yourself a detective? How utterly stupid of you."

Bending to retrieve something from the lower shelf, Collette's tone turned conversational again. The woman's moods changed as easily as the wind.

"We've always known Jeannie was related to the Barrett family in Juliet. But according to Grandma Betty Jean, they were dirt poor. Lorie Jean—or Jeannie, as she preferred—never knew her family had struck oil. I thought it best if she died not knowing what she was missing."

"So you killed her."

"I had to." Collette blinked her eyes, looking almost as innocent as she sounded. "She knew she had cousins. Once she heard about the family fortune, she might insist on sharing. She was funny that way, always wanting to do the right thing. It seemed easiest to thin the family forest down to a single branch."

Madison paled. "Barb62," she whispered. "Barbara Motte was her cousin. I–I told you where she lived." Realization washed over her, and she cried out in utter dismay, "You *didn't*!"

Collette put her hands to her mouth in an overplayed gesture of chagrin. "I did." The words came out guiltily, but her eyes danced with delight. "Again, I had to. She'd already made the connection to her uncle, and then she would be standing there with her hand out, wanting part of the inheritance. From what I understand, she runs some sort of inmate rehabilitation center in cahoots with her brother. He didn't really die in prison like I told you. Turns out, he's reformed and works in the center. They would probably take their millions and waste them on those undeserving prisoners," she used a dramatic tone, as if the thought were utterly tiresome, "and then it would cut into *my* share."

The more she talked, the harder Madison and Derron pulled on their restraints. Neither budged.

"By stroke of luck, my friend told me who you were. Once you and I became friends, you were so easy to manipulate! A pathetic look here, a sniffle or two there, and you fell all over yourself being nice to me. Once you invited me to the reception... well, my plans just fell into place."

Now she was smiling again, obviously quite pleased with how everything had worked out. "Like I said," she continued, "a plan of this magnitude took a great deal of planning. Right down to the tiniest of shrimp." She affected a pose, paraphrasing that famous line from *Oliver Twist*. "Please, sir, would you like some more?"

Derron's expression of disbelief said it all. The woman was insane.

"You killed Nigel," Madison belatedly realized. Where did that put the body count? Jeannie, Bobby Ray, Nigel, and possibly Barbara, if she didn't pull through. And unless they came up with a plan—and quick!—that number would soon increase by two. She struggled to get her hands free, but every movement tightened the chain. Her hands were now snug against the cannon's barrel.

"Again, I had to," Collette explained. She pushed Madison's bound hands aside and jabbed a wire into the vent hole as she continued, "Things were simply getting too complicated. The sooner it was all said and done, the better.

Originally, I had planned to wait him out. I mean, he was eighty-six, and he had cancer. How long could it have been?" She gestured with her hands. "But then he went and hired *you* to find his relatives! I tried running you off the road—"

"That was *you* in the burnt-orange car!"

"—which would have taken care of both you and Nigel in one easy step. When that didn't work, I tried handing you the answers on a silver platter. I thought it would look better if Nigel discovered us, rather than the other way around. I let you look up Jeannie at the courthouse. I flat out told you RR78 was the best match. I did everything I could to lead you down a straight, easy path to our family. But noooooo, you insisted on making things complicated!" She glared at Madison before she replaced the wire with a long, braided match cord, talking as she worked.

"When the DNA hits started popping up, I knew someone would get greedy and try to move in on my claim. That night at the reception, Tony Sanchez made it almost too easy. He gave me the perfect opportunity. While everyone was watching their big argument, all I had to do was slip a tiny little shrimp or two into Nigel's sandwich. All done."

Collette crossed her arms over her chest and glared at Madison again. "Or, it would have been, if you had only let things go! I could have suddenly 'discovered' the family connection between Nigel and my husband, and no one would have been the wiser. And no one else would have tried to horn in on the fortune I worked so hard to secure."

"How did you find out Nigel was loaded?" Derron wanted to know.

Madison answered before Collette had the chance. "She overheard him and Frank Fuller talking in the doctor's office. People often forget who might be listening to their conversation. In this case, it turned out to be a deadly mistake."

Collette nodded, confirming Madison's assessment. "I really hope that Frank is too slow to make the connection. Believe it or not, I don't like killing people. It's more of a necessary evil, like going to the dentist. As long as he doesn't remember their conversation and doesn't bring up the family Bible, I may just let him live."

If there was any doubt before —and there wasn't— Collette's statement confirmed she was certifiably insane. Sane people did not equate murder to a dental visit.

"Nigel brought his family Bible to the clinic, didn't he?" Madison guessed.

"Frank couldn't make it out to see him, so Nigel brought the Bible to him. And then he proudly showed it to me. When I saw the notes, the ones that confirmed the stipulations in the old deeds, I knew he was sitting on a fortune. That was about the time I realized that Jeannie's family and Nigel's family were one in the same, and that I was married to a goldmine. That was when my plan first came together."

Collette stood back from the cannon and the two people chained to it.

"If it's any consolation," she told Madison, "I think we really could have been friends. And you don't need to worry about Brash. I'll be there to console him and comfort him in his time of grief. I really feel we can form a tight bond, borne of our mutual grief for our beloved spouses. In time, with your house and my fortune, I think Chief Hottie and I can be quite happy together."

The growl came deep from within Madison's throat. Blinded by hatred for the evil woman and her heinous deeds, she lunged for her. She rammed her head into Collette's, knocking the other woman to the ground. If she weren't still chained to the cannon, Madison would have crawled over the table and gone after the woman again. She could ignore the throbbing pain in her forehead. The double vision from the head butt was a bit harder to cope with.

Collette scrambled to her feet with an angry curse. "Just for that, you can forget what I said about being friends! I won't even try to be a good stepmother to your little darlings." A hateful snarl curled her lip. "Now both of you listen to me very carefully. You're standing in a room full of gunpowder. It doesn't matter what strength it is. I'm about to light a match, and if you even think of making any fast moves or doing anything smart, we'll all be blown to smithereens."

"We will be anyway!" Derron cried.

"Some of us will be," Collette agreed smugly. "I've used a slow match fuse, same as they did back in the day, so I'll have time to get out to the car and be on my way before it goes off. You'll have time to make your peace with God. Good luck with anything after that."

Madison wasn't above groveling. "Collette. Collette, please, I beg you. I'm a mother."

"You can't do this to us!" screamed Derron, bucking against the table.

"Be still, you fool!" Collette hissed. "I've already lit the match."

31

Collette backed out of the room, deaf to their cries for mercy.

Madison wasn't sure what was loudest: the pounding of Collette's footsteps as she ran away, the maniacal laughter trailing behind her, or the echoes of their thudding hearts as she and Derron realized precious seconds ticked away.

"Help! Someone help us!"

With any luck, a neighbor would hear and come to their rescue, but time was running short.

Waiting wasn't an option. "We've got to do something!" she yelled at Derron.

"I know, but what?" he yelled back. They were only inches away from each other, and the room around them was silent, but the fear between them was deafening.

The tabletop weapon was built to scale and looked authentic, right down to the cannon wheels it sat upon. Each time Derron moved, the ropes binding him tightened more, biting into his flesh. Like the chain attached to Madison's handcuffs, the rope was woven through the spokes of the wheels. Neither he nor she could simply slip their hands down the barrel of the three-foot cannon and be free.

Madison looked around the room for some kind of tool they could use, some means of escape. There were instruments on Bobby Ray's reload table, but none looked particularly helpful. She mostly saw boxes of black powder stacked against the wall, waiting to explode.

"Black powder doesn't just explode on contact," she remembered. "I heard Brash explain it to Blake. It will flash and burn, but it won't explode unless it's under pressure. Something about the gasses. Unless it's in a tight, confined space or under extreme pressure, it burns out quickly."

"Is a cannon pressure enough?" Derron shrieked, using his chin to point to the vessel he hugged. The barrel pointed directly at the stack of boxes.

"Right." She gulped, trying to think of a solution. "We have to defuse it."

He stopped yelling for help long enough to ask, "But how?"

"We pull the fuse out."

"I don't know about you, but my hands are a little occupied at the moment." He turned his head and bellowed again for help.

"I'll try. I have a little wiggle room."

The chain held her hands close against the cannon, but by lifting her shoulders and shifting to the left, Madison managed to slide it sideways by a few links. It was enough to work the tips of her fingers over to the fuse. One end of the fuse was stuffed through the vent hole and into the charge. The other end was still a few inches away, but it sputtered and sparked like a firework on the Fourth of July.

Madison tugged, but bound so tightly against the barrel, her grip was tenuous and unsteady. Nothing happened.

"Pull harder!" Derron said.

"I'm trying!" she hissed. She wiggled some more, getting a fraction of an inch closer to the vent hole and its stem. Levering the strength of her upper body, Madison gripped the cord best she could and jerked her entire arm.

Hard.

The slow match popped out of the hole. Relief danced through her, weakening her knees, as the crisis was averted.

Madison's relief was short lived as she watched the fuse sail through the air.

Still sizzling, it landed on the carpet near the box of black powder.

The room now smelled of sulfur, melting synthetic fibers, and fear.

"Uh, Maddy," Derron stuttered, his voice sounding increasingly worried. "That—That didn't work so well."

"I can see that!"

"What now?"

"I'm open to suggestions."

Derron eyed the shortening fuse as it burned. Beneath the glittery sparks, the fibers of the carpet melted into a dark puddle, its edges already smoldering and spreading wider. Stomping out the fuse didn't mean stomping out the danger. Who knew how much gunpowder burrowed into the carpet and the padding below? Who knew how unstable it might be? The tufts of smoke churned ever closer to the boxes, silently ticking down the minutes of their lives.

Derron looked at the cannon and then to her tense shoulders. "How strong are you?" he asked.

"Are you thinking what I'm thinking?"

"I don't think we have another choice."

Blowing out a deep breath, Madison prepared herself for the task to come. "The back door is just down the hall. Think we can make it?"

"We have to." Derron gave her a weak smile. "We can do this, dollface. On three."

Her hands were bound too closely to get a good grip on the barrel, but she curled her hands the best she could and, on the count of three, heaved with all her might. Even though Derron pulled more than his share of the weight,

Madison could have sworn that all two hundred pounds of the cannon hung from the chains on her wrists. She stifled a cry as the metal bit into her skin.

Their progress was slow and awkward. Madison staggered backwards as they hefted the bulky load, inch by inch, across the room. Reaching the interior door was only the first challenge. Getting *through* the door was a feat unto itself.

"I—I need to rest," Madison rasped, leaning into the doorframe to gather a deep breath. She hiked her knee and tried to help balance the weight, nearly falling over when she did so.

"There's no time," Derron warned, looking over his shoulder. The smoke was getting thicker as the puddle of melting carpet grew. He had no desire to test Brash's theory on open flames and contained spaces. The boxes—and this room—were more than enough containment for him. "Explosion or not," he told her, "I'll take my chances of burning in hell, not here. Keep moving, dollface."

It took sheer determination and strained muscles, a generous dose of grunting and groaning, ripped clothes and ripped skin, but they managed to squeeze through the narrow opening.

"I swear," Madison panted, as they broke past the splintered doorframe and stumbled into the hall, "my arms are pulled from their sockets. I have to set it down."

"We'll push it from here," Derron agreed. "Easy down."

"Can't. Move back."

She dropped her end unceremoniously, forgetting that she was tethered to the heavy barrel. When it clattered to the ground, so did she. Derron staggered down with his end, collapsing on top of her. They indulged in a few brief seconds of respite, dragging in deep gulps of air and allowing their fatigued muscles to quiver in peace. But as the stench of melting carpet permeated the hallway, their rest was over. Crawling on their knees, they pushed the cannon as much as they rolled it. With the attached chain and rope constricting movement, the wheels couldn't turn the way they should.

Between the two of them, they managed to slide the bulky weapon to the nearest door. It wasn't until they opened it that they realized there was no porch, and the ground was at least four feet below.

Faced with yet another obstacle, Madison turned back to shout at her friend. She had to yell to be heard over the roar of their ragged breathing and their pounding hearts. "I'd rather have a broken arm," she yelled, "than one blown to kingdom come."

"I'll go first," he offered.

Madison shook her head. "Takes too long to turn around," she huffed out. She rested against the opened door for only a second. "I'm already here."

"Let the cannon fall. Don't try to hold it," Derron advised. "Make yourself limp and just go with the flow. I'll be right behind you."

"Literally." She tried to smile, but it required too much effort.

Using all the energy she had left, she pushed the cannon through the doorway and followed it down.

೮೮೮೮೮೮

The four-foot tumble was the longest yard and a half of both their lives. Despite the two-hundred-pound cannon hurtling them to the ground, Madison swore there was time to watch a movie during the descent—the movie of her life. She saw flashes of the highlights: the birth of the twins, her wedding to Brash, a snapshot of the five of them at the Big House.

All too soon—and yet long, agonizing seconds later—she smacked into the hard surface of the earth. The impact knocked the wind from her lungs and rattled stars from the rafters of her brain. Tears stung her eyes as she landed with her face in the dirt and one arm beneath the barrel. Just before Derron pummeled atop her, she realized the chain on the handcuffs had snapped in two.

Even though his body was petite for a man, it felt like a whale had crashed into her. She lay in stunned silence, trying to breathe, trying to move, and failing miserably at both. Between the pain in her arm, the roar in her ears, and the crushing weight upon her lungs, Madison clung to consciousness by a thread. As stars continued to burst in her head, she imagined holding on for dear life and riding them down.

"M—M—Move," she finally croaked. In her mind, she poked his shoulder.

Derron didn't budge. As Madison managed to squeeze air into her lungs, she pried an eyelid open. Derron's blond head rested against the cannon, his body sprawled atop hers. There was a bright red slash from the edge of his mussed hair down to his temple, and something poured down the side of his cheek.

It took a moment for the scene to register in her befuddled brain. That red stream was blood, and there was too much of it to be a simple scratch. "D—Derron. Move." With tremendous effort, Madison wiggled her shoulder enough to jostle the body atop hers. The movement sent off a wave of nausea, but she gritted her teeth and tried again. "Wake up. Derron, wake up."

She pulled her right arm from beneath him and clumsily shook his shoulder. The blood still flowed from his head, spilling over the side of his face and pooling in the collar of his shirt. "You—You're ruining your shirt," she mumbled, knowing how much pride he took in his appearance. "Come on, Derron. We have to move back. Have to... have to keep moving."

She wasn't quite sure of the details—her mind was still fuzzy, complicated by the pain in her left arm, the nausea in her stomach, and the roar floating among the stars—but she knew there was some sense of urgency. Some reason she had jumped out of a house wearing a two-hundred-pound parachute. Three-fifty, when she added the dead weight of her friend. For the life of her, she couldn't remember the particulars, but she knew it was imperative that they get safely away from the house.

A deafening trill broke through the roar in her head. In response to the mobile home's smoke alarm, neighborhood dogs began to bark. Each yap felt like a nail driven into her brain, but Madison reasoned that if she could move, she could get away from the terrible racket.

She pulled her arm from beneath the cannon barrel, which was beneath Derron's prone body. She screamed out in pain as she tugged herself free. Fighting another onset of nausea, she had to stop several times as she struggled out from under him and into a kneeling position. Her left arm hung limply at her side, no doubt broken. She vaguely remembered something about it being blown off.

No. Not blown off. But there had been the possibility of it...

Still fuzzyheaded, she knew the screeching alarm and the memory were trying to tell her something. Madison tried again to wake her friend, but he had chosen now to take a nap. She saw a severed rope around his chaffed wrist and noticed it, too, smeared with blood.

It was nothing like the blood still flowing from his head.

"Not joking. Move." She poked him in his ribs, a surefire way to get a response from the ticklish man. Still nothing. "Gotta be. Kidding me." With a grunt and a driving sense of urgency she still didn't understand, Madison pushed her friend, rolling him off the barrel and onto the ground. Using her one good hand, and sometimes her shoulder, sometimes her feet, Madison rolled Derron across the lawn until they were a least a dozen feet away from the house.

Smoke rolled from the open door of the mobile home, and she thought she smelt fire. Madison ignored the drama behind her, intent on rolling her friend to safety. When pain and exhaustion overtook her, she collapsed there on the ground beside her friend, their bodies draped across a stepping stone bearing the image of the Alamo.

Eventually, the black powder inside the house caught fire and went off with a huge bang. The reverberation was enough to engage her car alarm, but neither Madison nor Derron ever knew.

But with the boom came the fire department.

Help was on the way.

32

Madison awoke with a start. She felt disoriented and out of place, even though she recognized the pale sage green on the walls and the Egyptian cotton linens beneath her leaden limbs. The fresh bouquet of wildflowers on the nightstand stirred a warm feeling in her heart and evoked a memory seeded deep in her soul. This was her bedroom, and the warm body stretched out beside her belonged to Brash. She couldn't as easily identify the murky fog inside her head or the faint memory of... something. It was just beyond her reach, but she knew it posed an immediate danger. A bomb, perhaps?

She gasped, wondering why such a thought would enter her mind, even as her mother's instincts took over. Were the kids okay? Has something happened to Bethani and Blake? To Megan? She tried sitting up, but her left arm felt unusually heavy and stiff.

"Shh, sweetheart. Calm down." Brash was there beside her, gently stroking her forehead. "You're fine. You're safe."

"The—The kids? Are the kids okay? You're okay?" Her eyes were wild as she looked around for proof that her world was in order. She clutched at his arm with her right hand, wondering about the weakness in her limbs.

"Yes, of course, sweetheart. We're all fine," he crooned gently. "It's you that we're worried about."

"Me? Why me?"

"You don't remember what happened?"

Her forehead puckered. "No." But even as she managed a tiny shake of her head, the memories flooded in. Collette. Nigel. A homemade cannon. Black powder and blood. And Derron.

"Derron!" she cried in alarm. "How is he? Is he okay?"

"Yes, babe, Derron is going to be fine. He's in the hospital for observation, but the doctors say he's going to be just fine. He had a nasty gash on his head, and both of you have a concussion, but with time and rest, you'll both be good as new."

Madison looked down at the cast on her arm. "I broke my arm?" she asked needlessly. She thought back to the pain and the nausea after the fall. Definitely a break.

"Yes. But at least it's your left arm, and at least it wasn't any worse. I don't have to tell you how lucky you two were. You could have been killed, sweetheart." His voice dropped to a deep rumble as he spoke, and in his beautiful brown eyes, she saw the pain caused by the very thought of losing her.

"I know," she whispered, closing her eyes to the memory. They popped wide open again as she remembered the rest. "Collette! It was Collette all along. She killed them all, and she would have killed us. The woman is insane!"

"Shh, sweetheart, sit back. We have Collette in custody, and she's not going anywhere, anytime soon."

"How did you know?"

"You kept mumbling her name last night. Something about shrimp and a Bible and DNA tests. You wouldn't let the doctor treat you until he promised to write it all down and tell me. And you said he had to do it over the phone, before the orange car got away. I pieced enough of it together to put out a BOLO and bring her in for questioning."

"She's crazy, Brash." Madison's voice was steeped in sadness. "Stark-raving mad. She said killing people was a necessary evil, like going to the dentist. She believed Nigel's fortune rightfully belonged to her, and nothing and no one would get in her way."

"We've been piecing the details together all afternoon. It seems—"

"What time is it?" she broke in sharply.

"Almost eight at night. You've been out of it all day."

"Are you serious? I can't believe I slept that long."

"We didn't get back home until the wee hours of the morning. And the doctor gave you something to help you sleep," he assured her. "You can have more for the pain, if you need it."

She shook her head. "It's not too bad. Before I take anything more, I want to hear how things turned out, and I want to see the kids."

"I have several pieces of good news to share. All charges against Tony have been dropped, and the ADA has scheduled a press conference for Monday morning to issue a formal apology and announce pending charges against Collette."

"Only pending charges?"

"There's so many, they're still tallying them up. Murder, attempted murder, assault with a deadly weapon, assault with a motor vehicle... the list is extensive. But Barbara Barrett Motte pulled through surgery and, barring complications, should make a full recovery. She and her brother Earl, Jr. appear to be the heirs apparent for Nigel's estate."

"I feel so guilty about Barbara. I practically led Collette to her!"

"She knew Jeannie had a niece. I'm sure she was already on her hit list."

"Some investigator I've turned out to be," Madison groaned, pulling the covers up around herself in chagrin. "I couldn't find Jeannie, even with Collette pushing me in the right direction."

"It was a bit complicated," Brash admitted. "She had a son with a man she never married, and then took three husbands. That's a lot of different surnames, especially when she didn't go by her own given name."

"And I had some bad information," Madison murmured.

"Granny Bert had a feeling you might say that," Brash said with a grin. "She said to tell you that her intel was good. The Eric her sources mentioned obviously were referring to the man she didn't marry, the Erickson who fathered her child. And Winston was, in fact, the name of her last husband, even though his friends called him Stony. So she claims she's still batting a hundred."

An indulgent smile accompanied her groan. "That woman!" She shook her head at her grandmother's antics, even though the movement caused her pain. The smile soon fell as less-pleasant memories flooded back in. "You were right about Bobby Ray. He didn't die of natural causes. Collette killed him, too. But I was wrong about Joel Werner. I actually thought he might have been responsible for Nigel's death. I guess I owe the man an apology, if only mentally."

"Hold up on that," he advised. "I hear the Walker County Sheriff's office has uncovered new evidence and is reopening the suicide case he was suspected of being involved in. No matter how that comes out, we all know the man is underhanded and will stoop to unscrupulous means to get what he wants."

"Hey, where do you think you're going?" she asked when he stood and crossed the room.

"I promised the kids I'd let them know when you woke up. By the time they got in last night from their ski trip, you were already at the emergency room. They're anxious to see you, sweetheart." He went to the intercom and pressed a button. "Sleeping Beauty is now awake and seeing select dwarfs. Would Hungry, Cheery, and Perky please report to the inner chamber?"

Madison laughed at the names he had assigned their children. *Hungry* was the perfect moniker for Blake, and while Bethani and Megan were both cheerleaders, Megan was the perpetually perky one. All the names fit.

"Thank you for my flowers, by the way. They're beautiful."

"I thought you might like seeing those when you woke up." He swooped down to drop a kiss on her lips, but she snagged him around the neck with her good arm and held him there.

"Your face," she whispered, "was all I needed."

"Happy anniversary, Mrs. deCordova. One week today."

"And what a week it's been!"

Brash crawled atop the covers again and settled in beside her, careful of her arm. "Wonder if every week will be this eventful?"

"I hope not!" she laughed. "I don't think I can stand that much excitement all the time!"

"Are you referring to time spent under house arrest for skipping out on your honeymoon, or the other events of the week?" he wanted to know, nuzzling her hair.

"Definitely the other events," she assured him. "I'm thinking of turning myself in for a number of offenses, real or alleged, if it lands me under house arrest again."

"I'm sure that can be arranged." Brash gathered a handful of hair as he cupped her face and leaned in for a thorough kiss.

"Hey, I thought you told us to come in!" Blake's voice protested from the doorway. "None of that X-rated stuff. Not before dinner, anyway."

"Hey, Mom, how you feeling?" Bethani wanted to know, skipping across the room.

Megan was close on her heels. "You worried us, Momma

Maddy!"

"It's so good to see you!" Madison beamed as she stretched out her good arm for hugs. "Come on up here. There's plenty of room. I want to hear all about your ski trip!"

All three teenagers piled onto the bed with their parents, in what was a tangle of arms, legs, and laughter. The stories flowed, each told louder and faster than the last, each a competition for the best memory or the worst catastrophe.

The worries of the week paled in comparison to the joys of that moment, shared as a family.

They didn't know it then, but it was a new family tradition in the making. A lazy Saturday when they could lounge on the bed and rehash the events of the week. A quiet strengthening of their band of love and togetherness. As Brash taught his daughter long ago, that band could stretch to include others, but it always held close those dearest to the heart. This new Saturday tradition was a time to recharge and reconnect, and it was exactly what this family—every family—needed.

Over the tops of the teenager's heads, Brash caught his bride's eye and winked. Somehow, the girls had wormed in between them, and soon he and Blake were relegated to the foot of the bed, sprawled across the lumpy covers. On the air rode the scent of wildflowers and wild stories, and neither of the newlyweds had ever known a sweeter moment.

It might not be the honeymoon they had envisioned, but it was exactly the life they had dreamed of.

And the best was yet to come.

CRCBCBCR

The deCordova-Reynoldses and all their friends and family in The Sisters invite you to share in more adventures in the near future!

If you enjoyed this story, please leave a review on the site of your choice. It only takes a moment of your time but makes a huge impact on the success of a novel. Thank you for reading! You can connect with me at beckiwillis.ccp@gmail.com or https://www.facebook.com/beckiwillis.ccp/.

ABOUT THE AUTHOR

Becki Willis, best known for her popular The Sisters, Texas Mystery Series and Forgotten Boxes, always dreamed of being an author. In November of '13, that dream became a reality. Since that time, she has published numerous books, won first place honors for Best Mystery Series, Best Suspense Fiction, Best Women's Detective Fiction and Best Audio Book, won the 2018 RONE Award for Paranormal Fiction, and has introduced her imaginary friends to readers around the world.

An avid history buff, Becki likes to poke around in old places and learn about the past. Other addictions include reading, writing, junking, unraveling a good mystery, and coffee. She loves to travel, but believes coming home to her family and her Texas ranch is the best part of any trip. Becki is a member of the Association of Texas Authors, Writer's League of Texas, Sisters in Crime, the National Association of Professional Women, and the Brazos Writers organization. She attended Texas A&M University and majored in Journalism.

You can connect with her at http://www.beckiwillis.com/ and http://www.facebook.com/beckiwillis.ccp?ref=hl. Better yet, email her at beckiwillis.ccp@gmail.com. She loves to hear from readers and encourages feedback!

CPSIA information can be obtained
at www.ICGtesting.com
Printed in the USA
FFHW021159220519
52585221-58071FF